Winter Interlude

Sandy Loyd

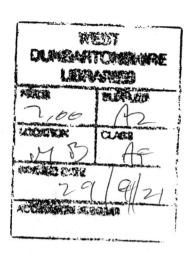
Published by Sandy Loyd
Copyright 2012 Sandy Loyd
Cover design by Inspire Creative Services

Other books by Sandy Loyd

Contemporary Romances
The California Series
Winter Interlude – Book One
Promises, Promises – Book Two
James – Book Three

Second Chances Series
Tropical Spice – Book One

Romantic Suspense
D.C. Bad Boys Series
The Sin Factor – Book One

Running Series
Running Out Of Fear – Book One

Dedication

Winter Interlude is dedicated to everyone who helped me on my journey. To my sister, Jeannette Antry and my husband Bill – both loved the rough 'first draft' and have been my ardent supporters ever since. To my critique partners, Leslie Lynch, Caroline Fyffe and Lisa Tapp, who helped smooth out those rough edges. And finally, to Pam Berehulke, my copy editor who took a good story and made it better. Thank you all!

Chapter 1

Kate Winters winced and resisted the urge to say "Careful!" as the big burly guy hit a bump on his way down the truck's ramp, jarring the Victorian-era rolltop desk. The second the wheels hit even ground, she released the breath she'd been holding and followed him inside her shop, Yesterday's Treasures.

Her cell phone rang. Glancing down, she frowned. She had a strong urge to ignore the caller and concentrate on her delivery. Instead, she sighed, pressed Answer, and said, "Hey, Mom. What's up?"

"Hi, sweetie. Chrissie just texted you the pictures of the bridesmaids' dresses she picked out. You're maid of honor, so she wants your approval. Will you take a look so we can order them today?"

"Sure. Hold on a minute." She tamped down the bit of envy that sprang free every time she thought of her sister's engagement, and brought up the text message to scroll through the photos. After all, Chrissie deserved to be happy. It's just that she always figured she would beat her younger sister to the altar. That she obviously wasn't going to had been a wake-up call.

"So," her mother said, interrupting her thoughts. "What do you think?"

Kate refocused on the dress and smiled at the color. Rose, Chrissie's favorite. "I love the style, and that shade of pink should enhance everyone's complexions." Even hers, she added mentally, while her mother chatted about the wedding plans. Thankfully, Tippy Winters didn't mention her true opinion regarding her older daughter's still-single status—that after dating the same man since college, it was well past time for marriage.

She glanced back at the truck. Peter, whose name was embroidered above the pocket of his work shirt, had already unloaded several pieces. "Look, Mom, I've got a deliveryman here and I need to tell him where to put my pieces." Tippy never tired of voicing her disapproval, and Kate didn't have time for the same old lecture about not getting any younger.

"Okay, dear. We'll talk later."

Kate disconnected. It was bad enough to hear her mom's voice inside her head saying her eggs wouldn't stay fresh forever. "Like I don't already have enough to worry about," she grumbled as she headed out to the truck.

Peter loaded up the last piece and scuttled down the ramp like he was going to a fire. Once inside, he angled the hand truck in the opposite corner of where she'd asked him to unload the furniture.

"Wait," she said in her firmest voice.

He slowed his forward momentum and spared her a glance.

She smiled sweetly, going for the 'poor little old me' routine, batted her eyes and pointed. "Would you mind placing it in that corner like I wanted?"

"I'm a delivery guy, not a mover," he said, his tone snide, and turned the hand truck containing the heavy eighteenth-century armoire toward the chest and other items he'd unloaded.

"You're also a jerk," she said under her breath. She counted to ten, but it did little good to ease her annoyance. "Back up, bucko." Determined he would honor her request, she squared her shoulders. "I suggest you put the armoire over there."

After throwing her another brief glance, he stopped, none too pleased with the interruption.

This time her expression said, *Don't mess with me.* "Otherwise, I'm calling your supervisor." It was an empty threat, but he didn't have to know that. A complaint to his boss would generate bad karma. She wasn't into causing anyone to lose a source of income in this economy. It was simply that moving the furniture to where she'd indicated would be far easier for him than for her. She was five foot two and weighed a hundred pounds, soaking wet. This guy had to be at least a hundred and fifty pounds heavier, and towered over her by nearly a foot.

He begrudgingly changed directions and she offered another smile, this one more fake than a Gucci knockoff. "I appreciate your help." At least Peter hadn't dropped or scratched anything. She wondered where her regular guy was. "Do you know if Tony will be back on the route soon?" She gritted her teeth to hold her smile in place, doing her darnedest to remain pleasant, the entire time praying Tony hadn't quit.

"How do I know? I'm just a—"

"Delivery guy. Yeah, I got that."

He yanked the hand truck out from under the armoire. "That should do it."

Kate signed the delivery release form and handed the clipboard back to him.

"I'll be sure to tell your supervisor how much help you were," she said to his departing back, as he trudged out the rear entrance. "When hell freezes over," she muttered, as she locked the door behind him, then grabbed her own hand truck. Peter could definitely use a few pointers from Tony on his customer service skills.

She returned to the showroom, kicked off her pointed-toe high heels, and began with the rolltop desk. The first step of leaning it back onto the hand truck took some doing. Holding the heavy piece firmly in place with one hand and pushing the awkward load with the other, she angled it toward the perfect corner. Nearly dropping it twice along the way, she slowly set the hand truck upright but quickly tightened her grip to stop the load from hitting the floor too hard. With a greater respect for Peter, she used as much strength as she could muster to inch the desk into place. Satisfied, she steered the hand truck back across the room to tackle the rest of the delivered pieces.

She set the last item, a Chippendale table, next to a Victorian sofa and stood back, sighing contentedly. She brushed the dust off her skirt and then made a slow circle around the new pieces, touching each one reverently, as she imagined others of bygone generations had done.

After all this time, my shop is in the black and doing well! Her dream was finally coming true. Even though it had been four years since she opened, the same feeling of accomplishment swept over her whenever she took stock of any new inventory. All of these antiques were hers, at least until they sold, which wouldn't take long.

She rolled her aching shoulders and stepped into her shoes on her way to the cash register. *One more chore, then I can get off my feet.* Her day started early. She hadn't stopped from the moment she arrived in the store that morning.

Not wanting to dwell on her mother's call or her sister's upcoming wedding, she counted out the day's receipts, happy with the week's gross. Yesterday's Treasures' customers didn't seem to mind that her shop was in a shabby section of San Bruno, a city on the outskirts of San Francisco. She had several ladies in mind who would probably snap up most of her recent purchases, and increase her profit margin at the same time.

Kate worked her tail off for years building her reputation. Now her sales were strong and steady, providing a decent salary, enough to live in one of the nicest areas of an expensive city. As long as she was frugal—which she was.

Done with her receipts, Kate let herself out and locked the front door after setting the state-of-the-art security system, her one big splurge. Before starting the car, she checked her smartphone to see if James had texted her. *Nothing.* A twinge of disappointment fluttered inside as she typed a quick message to say hi and to ask about their plans for the next day. After all, she had no problem communicating. Her long-term boyfriend did. As much as she tried to pretend his inattention didn't matter, thoughts of the decisions she'd made while on her buying trip kept intruding on her good mood. It had been over a month since they'd spent any quality time together, and even then, James had been distracted and distant.

This might not mean anything, she reminded herself, as she backed out of her parking space. *I knew he'd be busy working. He's on a deadline with his latest project, which is due on Monday morning. His lack of communication will not get me down.* Thankfully, her mental pep talk worked and, as she drove to the bank, she banished all thoughts of James Morrison from her mind.

Her deposits safely made, she sped toward San Francisco via Highway 101. Traffic was light for a Friday commute. She exited the freeway, weaved through city streets, and turned into the lot at the Safeway not far from her Marina District apartment in half of the usual twenty minutes. She headed into the grocery store, having almost forgotten her earlier promise to pick up a few items for her next-door neighbor.

Soon she was back on the road. At her street, she slowly circled the block three times, then sighed. The daily chore of searching for a parking spot was one of the downsides to living in the city. She turned to increase her circle by a block and spotted a space right away. As she quickly backed in, she sent up a huge thank-you to the parking gods. A space, even this far away, required more than luck on a weekday.

After grabbing the groceries and her handbag, she emerged from the car and started the two-block trek to her apartment building.

At Mrs. Pike's door, Kate pressed the buzzer. The TV inside blared as usual, so she didn't release her finger until the volume eventually lowered.

"Who's there?" came the cautious voice that always made her smile.

"It's me, Kate Winters." It didn't matter how many times she'd been at this same spot at this same time in the past year delivering groceries, her neighbor always asked the same question. "I have your milk and eggs."

Mrs. Pike opened the door and peeked through the space. "Oh, my. Aren't you a dear?" She opened it wider and moved to the side, pushing her walker out of the way.

Still smiling, Kate stepped past her and carried the heavy bag to the kitchen counter. "There you go."

"I hope it wasn't too much trouble." The older woman slowly followed her into the room, using the walker for support.

"None whatsoever." Kate placed the items in the fridge. "Let me know when you'll need anything else."

"You're an angel. I can't figure out what's wrong with that young man you've been dating. You two have had plenty of time to get married. In my day, boys didn't pussyfoot around when they had a good thing. They weren't afraid of marriage."

"I got you a couple of candy bars," Kate interjected, having come fully prepared to deflect the forthcoming lecture about not buying a cow when the milk is free. Mrs. Pike was worse than her mother at times. She emptied the bag and presented two Snickers bars.

Mrs. Pike's aged eyes lit up with pleasure and her wrinkled face broke out in huge smile. "Thank you." The older woman didn't just have one sweet tooth. Every remaining tooth in her mouth craved sugary snacks.

Kate said her good-byes and quickly let herself out, making a getaway while she could. The candy diversion wouldn't last long. She walked to her own apartment trying not to think about Mrs. Pike's comment. Unfortunately, it hit a nerve, thanks to her mom's phone call. Stuff like that never bothered her before. Chrissie's engagement announcement, however, had prompted her to wonder the same thing. What was James afraid of? She thought about it constantly for the last few weeks, and the answer had become obvious.

Commitment.

Don't dwell on it, she told herself, as she inserted her key into the lock. Hopefully, the plans she'd set into motion for the trip to Tahoe next weekend would change things. The second her front door clicked shut behind her, she glanced around. Ignoring her tightening stomach, she took a deep breath and focused on the scene before her—one that always lifted her spirits.

Various shades of blues and creams framed the windows and covered the upholstered furniture. The fabrics she chose blended with expensive antiques—of course she would own nothing less—and created a warm and inviting elegance that always made her feel like a princess, even if James' lack of attention was starting to make her feel like a toad.

An oversized off-white sofa flanked one side of the room, two upholstered navy chairs the other. Her wide-screen TV rested atop a long, dark wood sideboard, completing the *U*-shape. The antique sideboard had at one time graced a mansion in Seacliff, but Kate snapped it up at the estate sale after the owner had died. The grandkids' lack of appreciation for what they'd practically given away had been her good fortune.

Her gaze landed at her feet and she grimaced. Whoever created heels had to be a sadistic man. Kate kicked them off and dug her bare toes into the thick rug she'd picked up at a bargain. Covering her apartment's refinished turn-of-the-century hardwood floors went against her nature as a decorator. But the carpet's four corners defined the parameters of what she considered her living room, and kept noise at a minimum for the neighbor below her.

She stepped around the blue silk screen that separated the enormous area into two rooms. An antique four-poster bed and matching armoire took up most of the smaller space she considered her bedroom.

"Ah." She dropped onto the plush mattress, rubbing her aching arches and toes.

Fashion requires a hefty price.

The thought of putting her feet up and nestling in for the night flitted through her mind, but tonight she didn't have time for self-indulgence.

Judith Reid, one of her best friends, was treating her to a belated birthday meal. This was their first opportunity to get together for dinner since before Kate left on her buying trip. Tonight they planned to finalize the details of her proposed getaway. Unfortunately, Paul Morrison, Judith's boyfriend and James' younger brother, rounded out the foursome for the weekend. Willingly including him in any of her plans meant she was desperate. But desperate times called for desperate measures, she reminded herself, determining then and there not to let his little digs get to her.

She sighed, and rubbed her foot a little harder.

The guy wouldn't be so bad if he would just quit with the jokes at her expense. Of course, rising to his taunts most likely kept their sparring alive, she decided, remembering the last family get-together at Christmas. Paul's off-the-wall remark about James' present seeming a little impersonal after dating so long struck a nerve, as had so many others over the years. At that point, she'd grasped that responding wasn't the answer. But the knowledge hadn't mattered one bit because the minute the words were out of his mouth, something inside her subconscious kicked in. Even biting her tongue hadn't stopped her nasty retort.

And the worst part? Most of the anger she vented at Paul should have been directed at James for giving his brother the ammunition for his verbal barbs in the first place. Oven mitts and an apron were pretty much at the bottom of anyone's list of romantic presents. The gift definitely lacked intimacy, adding to her concerns, which spurred her to plan a weekend ski trip to make things better. It had to; it certainly couldn't make things worse.

With the kinks finally worked out of her feet, she padded to the armoire and pulled out jeans and a sweater. On the way to the bathroom to change, her cell phone beeped. *Please let it be a message from James.* She grabbed the phone, exhaled a relieved sigh, and read the text message while walking.

'Scored tickets to the Warriors game on Tuesday night.'

Yes! She gave herself a mental high five, excited that he'd come through for her. Basketball was her game. But her excitement died a quick death as she read on. He'd hit a snag on his project and had to cancel their plans for tomorrow night. Their usual Sunday brunch didn't look promising either.

She tried not to be too disappointed; in fact, she should have expected it. James, an architect and a perfectionist with his designs, worked long hours, something she didn't mind early on in their relationship. Heck, she'd put in years of eighty-hour weeks too. But now that her shop was doing well and her workload had leveled off, she realized how little time they actually spent together as a couple. She wanted more than the few dates a month James seemed perfectly happy with. And as far as the future went? They didn't appear to be on the same page any longer. Even Mrs. Pike noticed it.

Her recent goal assessment was an eye-opener, highlighting the years that had passed since she'd met James. Eight in all, and they'd been in a monogamous relationship for six of them. To be fair, she owned part of the reasons. Her shop came first and foremost for years, leaving her with little opportunity to think about marriage and a family. Now that Yesterday's Treasures was generating a decent income, it seemed as if time kept marching on and she wasn't getting any younger, as her mother kept reminding her.

"Don't think about it," she whispered. "Stick to your resolve." She'd vowed during her buying trip to change things.

They'd either get married, or she was finally ready to throw in the towel in order to be free to find someone else. At this point, she couldn't ignore that she'd spent most of her adult life playing the waiting game. A trip to the altar was the next logical step and it was well past time for it.

Aside from dealing with Paul, her biggest hurdle now was getting James away from work. But she didn't want to think about that now.

Banishing all disturbing thoughts from her mind, she slipped out of her skirt and stepped into more relaxing jeans. While tucking in her sweater, she caught her reflection in the mirror and noticed a few smudges of dirt.

She washed her face, ran a brush through her short dark hair, and applied fresh makeup. A touch of mascara framed what she considered her best feature, her brown eyes, making them appear bigger. She finished, not needing more than a bit of blush and a dab of lipstick, before eagerly dashing out the door.

Judith and dinner at her favorite restaurant on Union Street awaited.

~

"Hey, gorgeous," Paul Morrison said, after spotting Judith Reid seated at the bar. Miguel's was packed as usual. Not with tourists, but with neighborhood professionals, like him, ready to reel in the weekend with a drink and relaxation during happy hour.

"Hi, Paul. You're looking very GQ today. Business with a client?"

"Yeah." He grinned at her reference to his clothes. An Armani was definitely more formal than the worn-out jeans and sweatshirt he usually wore while working out of his home office. "Nathaniel A. Baker just left. I have to look the part, you know, if I'm to impress him enough to tell him where to put his money." Yep, appearance was everything when meeting anyone new, and he had to admit, he certainly felt the part. His grin spread. "And Mr. Baker handed me a million-dollar account, which means I'm buying."

"Thanks." She held up a glass of what had to be BV cabernet, since that was her favorite. "I already bought one and I plan to nurse it all night." Taking a sip, she kept her warm gaze on him as he grabbed the stool a stranger had just vacated.

"So, what's up with you?" he asked.

"Kate's meeting me for dinner." She smiled. "We're celebrating her birthday a little late. You're welcome to join us," Judith offered.

He nodded. "Thanks, but I'll pass." His time was limited and having dinner with Kate Winters was at the very bottom of his to-do list. "But I'll share a celebratory glass of wine and keep you company until she gets here." He waved to the bartender and ordered.

Judith sighed and gave him a disapproving frown. "I don't understand why you two don't like each other when you have so much in common."

His drink appeared. Paul picked up the wineglass and sipped while considering her words. "I can't speak for her, but for me it's a matter of taste," he finally said, scrunching up his nose. "She's definitely a go-getter, but she's too opinionated." While he appreciated her business acumen and her ability to sell antiques, her pushy personality always rubbed him the wrong way—which didn't make sense, considering he usually admired that type of person. Hell, he strived to be one himself.

Judith remained silent, eyeing him thoughtfully. "Are you sure you two can handle three days with each other at Lake Tahoe?"

"Sure." Kate had been the main instigator in organizing the getaway and Paul had jumped on the chance to spend an entire weekend with Judith. He'd known Judith since they were kids on the same summer swim team. In college, thanks to his efforts, they'd become good friends, yet he'd always wanted more. Judith had recently talked about marriage, so he'd mentioned taking their relationship to another level. She soon backed off, saying she didn't want anything to spoil their friendship. For Paul, it was damned frustrating to be relegated to 'friend' status after all this time. "Have you thought more about the trip?"

"Yeah." She nodded. "Apparently, it's important to Kate, so I'm working on clearing my schedule." She gave him a pointed look. "But *we're* going just as friends. We agreed, remember?"

"How could I forget?" he said, wishing she'd never brought up the *M* word. He should have known she'd be skittish about something so permanent, when it had taken him years to gain her friendship. He reminded himself that she *had* recently made the move to the city, which was a good thing. Baby steps. Now that she was only minutes away, rather than an hour's drive, they could spend more time together. He held up his wineglass. "Here's to clearing your schedule." He had three glorious days to change her mind about being more than friends by showing her how great they were together. Thank God, Kate's ballsy approach was finally useful for something besides irritating him. "When's she due?"

"Anytime. I'm a little early."

"Well, I'll clear out once she shows." Paul had to remain on his best behavior. It wouldn't do to hang around and verbally try to get a rise out of Kate, something he had a hard time resisting. He had to prove he could get along. Otherwise, Judith might add to her schedule rather than clear it. "So, how's work going?" he asked, switching to safer topics. She was a commercial designer who'd ventured out on her own after relocating from San Jose two months earlier.

Judith had just finished detailing her latest project when he glanced up to see Kate breeze through the restaurant's entrance. Once she spotted Judith, she jostled through the throng of bodies. A salmon had an easier time swimming upstream than she had working her way to the bar.

When her gaze hit his, she halted and her smile faded somewhat. "Hey, Paul."

Her unenthusiastic greeting rose above the din of the noisy bar.

Paul nodded. "Don't worry," he said, to put her mind at ease. "I'm finishing my drink, then I'm outta here."

"Don't rush off on my account," she purred, but her sweet tone was as phony as her too-tight smile. She turned to Judith, who'd stood, and offered a more natural smile.

As the two women exchanged hugs, he laughed. "I wouldn't dream of rushing."

"I'm so glad to see you," Judith said, sitting back down as Kate perched on the empty barstool on the other side of her. Her attention on Kate, she asked, "Would you like a drink?"

Kate nodded, then made eye contact with the bartender and pointed at Paul's glass. "I'll have white wine too. Chardonnay, please." She leaned forward to glance at Paul through the space between the bar and Judith. "I see you're dressed up today." The genuineness of her smile slipped a bit, hiding behind her salesperson's insincere mien. "You look very professional."

His jaw clenched at the part of the sentence she left off— *for a change.* After making too many comments about his laid-back work habits in the past, she didn't have to say it for him to know she was thinking it.

Their gazes remained locked, until he shook his head. He shouldn't care what she thought. Hell, he usually had three or four hours in by the time most people arrived at their jobs, including her. Besides, results mattered most in his business. And he provided results. His connections, together with his intellect and long hours, had proven to be quite profitable since starting his own firm, for both him and his clients. He didn't need Kate Winters' approval to validate his success.

"Our table should be ready soon," Judith said, drawing his attention. "So, how was your trip?"

"Great!" Kate replied. "I missed you, though."

"You've been on a trip?" Paul snared her gaze again and flashed a quick grin. "I didn't even realize you were gone."

She turned to Judith with eyes that said, *See what I have to deal with?*

When Judith glared at him, he shrugged his shoulders, and formed his features into an innocent expression that said, *What?*

"So when did you get in?" she asked, turning back to Kate as the bartender placed a glass of Murphy Goode chardonnay in front of her.

"Late Monday night." Kate took a sip and sighed. "Today was a backbreaker because one of the deliveries from my buying trip arrived."

The two women discussed Kate's antiques store, while Paul stayed silent. Finally finishing his wine, he stood and gave Judith a peck on the cheek. "I'll let you two continue talking business."

"You're sure you don't want to join us? You *are* welcome, you know," Judith offered, throwing Kate a warning glare, daring her to disagree.

"I know, but I've got stuff to do. I'll give you a call and catch up with you later, okay?"

"Okay."

"Bye, Paul," Kate said, in that same too-sugary voice.

"See ya, Kate." He smiled and waved.

~

As she watched Paul go, Kate whispered, "He stayed longer just to bug me."

"Cut it out!" Annoyance flared in Judith's eyes.

"What?" Kate huffed. "I didn't do anything but try to be nice." Paul scored a ten in the looks department, but that was mainly because he favored James. Both were striking blond men with the same sexy blue eyes and six-foot frame, but Paul was slightly leaner. Sporting a navy business suit, he looked as if he'd stepped out of a magazine.

Everyone but her saw Paul as a great guy—funny, intelligent, hardworking—a successful self-starter, so no one understood why the two of them were at odds. Heck, sometimes she had trouble understanding the reasons. Somehow, they just fell into their combative pattern and she had no clue as to how it happened. For as long as she could remember, Paul seemed to derive a lot of pleasure from pushing her hot buttons, and tonight had been no different.

"You heard him say he didn't realize I'd been gone."

"I doubt he meant it the way you took it." Judith stood, waded through several bodies toward the hostess, and asked about being seated.

Kate knew exactly how he meant it. He might have a decent sense of humor, but he also used subtlety like a weapon. When he aimed that subtle humor her way, she felt like some moronic bimbo who chased after his brother. Like he had room to joke about relationships. But Judith was right. His comments struck a nerve because she sometimes felt like a lone aggressor, the sole participant doing anything to maintain a relationship with James. It was definitely past time to put petty grievances aside, especially since they'd be spending a few days together. And if everything worked out, they would be related, which meant she had to work harder on changing her attitude toward him.

The hostess grabbed two menus and nodded. "Your table's ready. Right this way."

"Come on, let's sit down and you can tell me all about

your buying trip," Judith said, reaching for her drink.

Maintaining a contrite smile, Kate joined the procession through a maze of crowded tables. The hostess stopped at a small one in front of the main window overlooking the busy street.

After sitting, Judith opened her menu.

Kate sat opposite and tried to focus on her menu, but too excited by all her news, her enthusiasm sprang free. "Oh, Judith, it was such a great trip. I got more than I'd imagined. Some great deals and a few good contacts."

"I'm glad." Judith lowered her menu and smiled. "I know what success means to you."

"And this only adds to that success." She didn't struggle any longer, not like before, but she still had to budget. The salary she gave herself allowed for her two greatest pleasures— traveling and snow skiing. She used her buying trips to satisfy her traveling bug. As for her skiing passion, dating James had its perks. The two used the Morrison family lake house in the mountains for ski weekends. Only this year, he'd been too buried in projects to take a day off, so she'd gone without him too many times. And skiing alone was the pits.

"Tell me about your trip."

Kate nodded. "You wouldn't believe the places I've seen in the past two weeks." She recounted her trip to Charleston and Savannah, providing tidbits of her observations while scouting out auction houses and other resources for the most interesting pieces to buy. "A couple of times I was out in the middle of nowhere—well, not really because I was usually no more than an hour or two from any city. But, I have to admit, the tune from *Deliverance* kept going through my head on some of those back roads, considering the looming live oaks bordering them with moss hanging down on branches touching each other and blocking out the sky. I felt all alone and out of my element."

The waiter who'd taken their orders earlier returned with a tray full of food and began serving them.

"I don't know how you do it, but you can always make a mundane business trip sound like an adventure of a lifetime. I wish my life could be half as exciting," Judith stated, picking up her fork and digging into her salmon.

Silently, they ate.

"I'm bidding on a new project," Judith finally said, breaking their lull. "It's not big, but it's a start, and hopefully will lead to another job."

"Tell me about it." She listened intently while Judith chatted about designing the interior of a new store. Kate understood her desire to make something grow from nothing but an idea and a dream, as her friend was doing with her new commercial designing business.

"I still have several irons in the fire for more jobs, but the process takes time and I won't hear anything back for several days, maybe weeks."

Judith's voice faded to silence. The two continued eating.

"You haven't changed your mind about the ski trip next weekend, have you?" Kate asked, bringing up the subject after swallowing a bite.

"No. Paul's ecstatic. Unfortunately, I have a feeling spending three days with him as a foursome might be a big mistake."

"Wait," Kate said, holding up her hand. "I'm lost. I thought you guys were talking about marriage?" Heck, their situation was what started her discontent in the first place. That and Chrissie's engagement. Both made her realize her biological clock was ticking and she wanted a family more than anything.

"We were." Judith sighed and stirred the food around on her plate. "But suddenly I have huge misgivings. I told him how I felt and just want to keep things light, but I sense he's ccc

on a different schedule than me. I really wish we could go back to the way it was before I said anything." Her expression was torn. "So you see my dilemma." She hesitated before adding, "Why do you need us along, anyway?"

"Because if you and Paul don't go, James won't either, and it's important that he go." Kate cleared her throat. She couldn't admit her real reasons, when doing so would lead to questions she didn't want to think about, much less answer. "I kind of told him we needed to socialize more. And in doing so, may have inferred you and Paul needed the time together."

"Oh, great. I hope James doesn't repeat that to Paul."

"I'm sorry. I assumed it wasn't a big deal." She met Judith's eyes, hers pleading. "It won't be so bad."

"Aren't there other couples you could ask?"

"I tried." Kate shrugged. "No one else could make it." Which was why she'd turned to Judith and Paul in a last-ditch effort to salvage plans for next weekend. She felt James slipping away as it was and, if she waited longer, he'd most likely be enmeshed in another all-consuming project.

Judith searched her face for several beats. "So, let me get this straight. You decided to include us when you can barely stand Paul. Yet, you're willing to spend a weekend with him? What's with James anyway? Is everything okay?"

"Everything is fine. He just works too hard." Kate focused on her wineglass, uncomfortable with her friend's probing eyes. "I can handle Paul for a weekend—especially since we'll be skiing most of it." Besides, she'd already decided not to let his little verbal jabs get to her. She brought her glass to her lips and took a drink.

"You know, this might work out for the best. I mean, once all our marriage phobias are worked out, we'll be related. We all need to learn how to get along." Kate had good reason for disliking Paul, but she suspected Judith wasn't overly fond of James, an idea that started in college. "I know James isn't your favorite person." Over the years, she'd nixed too many of Kate's attempts at forming a foursome like best friends usually did. Of course, Judith rarely dated in college, which played a big part, as did being GUL—geographically undesirably located—for living an hour's drive away for most of that time. Still, even after moving to the city, she claimed to have plans if she knew James would be around. Judith treated him with the same reserve she did all other men, except Paul. And Kate had always wondered why.

"What do you mean?" Judith asked, drawing her gaze.

Kate eyed her thoughtfully. Although her friend feigned confusion, she didn't buy it. "Why don't you like him?"

"I don't dislike him." She frowned. "He just seems a little unapproachable."

"Unapproachable?" Taken aback, she thought about it for a moment and shrugged. "Maybe he's just mirroring you, which is all the more reason to come skiing. To become better friends. He may end up being your brother-in-law, you know." To be fair, if she expected it of Judith, she should be willing to do the same with Paul. "Don't worry. You'll survive and so will I," she soothed, squeezing Judith's hand. "You might even enjoy it and have fun."

A nice weekend away without distractions was what they all needed. She only had to remember that. And once James understood how serious she was, he'd propose. "We could both use some downtime." She grinned at Judith's skeptical expression, suddenly feeling more encouraged...more like her old, optimistic self. Her plan would work. It had to.

"What's so amusing?"

Kate shrugged. "It's too bad we can't flip-flop the guys' timing."

When Judith's expression turned questioning, she explained. "I know James loves me, but the white picket fence isn't a priority for him yet. Work is. You love Paul, and he's embracing happily-ever-after. You don't want marriage right now and I do. Wouldn't it be great if their timing matched ours?"

"Hmm, I never thought of it that way. Paul's a great guy, and I do love him, but I can't see myself married to him. Or anyone, for that matter."

"You're just not ready to marry."

Judith sighed. "I wish it was that easy."

"It has to be. James is perfect for me and I'm perfect for him."

"And a weekend in Tahoe is going to make him realize this?"

"Yes. He's so different when we're skiing and away from the daily grind." Her words and tone filtered past her ears, as she noticed a woman pushing a stroller past their table. In seconds, the yearning for more intensified and she wondered. Who was she trying to convince? Herself or Judith? Doubts returned. How pathetic to have them at all at this point.

Just then, their waiter interrupted, asking if they wanted another glass of wine.

"Yes, please," Kate said.

Judith shook her head and when he was out of earshot, added, "Maybe, but face it, Kate. You've been ready for commitment since you met him."

That wasn't totally true, but she didn't dispute the fact. As far as Judith knew, she'd decided James was perfect for her within hours of meeting him. Part of his appeal had been that he wasn't ready to settle down, which worked to give her time to accomplish her own goals. But now? James was in his early thirties and his business was going gangbusters, so it was time to cut back on work and think about their future. She only hoped she could convince him of that. Not wanting to think negatively, she smiled and said, "We're going to have so much fun. You'll see."

"I hope so," Judith said, rolling her eyes. "I'll have a hard enough time getting Paul to back off after this." She started drumming her fingers on the table, thinking. "Relationships just shouldn't be so much work," she finally said.

By the time the check arrived, their plans for the next weekend were set and the conversation switched to a new art gallery opening. The two decided to check it out during the week.

They left the restaurant and strolled down the block, looking at the passersby. It was a beautiful clear night with a light wind, a little on the chilly side for ambling, but Kate thought it was a perfect end to a wonderful dinner.

Neither spoke until they reached the street where the two separated to go in different directions.

"Thanks for agreeing to the trip," Kate said.

Judith smiled. "Hopefully, the weekend will be all you want it to be."

They hugged, added kisses, and said their good-byes.

"I'll let you know the time on Wednesday for the gallery. I'll drive so you won't have to hassle with it, okay?" Judith said over her shoulder.

Kate nodded and hurried away, not wanting to think about the doubts now clouding her mind, most of them centering on one question. Would her plan lead her to the altar?

Judith is right. She frowned. *Relationships shouldn't be this much work.*

Chapter 2

James Morrison braked hard and swore under his breath at the driver in front of him who was paying more attention to his cell phone conversation than to the heavy traffic. He wished he had one of those signs that read, 'DRIVE, DON'T TALK.' The bozo in front of him needed a warning. He was still yakking, with no idea his veering out of his lane had almost caused a pileup.

Unfortunately, clueless drivers and an upcoming traffic snarl weren't James' only concerns.

The entire time his Toyota Sequoia inched along I-275 on his way into the city to pick up Kate, he wondered why it felt as if the world was closing in on him, much like the cars surrounding him.

Face it, Morrison! It doesn't take a genius to understand why.

Kate was excited about their upcoming weekend in Tahoe. Not that he didn't want to go, but he knew what was in store once he got there. She'd push the commitment button again. She wanted marriage. She'd been vocal about it ever since her sister announced her wedding plans.

He should be totally ready for wedded bliss after six years. Yet, the idea of *till death do us part* scared the hell out of him. What if she wasn't 'the one'? The more he thought about it, the more he questioned their relationship.

Unfortunately, Kate was tenacious when chasing a goal. In the past, he'd always gone along with her demands because it was easier than all-out confrontation. He couldn't do that this time. He didn't want to hurt her, but he didn't want marriage either. James hadn't known how to voice his reservations, so he'd taken the coward's way out and backed off, which only made him feel guiltier.

Now he needed to grow a spine.

Despite her bulldog nature, he did love Kate and enjoyed being with her. What wasn't to love? She was gorgeous, bright, supportive, and successful. A woman any man would give his right arm to have standing by his side.

The traffic started flowing again and he sped up. As he drove, his thoughts swirled. The only solution to his predicament, he decided, was to take time this weekend to explain his feelings to Kate. As he wound his way through Golden Gate Park, his grip on the steering wheel tightened. He had to prepare himself for the prospect of letting her go. If he couldn't commit, she deserved the chance to find someone who would. It was only right, he decided, as he headed through the Presidio and eventually took the turnoff to Marina Boulevard.

Once on Kate's street, every square inch of curb space held a car. He drove around the block searching for a parking spot, only to become more edgy and frustrated. The ordeal reminded him of why he left San Francisco and moved south to San Mateo.

After another lap, he finally parked illegally. He jumped out, leaving the car running, stalked to the door, and jabbed the buzzer to Kate's apartment.

"James? Is that you?"

"Yeah, I couldn't find a spot, so can you just come down? I'm in your building's driveway."

"Sure, I'll be right there," shot through the intercom.

~

Kate sighed, wondering why he sounded so grouchy when his client had raved about his designs the day before.

As she walked to meet him, her thoughts drifted back to their last date, right before she left on her buying trip. He hadn't spent the night and was rather distant. Work. That was the problem. He really needed a break.

She turned the corner of the stairwell and spied James through the glass door of her apartment building's lobby, pacing impatiently. When he saw her, he waited until she unlatched the lock, helped her guide the heavy door open, and held it as she stepped through.

They both hopped into the SUV at the same time.

"Traffic's a bitch and there weren't any open spaces," he said, as he put the car in gear and backed out. "God, I hate coming into the city."

His words and annoyed manner had her grasping for patience. *Okay. He hasn't kissed me hello, even though it's been a while since we were last together. Plus, he's complaining about traffic.* Both only strengthened her resolve to get him to relax. In an effort to cheer him up, she began recounting her buying spree back east, happy to note after a couple of blocks he was smiling.

She had him laughing by the time they entered the entrance to the Bay Bridge. Her story ended at the same time he turned into the arena garage. As he drove up the ramp, she eyed him carefully, wondering whether to finalize their plans for the ski trip. No. Not yet. She'd wait until after the game.

After exiting the parked car, Kate took hold of James' hand and pulled him along. "Let's hurry. I don't want to miss the tip-off."

"Kate, slow down," he said, laughing. "We have plenty of time."

"Not if we want to get something to eat before it starts," she said, relieved to see him finally unwind.

"Oh, that's right. It's going to cost me an arm and a leg just to satisfy your junk food craving. Where do you put it all?" he teased. His gaze took a suggestive trip over her body, going up, then down, and back up again.

"Just consider this a cheap date. You won't have to take me out afterward." Oh, how she wished James would be this easygoing all the time.

"Sold."

Once inside, James pulled the tickets out of his pockets and handed her one. "Tell me what you want and I'll get it— you go sit down."

"Two hot dogs with the works, nachos with lots of cheese, and a beer," she rattled off. She looked at him and smiled. "I may want more later, but that should tide me over."

"Got it." He shook his head and returned her smile. "I know you'll eat every bite."

"Of course I will," she said, mirroring his teasing voice.

"I'm a growing girl."

"It's amazing."

"What's amazing?"

"In all the years I've known you, you've never gained an ounce though you eat like a truck driver at times." He turned and walked away, still shaking his head.

James returned with hot dogs, nachos, and beer, and for the next two hours, neither mentioned anything more serious than what the players were doing on the court. The game ended with a victory for her team.

Even the stop-and-go traffic on the way out of the parking garage didn't mar James' good mood. He was definitely relaxed.

On the drive back, he opened up a little more about his completed project and how smoothly his meeting went. By the time they neared her neighborhood, she decided it was silly to be worried, since this James was the man she'd come to love, not the other one who kept distancing himself with work. "We need to firm up plans for the weekend. What time are we leaving on Thursday?"

"I wanted to discuss that with you." James cleared his throat. "I can't leave on Thursday."

"Why not?" Kate eyed him suspiciously. "It's supposed to be a three-day weekend and I thought you were looking forward to skiing on Friday without the crowds. Plus, they're predicting snow." They'd bought their usual season passes together earlier last summer. While the money wasn't a problem for him, it had been a chunk of change for her, which meant careful budgeting. Buying a pass in advance usually paid off, since in the past the two went up often enough to more than break even. But this year, he'd barely used his. "We'll be skiing powder. You haven't been skiing since before Christmas."

In her situation, she couldn't afford to be so lax. Every weekend she didn't go meant wasted money. Some people went on exotic two-week trips where, once it was over, it was over. Snow skiing was her exotic vacation that lasted the entire winter. Still, it bugged her that James kept backing out.

"I know, but something came up with work."

Of course, something came up with work. Doesn't it always? Instead of voicing her first reaction, she countered, "Your project's done, James. You've been working nonstop for months…you need a break."

He sighed and ran a hand through his hair. "The partners are having a meeting Friday morning."

"Can you reschedule?"

"No," he said firmly.

"Why not?" Her gaze narrowed. "You're one of the head honchos." He was a senior partner of Morrison, Morgan, and Stone, an architectural firm located in San Mateo, twenty minutes south of San Francisco.

"It's the only time everyone can meet, and it's important. Besides, I planned to leave right after the meeting. We'll still have Friday afternoon and the rest of the weekend together."

She turned and looked blindly out the passenger window, her thoughts suddenly jumbled. Her plans were going south fast. It would be torture to spend an evening with Paul and Judith as a third wheel, so much so she might decide against going up early. What if Judith and Paul decided to cancel, making it a moot point? On the practical side, she'd already arranged for someone else to cover her at her shop. By keeping to her original plans, she'd knock out another awesome powder day on the slopes—an uncrowded one, at that. But she'd be skiing alone…again.

She glanced back at him and pleaded, "Are you sure you can't leave Thursday night?"

"I'm sure. Let's plan another three-day weekend if it means so much to you."

Fat chance of that happening. By then, he'd be involved in a new project and have another reason to cancel. "You could rearrange your meeting if you wanted," she accused, not backing down this time.

"Quit pushing," he barked.

Kate froze, staring mutely at him. There was no hiding the fact his actions and words had stung.

A deafening silence hung in the air until he sighed. "You've been up there plenty of times by yourself before, so why not now?" he finally asked, his voice and manner softer.

"It's only one night."

"Paul will be there."

James turned onto her street. "So? He's not that bad."

Her jaw dropped a good inch. Easy for him to say when he wasn't on the receiving end of the guy's razor wit. "I'd rather not deal with him alone if I don't have to."

"You should've thought about that before you invited him." When she remained silent, he added, "The house is big enough that you don't have to see him if you don't want to. Just stay in the guesthouse tomorrow night. I'll break away as soon as I can on Friday." Though he was attempting to smooth things over, she noted a bit of tension in his eyes. Frustration came out in his long sigh. "I'm looking forward to getting away for the weekend."

Her hurt slowly dissipated. He was trying, which helped. "Okay," she said, nodding. "I guess I can head up alone." She'd done so many times. Besides, if it did snow, she'd regret missing the opportunity to make first tracks down the mountain in fresh powder, something diehard skiers like her lived for. And she *had* vowed to make friends with Paul. With Judith there, it would be easier.

"Can we cook in Friday night and go out Saturday?" James slowed the car. "This way we can be more flexible. The restaurants are always so crowded."

"Sure. I'll hit the store after skiing. What time do you think you'll be there?"

"The meeting should be over by ten," he said, pulling into her apartment driveway, leaving the motor running. "So let's plan on two...three at the latest, depending on traffic."

"Okay, we're on." Kate heaved a relieved sigh, happy he was cooperating with at least part of her plans. But the mood only lasted until it became obvious he meant to drop her off and not spend the night. She sent him a questioning look.

"Cut me a break here, will you? I have an early appointment with a new client in the morning, and I still have about three hours of work left before I can meet with him."

Yep, he was definitely backing off. Kate now recognized the signals. He *was* using work to distance himself.

He turned to stare out the window, avoiding her gaze, and

said, "I'll give you a call."

She grabbed the handle, shoved the door open, and glanced back at him.

He didn't move.

"Sure, no problem," she choked out. She hurried out of the car and headed into her building as fast as her feet would carry her before she lost it and told him where he could stuff his demanding workload.

"Damn the man!" she thought, brushing a tear away and feeling him slip away even more.

~

The next evening, Kate watched from the lobby's glass door of her apartment building for Judith. When her dark green Murano pulled to a stop, double-parking beside another car, she ran and jumped inside.

"Right on time, I see," Judith said, letting her foot off the brake.

"Thanks for driving." She reached for her seatbelt.

"No problem."

Kate grimaced as she fastened the buckle, remembering her news. "Oh, by the way, James isn't going up until Friday afternoon, so I'm on my own tomorrow."

"That's a drag." She flashed her a sympathetic look. "Sorry about that. Are you sure you still want to go?"

"Of course." Smiling, and trying to act like it was no big deal, she shrugged. "There's no reason not to. He's the one with the meeting he can't get out of."

Judith nodded and refocused on traffic. A few blocks later, she glanced at Kate. "Why not drive up with us, then?"

"It's no biggie." Kate shook her head. "I can make the trip alone." She crossed her fingers, hoping Judith would accept her at her word. Sharing a two-thousand-square-foot house was one thing, but being stuck with Paul on a long car trip was another matter entirely, one she had every intention of avoiding. Even her endurance had limits.

"No," Judith said, tossing the idea away with the wave of her hand. "That's impractical, and a waste of gasoline when we're all going to the same place." She offered a satisfied smile. "This way you can ride back with James and having you along will keep things light with Paul. So it's a win-win."

Kate gritted her teeth and forced out a smile, silently searching for a way out. She stared, unseeing, out the window, as the Nissan wound through the streets of San Francisco in the direction of the downtown art gallery. "I doubt he'll want to include me," she finally said, using the only excuse that came to her.

"Let me worry about him." She turned into the lot provided for the gallery, then parked.

"I don't want to mess up his plans."

Judith switched off the ignition. "Paul lives right down the street from you, and we're planning to leave around the same time. So I don't see a problem." She emerged from the car and, holding the door open, bent back inside. "Weren't you the one who said we should all learn to get along?"

Kate hopped out of the car, and slammed the door. "I know what I said, but I really don't want to ride with him."

"What better opportunity to practice?" She hit the keyless lock. "Unless you're not serious about being friends with Paul."

She followed Judith to the entrance, as the noose around her neck tightened.

"So, we're in agreement, right?" With eyebrows raised, Judith opened the outer glass door and waited for her to go ahead before stepping inside.

"You might want to wait until he agrees before you set it in stone."

"I'm sure he'll be reasonable." She headed toward the first grouping of pictures.

Kate sighed heavily and nodded. Her plans just kept going from bad to worse. At least the skiing promised to be good on Friday. Fresh powder only occurred a couple of times a year in the Sierras. Most of the time, skiers called the hard pack 'Sierra cement.' "The snow better be worth it," she grumbled.

"And you won't throw out any sarcastic comments?" Judith said, glancing back at her.

"Of course not, but make sure he doesn't either." Kate hurried to catch up to her.

"I'll deal with Paul, you just deal with Kate. I mean it—be

nice. This is *your* weekend, remember."

"Judith, I'm always nice." *He was the one with the problem.*

"Ha! I've seen you in action, so cut the crap." Judith's brow shot up and she gave her the look. The same look mothers always saved for those special occasions when they knew they'd caught their naughty kids in the act. "I'm expecting you both to get along with each other."

"Okay," Kate said sheepishly, unable to stop the guilt from seeping out in her expression. Judith knew her too well. "We'll become the best of buddies."

"Good. Now that it's finally settled, let's enjoy the show. Come on. We're causing a scene." Judith grabbed Kate's hand and pulled her to the next exhibit.

~

"You what?" Paul shouted into the phone late Wednesday night. *How could she?*

"I told Kate she could ride with us to Tahoe," she repeated. Unfortunately, before hitting a bulls-eye with that news, she'd fired an earlier round—this one reiterating they were only going as friends.

Nothing new, there! It was all too much. "Why would you promise something like that without talking to me first? Especially when you know she irritates the hell out of me?"

"It's only a ride," she stated in an exasperated tone. "You know it's only for a couple of hours."

Which was a couple of hours too many for his liking when he'd planned to share the time with Judith. Alone. Paul rubbed his neck and sighed, thankful she hadn't canceled outright—his first thought upon answering her call.

For as long as he'd known her, Judith kept up a wall around her heart and never let him get too close, even going so far as to define their relationship as *friendship*. To him, she was more than a friend—always had been—from the moment ten-year-old Paul first caught a glimpse of the shy girl on his neighborhood swim team. He'd been smitten ever since.

Like Judith, Paul had been shy, much too shy to approach her, but he never tired of just being around her during those many summers of daily swim practice. He watched as she matured over that decade, and was reminded of a butterfly emerging from a cocoon. Like all beautiful butterflies, she had a fragility about her, a fragility that brought out his protective side. Quiet and introverted, she rarely spoke unless she felt totally comfortable in the situation.

That aspect never changed even after he came out of his shell in high school. Yet, when he observed her at that point, he noticed something new. She missed nothing in her world; she just chose not to engage in it. This intrigued him, and over time she became a challenge. He wanted to be the one to break through the thin barrier she presented to the world, and he wanted her to love him, as he'd always loved her.

During most of his teens, Judith had no clue he even existed. Despite that, she'd always been close to him, in his mind and heart, and for too many years Paul had kept his feelings secret.

"I don't get it," she asked, yanking him back to the present. "What is it with you two?"

"Nothing, I just don't like her."

"Why? She's never done anything to you to deserve such treatment and, according to Kate, you're always on her case. I've never understood why."

"She's always chasing after James, and never picks up on the truth. It's not going to happen with him."

"But, Paul, that's her business—it's between her and James."

"I know. It just makes me mad to watch."

"Aren't you being judgmental?"

"Maybe, but it's how I see it." A slight edge of guilt slipped into his consciousness and he couldn't ignore the niggling voice that told him she had a point. What was worse, his opinionated apple didn't fall far from the tree. But he didn't want to think about that.

"Well, you're both acting like children. It's very immature and tiring to deal with. Now promise me she can go with us and you'll be nice to her."

"God, why do I let you talk me into these things?" he asked, realizing he was fighting a losing battle.

Paul could hear the smile in her voice as she said, "Because you're a really nice guy underneath all that sarcasm and wit."

"Yeah?" The edges of his lips curled as he let out a long, slow breath. "Well, don't let anyone in on the secret. It'll spoil the effect." Knowing he'd lost, he surrendered good-naturedly. "Okay, tell her to be ready by two. I'll pick you up fifteen minutes later. I want to get out of the city before traffic hits. I'll be in my office at five thirty and working up until then to get in a full day."

"Thanks. I knew I could count on you."

Paul said good-bye and hung up, not at all happy about the turn of events. Being in love with that particular woman sucked at times. Judith expected people to be better than they were, it was something he'd always admired about her. She demanded his best and he usually rose to meet those expectations. He couldn't stomach the idea of disappointing her and truly appreciated being considered worthy of her esteem. But the fact that he now had to endure an extended car ride with Kate along because she required it of him, chafed.

At least she hadn't canceled. Paul chose to focus on the one bright spot in this whole mess, rather than dwell on her insistence of their maintaining a friendly relationship.

He sighed, fought to push the memories aside, and grabbed the remote. The TV burst to life, as his thoughts strayed back to the woman he'd spent a lifetime loving, rather than on the show in front of him.

In college, Paul decided to make his feelings known and steadfastly pursued Judith. Over time, their friendship grew and he came to love the real Judith, not just the idea of her in his mind. Yet, she continually resisted his every attempt at intimacy, saying she loved him as a friend. At that point, he'd backed off and dated others. Hell, he had to because Judith expected it of him. But no one really interested him enough to change his mind about her, especially since she'd never shown interest in dating anyone and always made time for him.

All this time he'd respected her wishes, figuring she just wasn't ready for a committed relationship. He could wait a little longer. Why give up now when she'd finally relocated to the city? Judith was the one who made the comment about settling down and having kids, even warming to the idea of a stronger relationship...he had simply followed up on it. But he realized too late he'd moved too fast. He should have held off a bit before mentioning marriage.

He prayed this weekend would bring him closer to his goal of having Judith realize they were meant to be more than friends.

The only damper was spending time with Kate. Paul's thoughts then shifted to the irritating woman. He snorted! How in the world had he gotten himself into this mess? He needed a drink.

"God help me, I need the whole damned bottle to deal with her," he muttered. Why did relationships have to be so difficult?

He padded to the kitchen to pour himself a glass of wine and wondered why his aversion to the woman was so intense. She always rubbed him the wrong way, like sandpaper over an open blister, right from the first moment he met her. He usually ignored people like that, but Paul found he could never ignore Kate, especially when he saw her with James. At those times, he always had a sarcastic comment for her, which was also something Judith gave him a hard time about.

He sighed and took a hefty swig of wine, working to drown his misery. Nothing about the weekend was going as expected. He grabbed the bottle, retraced his steps to the living room, and plopped onto the sofa.

His gaze circled the living room, a room that cost a month's salary to redo after he'd hired a decorator in hopes of impressing the woman he loved…and she hadn't even seen it yet.

He shot back another large mouthful of Murphy Goode without tasting the unusual nuances in his favorite chardonnay. His expensive surroundings felt empty without someone to share it with.

Deciding to view Judith's news as a small setback, he dismissed all negative thoughts from his mind and reached for the latest business prospectus he'd been reading. His attention drifted to it while the television blared in the background—a filler noise keeping him company.

Chapter 3

Paul rang Kate's buzzer promptly at one fifty-five the next afternoon.

Her voice shot through the intercom. "I'll be right down."

"Hurry," he replied. "I'm ready to get on the road and we still need to pick up Judith."

"You're five minutes early, so cool it, bucko."

He chuckled and bantered back to the box, "Judith said you were supposed to be nice to me."

Moments later, she came into view through the glass door. His grin widened to see such a short dynamo bogged down with skis, poles, and boots, along with an overnight bag slung over her shoulder that kept hitting her hip as she walked.

He wanted to rush to help, remembering the feel his mother's flick on his ear when he didn't jump fast enough to be courteous to a woman in need. Unfortunately, he was stuck on the other side of the locked door.

She had on snug jeans and a tight sweater that hugged her compact body underneath an open ski parka. The bulky jacket did little to hide her curves. Curves in all the right places that any male who wasn't dead couldn't fail to notice. And he noticed. He'd always thought she was put together well.

Kate made it to the entrance, dropped the boots, and leaned the skis up against the wall. Now having a free hand to open the heavy door, she pulled it at the same time Paul pushed, which almost knocked her down.

Oops, he thought, letting go and stepping back, only to realize the doorknob she held almost jerked out of her hand as the door started to slam shut.

"Sorry, I was trying to help," he said, halting it in the nick of time with his foot.

"Wait, take these." Kate pushed the door open wider and held it with that sexy tush, then reached in for her skis and handed them to him, following suit with the boots.

Carrying them with ease, Paul headed toward his car. He opened the trunk, dropped the boots inside, then turned and undid the straps to the ski rack. Kate walked up beside him as he lifted the skis to the top of the car, fastening them into place along with her poles.

Paul glanced down and, seeing the bag she still held, grabbed it and placed it next to the boots.

He closed the lid. "Is that it?"

She nodded.

"Let's get this show on the road. We're burning daylight." He moved to open the passenger door and bowed. "Your chariot awaits, my lady."

"Thanks, but don't you think you're overdoing it a bit?" She took off her jacket, laid it in the backseat, then slipped into the car.

"Just following orders," Paul said, before closing her door and running around to the driver's side. Seconds later, the BMW shot off into traffic.

"I didn't know you could afford such a sleek car." Kate's eyebrows rose as she glanced around at the car's interior. "Still smells new."

"I've had it a few months," Paul murmured, sensing her first comment was somehow meant as a put-down, but refusing to take it as one. He shrugged. "It gets me where I want to go."

"All cars do that, but one like this does it in style." Her tone held a touch of admiration and she ran a hand along the leather. "Who knew you had it in you?" She sat back, and said under her breath but loud enough for him to hear, "This might not be so bad. At least the ride'll be smooth."

Rather than annoy him, as it once would have, her comment only pleased him. He couldn't figure out why, so he stayed silent, mentally agreeing with her. *This may not be so bad. She likes my car.* He slowed for a red light as his phone beeped with an incoming text. After coming to a complete stop, he checked to see if it was important.

"It's a message from Judith," he said, glancing at Kate. He brought up the text screen and read the message. "There's a problem with one of her projects and she's stuck at the work site."

"You're kidding, right?"

He shook his head and handed her the phone. "I wish I was." The light changed, and he drove until he spotted a place to park while she read the message.

Her face scrunched up in dismay. "Damn. What do we do now?"

He sighed. "Let me call her and see what's up."

Judith answered right away and said, "I'm really sorry."

"No problem. We can wait," he said, glancing at Kate, who nodded. "What time do you think you'll be done?"

"This glitch is snowballing and I may end up working the weekend."

"The whole weekend?"

"At this point, I can't say." She hesitated. "I know you were looking forward to skiing. No sense spoiling your plans for tomorrow. If I can break away, I will, but for now, I have no choice but to take care of business. Tell Kate I'm sorry."

"Don't worry about it. We understand," he said, as disappointment welled up inside him. Her news didn't surprise him. Hadn't he expected something like this all along? If he waited until tomorrow, she'd probably find another excuse and the excuses were starting to get to him. He had no idea what she was afraid of, but until she was ready to face her demons, there was nothing he could do to change things. Sometimes the futility of his situation got to him. They said their good-byes amidst more of her apologies. He hung up with thoughts about turning around and canceling the weekend. But he'd already planned it and probably wouldn't see Judith for days, judging from her phone conversation. At least if he were skiing, he'd be doing something that would take his mind off his anger at Judith, even if it meant spending time with Kate.

"Well?" Kate asked. "What's going on?"

Paul filled her in on his conversation with Judith, and ended with, "I'm still heading up to Tahoe. You're welcome to come along, but I'll understand if you'd rather not."

"I'm here now and tomorrow does promise to be a decent day." She sighed and offered a smile. "If you're willing to take me, I'm willing to keep going."

He nodded and pulled away from the curb, making a U-turn.

Neither spoke as they drove out of the city.

Paul kept his focus on the road, but every once in a while he'd glance at Kate. She ignored him, had dragged out her smartphone, in fact. On his last peek, she was absorbed in playing a game, at which point he turned on the radio.

Twenty minutes later, Kate sighed heavily and stuck her phone back in her pocket. "Look, I hate our not talking."

Paul chanced a brief glance. "What do you mean?"

"I mean, are we going to just sit here for the next three hours and not say anything?" She crossed her arms. "Shouldn't we at least attempt to amuse ourselves with something besides listening to music or playing Angry Birds?"

His eyebrows shot up. "Sounds interesting." He shrugged. "What'd you have in mind?"

"Road games."

"Road games?"

"Yeah, you know." She nodded. "Like Truth or Dare."

"Dream on," he said in a grunt of disapproval.

Kate grinned. "Okay, not into telling secrets? Then what about Twenty Questions?"

When he looked over at her, his gaze narrowing, she snorted. "What? You've never played Twenty Questions when you went on road trips while growing up?"

Smiling, he shook his head.

"You're kidding?"

"We never took any road trips," he explained, his smile widening. "We always flew."

"Really?" Her eyes grew rounder. "I never knew that."

His hand went to his chest like he was clutching his heart. "You mean there's something you don't know about James' childhood?"

"The subject never came up." She turned to regard the scenery out the passenger window, and tried to act as if his revelation hadn't bothered her.

But he could tell it had.

Finally, she faced him again. "I don't know. Somehow, it seems un-American to never take road trips."

"Why?" He gave her a curious stare. "Because my parents weren't the type to drive to the Grand Canyon?"

She cleared her throat. "I didn't mean that as an insult." Averting her gaze, she brushed a strand of hair behind her ear.

He chuckled, enjoying her discomfort as well as the blush creeping across her cheeks. "I'm amused, not insulted."

"Oh?" She glanced back at him with questioning eyes.

"Yeah! You're assuming I missed out on something."

"No, I'm not," she denied too quickly, shaking her head. "I know you had a privileged childhood." Her gaze shifted to the window again.

"Then why is flying on vacations un-American?" He eyed her briefly before letting his attention go back to the road. "Admit it. You think I missed something. I hear it in your voice."

"Not really." She sighed. "It's just that I didn't think there was anyone out there who didn't drive somewhere on trips." She broke off. After a long pause, she nodded. "Okay, maybe I do feel you lost out. Some of my best experiences with my family were on road trips." She uncrossed her legs and stretched them out. "Maybe it's a midwestern thing. I mean, there are several cities within a five-hour drive from Chicago. My sister and I especially loved long weekends—or three-day adventures, as my dad called them."

"Let me assure you," he said with a self-satisfied smile, "that despite being a Californian whose dad rarely took long weekends, I don't feel I missed out on anything. James and I had a damn good upbringing."

"Of course you did."

"My parents are great."

"I didn't mean to suggest otherwise." She exhaled a long breath. "Maybe I should just keep my mouth shut and stick to playing Angry Birds. I promised Judith I'd be nice and I can't do that if you're going to find fault with everything I say."

"I'm not finding fault."

"Yes, you are. If you didn't like my suggestion about

playing games, you only had to say so."

"Is that what we're doing, Kate? Playing games?" The words just popped out of his mouth. He wished he could take them back when he looked over and saw her stunned face.

Eventually, the shock wore off, but she still didn't respond right away. Instead, she took her time, clearly weighing her answer. Finally, her gaze pierced his and she said, with a voice full of challenge, "I don't know, Paul. Are we?"

His bark of laughter filled the air. "Okay, the ice is broken. Now you can tell me about your *game*," he parried back

"Oh, shut up." She crossed her arms and glared out the window. "I've changed my mind. I'm not playing any games with you."

Paul looked over and watched her for a moment. He always thought of her as pushy and obnoxious, never silently subdued like now. She was kind of cute when she stewed.

Figuring he'd gone a little too far, he decided to strive for amicability. "What I mean is, tell me about Twenty Questions." He *had* promised Judith to behave.

The silence was deafening as she completely ignored him.

Long minutes went by before he tried again. "Come on, it just slipped out. I'm trying here, but you never make it easy."

Her entire body stiffened and color infused her face. "Oh, now I've heard everything," she huffed. Her tightened jaw jutted out. "So tell me! Why do I make it so hard?"

"God, you tempt me," Paul replied, and shook his head, totally unprepared for the thoughts streaking through his brain that allowed the comment to just slip out. Damn his quick, twisted mind. How in the hell could he even think of saying that to someone other than Judith? The fact that it was Kate was a double whammy. Even though her words had taken him by surprise, he found he couldn't let them go. "And here I promised to mind my manners."

He caught the exact moment realization hit. Her face went from blushing pink to beet red. She moved to stare out the window, without saying another word.

"So I guess Twenty Questions is out?" Paul asked a little while later, risking another quick glance at her. He grinned, holding on to a chuckle. She'd crossed her arms and legs again, closing up like a hedgehog with quills, steadfastly refusing to acknowledge him any further.

Laughing at this point wouldn't be wise. He resisted the urge to toss out a snide comment, determined to honor his word. At the same time, he couldn't help feeling a twinge of satisfaction that, despite her barbed exterior, he was getting under her skin, digging his way in as easily as an earthworm plows through moist dirt. Why that gave him so much enjoyment, he had no idea. The thought stopped him cold and he threw her another sideways glance. Since when had he started thinking of sparring with Kate Winters as entertaining?

~

As Kate fumed, she wished Paul could fall into one of the potholes in the road and be swallowed up. Of course, her wish included him leaving his car behind so she could drive it the rest of the way.

This ride wasn't going the way she'd planned. *At all!* Her reaction, not his words, was the real problem. For some idiotic reason, their limited conversation had been fun in an invigorating, almost naughty fashion, which totally threw her off-kilter. Anger was the only way to regain even a little bit of balance. He was her enemy, not someone to find exciting. She needed to remember that for the rest of the trip. She reached for her cell phone and retrieved the app for Spider Solitaire, deciding it best to ignore him from here on out.

"I need a diversion." Paul's voice broke into her thoughts a half hour later.

When she spared him a brief glance, he smiled. "Tell me about Twenty Questions."

She gave a disbelieving snort, ignoring the butterfly wings flapping inside her tummy at his teasing voice. "Like I'm going to touch that remark?" His silly expression wasn't about to lure her in either.

"Touché! You've won round one." His grin spread, drawing her focus like an invisible force. It was James' smile, but so much more infectious. "Come on," he pleaded. "Tell me and we'll play." His eyebrows rose up and down several times.

Kate couldn't withhold her laughter any longer, completely

destroying her resolve of not engaging. She shouldn't want to respond, but why deny herself when he looked so innocent, yet full of mischief.

So with her own gleam and innocent smile forming, she shot back, "Okay, but let me warn you, I'm not someone who's easy to take down. Don't forget, I've been dodging your verbal blows for years."

"You always got in a few good punches, if my memory is correct," he countered, still grinning like an idiot.

"You left me no choice." Her smile died, as memories of all his jokes came back—one by one—allowing her good sense to return. Looking at him like this, she couldn't imagine he was the same man who'd hurled so many insults her way. She couldn't help asking, "Why do you hate me so much?"

He stiffened and his glance went from her to the road and back again. He definitely hadn't expected the question, considering the expression that settled over his features. Remaining silent, he refocused on driving, as if he couldn't find the words to answer her question. A drawn-out moment passed before he said quietly, "I don't hate you."

Confused, Kate shook her head. "Then what have I ever done to you to deserve such venom?" she blurted out, unable to halt the words because she really wanted to know.

With all of her defenses lowered, she couldn't erase the hurt from her voice or keep pain from showing on her face.

Unfortunately, Paul chose that moment to glance over. When he swore under his breath and resumed staring at the road ahead, she groaned inwardly, dying to disappear. Why had she opened her mouth? She'd probably never hear the end of this.

He drove for several miles before offering in a contrite voice, one that was totally devoid of his usual mocking tone, "I don't know."

Still shaken from her initial question, she frowned. His reply, given so humbly, only irritated her. "That's not an answer, that's a cop-out."

"No, it's not," he shot back defensively. "I really have no idea."

The silence in the car became deafening once again, until

she waved a hand. "Forget it. I don't know why I asked." Her words came out in a rush. "It's not as if anything's going to change," Kate said, wanting the subject dropped.

More silence followed.

"Before you continue to make me feel worse," he said in a lower, more penitent voice a moment later. "I want you to know I never thought about the effect of my words before. It's not pleasant now to realize they may have hurt you, and for what it's worth, I'm sorry."

Mollified a little by his apology, she nodded, wishing now more than ever she'd kept her mouth shut. An annoying Paul was someone she could handle. A contrite Paul was someone she'd never seen before. His sincere regret played havoc on her senses.

"Look," he said, a few miles further down the road. "Since we're being honest here, I have to say I think you take too much shit from my brother. You're better than that."

Her jaw dropped open in disbelief. He was as bad as she in his pursuit of Judith. Since she had already said more than enough, she kept the words to herself, unwilling to open Pandora's box.

For endless miles, the only sound came from the low hum of the radio.

"The music's starting to get on my nerves," Paul said, and turned off the radio after they'd driven for almost an hour without a word between them. They were on the outskirts of Sacramento, headed into the mountains. "I just made up my own version of Twenty Questions. I ask the questions and you answer. Then you get a turn."

"That sounds a lot like Truth or Dare." Crossing her arms, Kate had no intention of answering any more of his questions. "I think we've had enough truth for one afternoon and I'm not about to dare you to do anything. I recognize a worthy adversary when I see one."

"Come on. What have you got to lose?" he countered, grinning. "I can't be mean, I promised Judith—and neither can you."

He seemed so earnest in his request…and that engaging smile, now aimed at her, was too hard to ignore. Encouraging him even the least little bit was surely asking for trouble, but she couldn't resist. Not when sincerity spilled out of that sexy blue gaze, so similar to James', yet strangely, nothing like his.

Besides, he was right about one thing. It would help with boredom. "Okay," she said, and nodded.

His grin expanded, and the mischievous glint in his eyes had her returning the smile. Even though she was a risk-taker, she might regret her decision. Those crinkles around his eyes that transformed his face, giving him a devilish appearance, sucked her right in to agreeing to the game. She had to admit, the guy had an intriguing side she never expected. Time for a little defense, she thought. "I have the right to refuse to answer."

"Same here. Let's see…" He broke off, clearly warming to the idea. "We should make some ground rules so that it's a fair contest."

"Okay. What'd you have in mind?" Kate eased back into the seat.

"We each get to ask a question until we stump each other. Then the other person has the floor, so to speak. If you don't want to answer, it's your turn to ask. How's that?"

"That's silly!" She rolled her eyes. "We'll just keep passing the questions back and forth because neither one of us will answer."

"Hmm, you're right," he agreed, and after taking a few minutes to think, he added, "Okay, I got it. The winner is the person who answers the most questions."

"Now you're being ridiculous." Kate smirked. "I'm sorry, but you really are pathetic when it comes to games." Her words earned another laugh out of him. She joined in. "I'm beginning to like the way your mind works, Morrison, and that's not a good thing. We're much better off as enemies, so let's just stay that way."

"Oh, come on. Lighten up. If you don't like my rules, let's see if you can do better."

She thought for a few minutes. "Okay, how about this. Any question asked is fair game. We each keep asking until the other person refuses to answer. If that happens, then whoever asked the question has to answer the other person's next question honestly and vice versa without refusing. Does that sound fair?"

"Sounds like a good way to kill the next hour or so," he said, and shot her another grin. "Okay, fire away."

Kate laughed. "Oh no, you don't, you started it. You ask first."

"Ah! You're on to me. I should've known you'd see through my ploy to get you at a disadvantage," he teased. "Let's see. I've got to think of a question to ask that won't be a risk in case you don't want to answer. Give me a minute, this is going to require some thought." After much contemplation, he smiled. "Okay, I've got it. I'll stay on easy stuff for a while. What's your favorite color?"

She grinned. "This I can handle. Blue."

"Favorite singing group or vocalist?"

"Cher!"

"You're joking, right?" he snorted, then chuckled at her indignant look.

"No. I told you, Cher. And stop laughing at my answer," she shot back, unable to hold on to her giggle. "I saw her in Vegas, and she puts on a hell of a show."

"I think I can learn more about you than I thought from these innocuous questions."

Sobering, she straightened. "This is strictly to pass time, bucko—not to get to know each other."

"Pipe down, I know what we're doing." He paused a second. "Okay, favorite food?"

"Pasta."

"Favorite animal?"

"Cats. I love cats."

"Favorite moment in time?"

"Too easy! Christmas the year after I graduated from college."

"Why?"

"That's when James told me he loved me," she blurted before realizing that her words alluded to something she didn't necessarily want him to know about her. She wished she could take them back, especially after glimpsing his face scrunch up in condemnation. "You obviously don't approve. So tell me why."

"I'm still asking the questions here," he said in a jovial manner, as if trying to move things back to smoother ground. His next words belied this. "Do you still think he loves you?"

Pain ripped through her when she thought about his question. *Question of the year.* If she knew the answer, she'd be one happy person. She shook her head. "I'm not answering. Now it's my turn. Why?"

"Why what?"

"Why don't you approve and why do you want to know if I think he still loves me? For your information, you agreed to the rules, so you need to reply honestly."

"That's two questions."

"Okay, answer the second one. Why do you want to know?"

Paul was silent for a moment, then shrugged. "Okay, since you want the truth, here goes. I'm just curious how you could think he loves you when he can't commit."

The same question had been going through her mind too often lately. The brutal veracity of his words suddenly struck her with full force. How much longer could she wait?

She answered, even though it wasn't her turn, as honestly as she could. "He loves me. He says he's not ready for commitment. I can't shut off how I feel, so I have no choice but to wait till he is." Having said too much and not wanting to think about her relationship with James, she quickly changed gears. "But since I'm still asking the questions, and we're being honest, answer me this. What about you and Judith?"

"What about us?" he queried, moving his attention back to the road.

"Do you think she loves you?"

"Yes."

"But you guys have been together almost as long as James and I, so what's the difference?"

"None. I guess." He glanced over at her, and a sheepish smile followed his words.

Her eyebrows rose.

"Okay, I get it. She's no more ready for commitment than James."

"Doesn't it hurt to know she's not still ready?" Judith loved Paul just like James loved her. Still, it amazed her that he could talk about it so calmly.

"Yeah, it hurts like hell," Paul blurted out. "But I'm in your boat. I've always loved her, from the first moment I saw her when I was ten years old. I can't just turn it off either."

With his outburst, the game came to a natural end. Neither spoke. They'd divulged personal information to each other, and Kate surmised he was just as uneasy with those revelations as she. It was like each had been talking to a stranger and could be more honest because he or she would never see that person again. Only this wasn't the case.

When they were close to the turnoff, Paul glanced her way. "Are you hungry?"

"No, I had a big lunch," Kate said distractedly, keeping her gaze on the pine trees.

"We're making pretty good time," he said. "We should be in Tahoe City in less than an hour." He added, in an obvious attempt at keeping the conversation alive, "You know they're predicting snow for tomorrow and the skiing should be great."

"I know. I can't wait," she answered, only too happy to reciprocate, glad to have something in common to talk about that didn't focus on either her or James. "Saturday should be an awesome day too—except for the lines. But if we get up early and get to the slopes right at opening time, we can get a few good runs on fresh powder before the masses invade."

"Hey, I'm all for fresh tracks down the mountain," he agreed. "I'll be ready. So will James, but somehow I doubt Judith'll will make it now. Especially since she's not much of a skier," Paul said. "Even though she said it was important to you, I'm surprised she agreed to it, considering she was so clear about us just being friends."

"Yeah," Kate spoke up. "I'm beginning to wish I'd never planned anything."

"Why?" Curiosity filled his eyes.

With nothing to lose, she decided to answer honestly. This was Paul, she reminded herself, who thought she was the lowest form on earth, so what difference would it make if he knew? "I was hoping a weekend away with James would help.

But I can't help thinking, if he's not ready to commit after so many years, I'm only delaying the inevitable." She smiled, then added, "Who knows, maybe he'll see the light this weekend!"

At Paul's raised eyebrows, she laughed. "You never know. Let's talk about something else. I'm tired of obsessing over James' lack of commitment."

"You're right," Paul agreed, shrugging. "Dwelling on my relationship won't change things."

For the last leg of the journey, they talked about their jobs and how much energy both put into them. Kate found they had common ground, which led to other areas. Soon both were laughing and joking about how compulsive each was. He ran several times a week to stay in shape and she took Zumba classes for the same reasons. They both realized they liked finding good restaurants, but Paul preferred Italian to her Chinese obsession.

By the time they veered off the winding main road and slowed as they neared the house, the two had come to a truce of sorts.

Kate glanced at him after he'd stopped the car and turned off the motor in the driveway. While he appeared to mull over his thoughts, she was stunned at how comfortable it felt to sit next to him.

"Look," he said a moment later. "I know we may never be BFFs, but can we at least agree to get along while we're here together?"

"I can manage it, if you can." His suggestion warmed her insides. More than it should have.

"Good, because I hate being alone. What do you say to going out to dinner tonight, since we're both here and single?"

"Okay." And because he had taken the first step, she offered, "I guess we can ski together, too, since you'll be giving me a ride tomorrow." Suddenly not sure, she searched his face to see his reaction. "You are going to, aren't you?"

"Yeah, I figured that was included in the deal when Judith recruited me. You want to shake on it?" Paul said at the same time he stuck out his right hand.

"Sure." When her hand disappeared inside his bigger one, warmth immediately engulfed her fingers, spreading all the way to her core. She ignored the tug of attraction she felt after spying his smile, a smile that reached those crinkling baby blues. Not wanting to dwell on the way his touch or his affable, teasing smile affected her in a dangerous way, she gave her head a slight, sobering shake. She was in love with James, and had no business finding his brother attractive. "Also, after skiing can you drop me off at the store to stock up on food?"

"Why don't we do that tonight after dinner?"

"Sounds like a plan." Despite her mind's warning, she gave in to the impulse and flashed her own smile, mirroring him. His grin, aimed exclusively at her, was too engaging to ignore for long. "We should easily survive the next twenty-four hours without killing each other."

~

Grunting, Paul got out of the car, then ran around and held her door open while she got out. He then turned to the task of unloading, with his thoughts on Kate and why all of a sudden he found her attractive. He couldn't erase the image of her just after they shook on their agreement. Nor could he ignore the result of her touch. He'd definitely felt a jolt, which had knotted his insides. When she smiled, her entire face lit up, reminding him of a burst of sunshine peeking out from behind a cloud on a rainy day.

Damn, now he was thinking like some kind of lovesick poet, he thought, as Kate came up to stand beside him. He handed her the keys. "Why don't you go unlock the door and hit the light switches?"

He shouldn't be affected. He snorted. Of course, he wasn't affected. His heart belonged to Judith. He might find Kate attractive, but he could deal with it. He would certainly never act on it.

Despite his mental pep talk, he sighed, not completely agreeing with Kate's last comment. "I'll unload, get the water on, and turn up the heat." The next twenty-four hours might be harder to survive than he imagined. Mainly because he was starting to like her.

"Okay." Kate nodded, paying rapt attention to the keys in her hand. "By the way, I'm staying in the guesthouse."

Something in her movements caught his attention and he

eyed her closely. The woman was actually nervous. He grinned. In a heartbeat, his amusement increased, while his trepidation at finding her attractive diminished. "No problem. I'll take the master with the wood-burning fireplace. I like real fires. The gas fireplace in the living room just doesn't cut it for me."

"Sounds good."

"Was it something I said?" he teased, chuckling.

"What do you mean?"

Despite her chin lifting a good two inches, she still wouldn't meet his gaze, which meant only one thing.

"I don't know." He shrugged. "You seem a little uneasy. You're not afraid to be alone with me, are you?"

"No way!" She stiffened, finally chanced a glance his way, and offered a nervous half laugh. "Why would you think that?"

Loaded down with bags and boots, he pierced her stare with a knowing look and mocked, "I can't imagine what has given me the impression."

"You give yourself too much credit, Morrison," she said huffily, before storming up the walk to unlock the door. "I'm not afraid of you."

Paul followed in her footsteps, still grinning. "Whatever you say, Kate."

On the stoop, he crowded her a bit, just to gauge her reaction and to prove his point. When she bristled, he took pity on her and stepped back, giving her plenty of room to open the door.

Once inside the main house, Kate turned on lights as she went, heading to the door that led to the guesthouse, which consisted of a separate bedroom and bath, complete with a couple of chairs and a television. The two rooms were only accessible from the deck outside through a connecting covered walkway. The guesthouse added the final leg of the U to the main house that had originally started out as L-shaped. Along the center of the U, a wall of glass doors provided a spectacular view of Lake Tahoe. A huge outdoor deck, about five feet lower than the house and sporting a hot tub in one corner, wrapped around the back half of the house and guesthouse.

Paul dropped Kate's boots and her bag in the middle of

the living room, placed her coat on top of the pile, and then went back for the skis.

Now loaded down again, he passed the patio door on his way to the mudroom and caught a glimpse of Kate unlocking the guesthouse. Leaving it open, she walked toward the living room to retrieve her things.

He flipped on the light in the mudroom, adjacent the two-car garage where all the main switches were housed. Once divested of his load, he focused on turning on the heat and the water.

While he fiddled with the dials, she yelled, "I think I'll go and take a rest, maybe shower and stuff. What time do you want to go to dinner?"

Paul glanced at his watch, ignoring the stab of disappointment at realizing she was disappearing so quickly. He should be relieved, not disappointed. "It's almost six now. How about seven thirty," he shouted back, and added, "The water should be hot enough for your shower in about ten minutes. The heat'll take a couple of hours to be comfortable, but it will feel warm coming out of the vent."

Kate's thanks rang in the air when he exited the utility room. With everything turned on, he made his way back to the living room to pick up his bag and headed for the master bedroom. He had plenty to keep him busy.

First on his list? Bring in wood to fill the bin and lay a fire for later tonight.

As he worked, his thoughts shifted to Kate. Maybe he could talk her into joining him in the hot tub, but the minute the thought was out, he discarded it. Not a good idea to get too chummy.

Remnants of their earlier conversation floated back, and he remembered her hurt look, so totally different from what he'd expected. She'd always been as bold as brass and twice as ballsy, pushing her way through and chasing after James like she did. Nothing had ever seemed to faze her. He didn't like the feeling of knowing his humor had made her feel bad. Hell, she always returned his taunts and they were so cutting, he just assumed his words were ignored. Verbal jabs, thrown back and forth, had been the habit between them for too many years to count, so it would be hard not to want to lob a few. But he was willing to make the attempt because he never wanted his words to hurt her again.

Besides, after spending the past few hours in Kate's company, he realized Judith was right. Who was he to judge when his situation wasn't much different from hers?

That thought brought him full circle to his own predicament. In seconds, he was depressed. He placed the last piece of wood in the bin and reached for the TV remote. Seven thirty couldn't come soon enough. Pushing both Judith and Kate out of his mind, he sat back on the bed, and flipped through channels. He settled on a basketball game and tried to ignore the lameness of his default activity of late—watching sports. By himself.

Chapter 4

"I love the burgers in this place," Kate said, as Paul helped take off her coat. It was such a gentlemanly thing to do and it flustered her a bit. James never bothered with stuff like that. She turned her face to hide her reaction as she slid into the booth. "Not crowded, either."

"Tomorrow, it'll be packed." Paul shrugged out of his parka and placed it with Kate's on the bench before sliding in next to them.

Kate nodded and peered out over Lake Tahoe. The restaurant's floor-to-ceiling windows gave her a good vantage point to enjoy the moonlight's reflection shimmering on the water. "It's beautiful here, especially the view tonight." Romantic even, except the person she was sharing it with happened to be the wrong Morrison.

"Looks like the storm's moving in."

She smiled, thankful to have something to think about besides what she was missing with James. "Yeah! Fresh powder if it stays cold and doesn't rain."

In between the attentions of their waitress, they discussed the next day's skiing. Eventually, the woman returned to place their plates, each loaded with steaming fries and a burger, in front of them.

A tantalizing aroma wafted under Kate's nose and her stomach made funny gurgling noises. She laughed to cover the sound, then quickly dug into the thick, juicy cheeseburger.

Kate took a bite and closed her eyes, savoring the

taste. When she opened them, she caught Paul watching her, a lopsided grin plastered on his face.

"What?" Self-conscious all of a sudden, she traced the edges of her mouth with her tongue, then wiped her lips with her napkin.

Still grinning from ear to ear, he shook his head.

When his slow rumble of a chuckle erupted, she glanced down to make sure there was no ketchup on her turtleneck. "What's so amusing?" she asked, meeting his gaze. "Don't tell me it's nothing because you're grinning like an idiot."

"You're inhaling your food with gusto." He indicated her plate with a nod. "I was just wondering where you put it all in that minuscule body. What are you? Five feet and maybe a hundred pounds?"

"I'm five two," she corrected. "And no woman reveals her true weight. Ever." She was too vain to tell him to add eight pounds. Let him think she weighed less than she really did. Why the thought pleased her, she had no idea.

"I see." He nodded slowly. "Still, it's nice to be around a woman who can enjoy her food without worrying about dieting and all that nonsense."

A flush of heat washed over her as the approval in his voice wrapped around her like a warm blanket. She looked down at her plate, not liking the tingling sensation on her neck those enthralling, liquid pools of blue generated. She studied her burger, working to keep both from affecting her further. Finally, she was able to say with a modicum of normalcy, "I guess I'm lucky. I never gain an ounce and I love to eat." She took a bite and slowly chewed until the feelings dissipated, before swallowing. Once they did, she spoke with more conviction. "I think it's all that nervous energy I expend." She shrugged. Her focus landed on his plate. "It looks as if we both appreciate a good burger."

"What's not to like?" His beguiling smile was back. He captured her gaze once more and, not letting her look away, added, "I've always had an appetite for the finer things in life."

Another warm flush seeped from her belly to her extremities. To break the spell he innocently cast, she glanced out at the water and took deep breaths, without noticing the view this time. If she didn't know better, she could have sworn he was flirting. But she did know better. Paul Morrison never flirted with anyone, not even Judith, whom he loved more than life itself. More likely, he was trying to rattle her.

As her gaze remained fastened on the scene outside, big white feathers began floating in the air, increasing in density by the second. Her attention refocused on the view. She pointed. "Look, it's snowing."

"Really?" His gaze followed her finger, to see snow now falling in earnest, but the flakes dissolved as soon as they hit the water. "Wow! Look at it. I hope it keeps up."

"Maybe we should do the snow dance," she teased, glad see that his thoughts had moved to something else besides tormenting her.

"Snow dance?" His eyes narrowed.

"Yeah. It's a lot like the rain dance only it produces snow, not rain." Tsking, she shook her head. "Surely, you've done one?"

He laughed. "No, you'll have to educate me."

"I'm sure there's not much I can teach you." She mentally groaned at the unintended double entendre. *Good job, Kate.* Why not give him an open invitation to torment her more?

"Oh? I'm sure you're full of surprises and could teach me a lot," he said, without missing a beat.

His mischievous voice, full of innuendo, sent a small thrill up her spine. If that wasn't enough to worry her, another infectious grin reaching all the way to his eyes had her stomach turning somersaults. For heaven's sake, he belonged to her best friend and just because Judith's biological clock wasn't ticking as loudly as hers didn't change that fact.

Don't look at him. He reminds you of James. That's why your insides are twisting like a pretzel.

"Whoa, back up, bucko," she said, once she found her equilibrium. "We're getting way off base."

"Oh, come on. We're just having a little fun. It doesn't mean anything. You can't tell me you're not enjoying this as much as I am." His eyes flashed pure amusement, sending enough warmth to her core to further impair rational thought.

She couldn't stop the smile from forming. "That may be so." Why deny it? She *was* enjoying him for once in her life. But she wasn't without some sense. This was Paul, and he and Judith loved each other. "We're still sworn enemies. I'm willing to be nice, but I don't think I'm ready to bury the hatchet yet."

He shrugged. "Okay, it's your loss." He sighed and took a sip of his drink. "But let me know when you've buried it deep enough because I find I don't mind playing nice with you."

Twisting her napkin in her lap with one hand, she cleared her throat and concentrated on bringing a fry to her mouth with the other. To answer him would be pure madness. Oh, he was good. So good at rattling her. Instead of humor and snide remarks, he was now using the infamous Morrison sex appeal and charm.

The man is not attractive. Repeat ten times and stop stealing glances at him. He was James' brother, for Pete's sake. She needed to ignore him. She needed to remember he was Paul Morrison, her hated enemy. She needed a drink. No, what she needed most was distance.

Remaining silent, she sighed and resumed eating.

Paul didn't seem to notice her newfound absorption

in her food. He continued talking while she pretended not to notice the cute way his eyes crinkled at the edges when he smiled or the devilish gleam in them when he found humor in something and shared it with her. Feeling trapped like a charmed cobra unable to break away from the charmer, she breathed a sigh of relief when he got up to go to the restroom.

She couldn't wait until the meal was over so she could escape to her secluded room.

~

Paul washed his hands and glanced into the mirror. What the hell was he doing?

He snorted.

Flirting.

That's exactly what he'd been doing. With Kate Winters! His brother's problem. The same Kate who gave back in triplicate everything he threw at her. How had their game changed? Had the earth turned on its axis? He hadn't been able to stop himself, the words just flew out of his mouth. Now, searching his reflection, he couldn't deny one fact. She intrigued him, made him want to keep flirting. No woman had ever intrigued him like this. Except Judith, and he never flirted with Judith.

He started out of the restroom and halted. Why was he in such a hurry? He shook his head. No way. He couldn't be attracted to her. Never in a million years would he think he'd ever enjoy her company, and never in a gazillion years would he think she'd attract him.

"Not good, Morrison," he muttered. Although he didn't think James would ever commit to Kate, he had no business encroaching on his brother's girlfriend. He had no business finding her attractive. *Remember, she's the enemy*—her words, not his—so he should avoid her.

Instead of listening to his mind's warning, he grinned as he walked toward the table when she glanced up at him. He was just having a good time, something he hadn't had in a long while. He could handle Kate.

Still, he wasn't a total fool. He'd keep the conversation going, but restrain from any and all sexual innuendos. No eye gazing. No charming smiles.

He sat back down and for the rest of the meal did just that. He had no idea if she was following his lead or not, but he was grateful all the same that she restricted her tongue as well.

Finally, after paying the check, he stood and helped her into her coat.

Thank God the ordeal was over, he thought as they headed toward his car. The snow was still coming down, but wasn't sticking to the ground. Yet.

"Can I tag along in the store?" He clicked the keyless entry as they neared his BMW.

He glanced at her, realizing by her puzzled look she hadn't caught his words. He repeated his question and opened her door. "I want to get some wine."

"No problem," she murmured, looking none too pleased. "I forgot we were going to stop."

He waited until she was inside to shut her door, then ran around to the driver's side, climbed in next to her, and started the engine. "We don't have to, if you'd rather not." He pulled onto the road.

"No." She offered a tired sigh. "Shopping tonight would be more convenient."

Paul slowed the car when the Safeway sign came into view. After parking, both emerged at the same time. He hit the keypad to lock the car and then turned toward the store's entrance. As she rushed to catch up with him, he glanced around and noted snow swirling everywhere. In the few minutes it took to drive to the store, the temperature dropped and the ground cooled enough for the snow to begin accumulating. Once inside the automatic doors, they stamped their feet and shook the flakes off their heads and clothes.

"Look at it come down," he said with a laugh. He caught Kate's excited gaze with raised eyebrows and a grin. "Powder day tomorrow!"

She grinned back. "Definitely compensates for being stuck here with you."

"Be nice," he warned, grabbing a cart. "Otherwise I'll have to rat you out to Judith."

"I am being nice. Far be it from me to ruin our truce since dinner went so well." She took control of the cart and headed for the far aisle. He hurried to keep up as she said, "We need basics. What do you need?"

"Me? I thought you were cooking."

"Why? Because I'm the little woman?"

"Well, you are little and you are a woman." He grinned, letting his eyebrows rise and fall and looking her up and down suggestively.

She snorted. "Funny." She grabbed something off the shelf and tossed it in the cart. "I never thought of you as a chauvinist."

"Wishful thinking." He shrugged, studying the items she'd added to the cart with the precision of a NASCAR auto mechanic. "Just making conversation. I don't cook. Can barely boil water. Judith isn't much better, so I was hoping more than anything you could. You have to admit, you look like you know what you're doing, given all that food," he said, indicating the basket.

His comments seemed to satisfy her. She nodded. "I guess we can make it a foursome tomorrow night." She paused, holding a wedge of cheese in her hand, and turned to him. "What do you like for breakfast?"

"Surprise me," he said, grinning. He picked up the Romano cheese along with some green stuff she'd just placed in the cart and quirked a brow. "What do you plan to make?"

"Something I mastered in my French cooking class

and one of James' favorites."

"I guess there are worse things than being stuck with someone who actually knows how to make an omelet." He ignored the glare she sent him and pointed to the eggs in her hand. "I'm perfectly happy with scrambled eggs."

"Shows you how much you know. I'm making a soufflé."

"I stand corrected. Soufflé," he joked, not wanting to think about how following behind her while she pushed a cart up and down the grocery aisles seemed cozy somehow, like they'd been doing it for years. He mentally groaned and tossed the silly thought from his brain.

When she stopped at the coffee bean display, he watched in horror as she haphazardly mixed different beans together into the small bag: first Columbian, then dark roast, and finally Kona, then repeating the process.

"What're you doing?" he shouted. He reached out and grabbed her wrist to stop her.

"Don't look so appalled." She threw out an amused laugh as she pulled out of his grasp and continued mixing. "Trust me, you'll enjoy it." When done, she caught his gaze with hers and winked, then added in a teasing voice, "And just to make sure there's no misunderstanding between us, I'm talking about the coffee, not sex."

The look and playful words caught him off guard. Out of nowhere, a quick flash of lust hit. Images of her dancing stark naked in front of him invaded his senses, as she stood so defiantly with her hair in disarray and a challenging grin plastered over her face. He swallowed hard, momentarily speechless. Though petite, she had all the right equipment in all the right places to incite anyone's lust. Heaven help him! *Get a grip! This is Kate Winters you're lusting over. Your brother's girl.*

He pushed away the errant thoughts, but they hung on with a tenacity that clearly suggested he'd been without sex too long. Abstinence was definitely playing tricks on his body.

"I'll grab some milk and half-and-half." He did an about-face and headed in the opposite direction, hoping time and distance would cool his overactive libido.

"Get enough for several days for everyone, okay?"

He gave a backward wave and nodded. Thankfully, his self-appointed task gave him the space necessary to bring his wacky mental images under control. He dismissed the unwanted desire as circumstantial.

"Face it, Morrison," he muttered under his breath. "It's been awhile." He sighed, thinking he'd have to rectify the situation. The thought depressed him. He hadn't dated anyone new in over a year, since Judith started talking about relocating to the city.

Like any male, he had a fairly strong sex drive, but sex was something he could take or leave, given the person he was sharing it with was never Judith. Back when she expected him to date, he honored her wishes, but he never found anyone he was serious about other than Judith—if you could count her as serious. Once the relationship got to a certain point, he'd break things off in an effort to avoid hurting anyone, but invariably too many got hurt anyway. None knew that someone else held his heart. Secretly, he'd hoped that maybe one of them would break the spell Judith held over him. Deep down, he knew he never gave anyone he met the opportunity. Tired of it all, he decided it wasn't worth another person's heartache.

Remembering, he sighed. How had his life become so pathetic?

He snatched a gallon of milk, along with a quart of half-and-half, and went to find Kate, determined not to think about her.

He'd just get back to the house without any more incidents and immerse himself in work.

Work always took his mind off his troubles. His

thoughts were interrupted when he spied the very woman currently so prevalent in them pushing the cart across the aisle at the other end of the store. He strode in her direction.

"I almost forgot the wine." Once he reached her, he stuck his items in the basket. "Judith and James like red. I prefer chardonnay, but I'll drink red if it's the only thing available."

"We're doing a French theme, so make sure both are French wines, okay?"

He nodded and started for the wine section as she headed toward the checkout stand.

Paul walked up as the last item was being scanned and placed the bottles on the belt. They were quickly added to the rest of the groceries and bagged.

When Kate reached into her purse, Paul put his hand over hers. "No way am I letting you pay for this."

"You paid for dinner," she said in a firm tone, shaking her head. "Quit trying to be Macho Man and let me buy the food."

"I really don't think you want to go head-to-head with me here in the checkout lane." He ran his MasterCard through the slot and dared her to protest with his stare.

"Men!" She rolled her eyes. "You know we're quite capable of earning money and paying for groceries without your help."

He grinned. "Accept the gift and say thank you. As long as I'm present, I'll never let you pay." His grin broadened and he amended his words. "Far be it from me to ruin your view of me as a chauvinist."

"Aargh!" she grunted. "Leave it to a Neanderthal like you to say something so stupid."

"I do aim to please," he said, in between chuckles. Kate glowered at him while he signed the sales slip. When done, he looked at her with raised eyebrows, and asked in an innocent tone, "Do you want to help me carry these? I mean, since you're so into equality."

"Oh, shut up." She grabbed half of the bags, turned, and stomped out of the store. His bark of laughter erupted. She was damned cute when annoyed.

At the car, she stopped, then turned, and began tapping an impatient foot. He hit the automatic locks. The lights flashed twice and the locks flipped up. She opened the back door, placed the groceries on the seat, and spun around, almost bumping into him after he'd followed on her heels. He held his ground just to see what she'd do. Since he wasn't moving, she abruptly snatched the bags out of his hands and stuck them inside the car with the others.

She turned and glared at him. "Do you mind?"

He grinned and backed up. As she slammed the car's back door, he stepped over and opened the passenger door. "Allow me." Holding on to his smile, he made an exaggerated bow.

She shook off snow, which was vigorously coming down at this point, and sent him another look that could freeze fire before sliding into the front seat.

Still grinning, he got in beside her.

Neither spoke as he started the engine and pulled onto the highway.

"So is our truce off because I paid for groceries?" he asked after driving a few miles.

She crossed her arms and snorted. "You know why I'm irritated, so don't try to use those sexy baby blues to get yourself out of it."

"You think I have sexy eyes?" He batted his eyelids and increased the wattage of his smile. "Ah, shucks."

"Humph. Don't read anything into it." Her steadfast gaze remained glued to the passenger window. "You happen to have James' eyes."

Paul stole glances at her while driving. Despite the fact that he hated to be compared with his brother, his smile stayed in place. Yep! He was getting under her skin. He had to admit, he hadn't expected a simple grocery stop to provide so much entertainment. And this kind of sparring certainly took his mind off sex, which was good.

"It's really coming down now," he said, in an effort to draw her into conversation minutes later. The snow was making the road slippery. "Storm must've come in early." He chuckled lightly when she ignored his comment. "Hopefully, the plows will keep up with it so I won't need chains in the morning. Such a pain to put them on."

When she still didn't respond, he sighed, thinking it was just as well. He followed her example and kept quiet for the rest of the drive.

Paul exhaled a sigh of relief as the house finally came into view. He turned into the driveway and pushed the electronic control for the garage door opener at the same time.

"Before you escape my annoying presence, will you help me with the groceries?"

"Sure," she murmured, before hopping out.

Together they made quick work of the chore. When everything was put away and she started toward the guesthouse, he couldn't stop from asking, "You wouldn't be interested in a glass of wine before you call it a night, would you?" No one could miss the pleading in his voice.

When she paused and glanced over her shoulder, he wished he'd never broached the question, especially after spying her torn expression, reading it as clearly as the morning paper's headline.

"Not tonight," she replied, offering a wan smile. "I think I'll turn in. I'm tired. Thanks for dinner and the groceries. It was nice of you to buy, even though you didn't need to."

He nodded, feeling both disappointed and relieved by her refusal.

Not wanting to dwell on what that meant, he opened

the bottle of wine, poured a hefty glass, and headed to his room. He put the glass on his nightstand, then turned to light the fire he'd laid earlier. The kindling caught and flared, eventually lighting up the bigger pieces. In a matter of moments, the fireplace was ablaze.

Paul stared into the flames as if they held the answers to all of his questions. He felt lonely as reality sank in. He wished with all his heart that things could be different; he was so tired of loving someone who would never return his feelings. The process of letting Judith go from his heart, which had begun a few months ago when he'd discovered he wanted to marry and she wasn't going along, was picking up speed, like a boulder tumbling from a cliff.

He sighed and turned back to the bed, dismissing his thoughts. They were all too depressing.

He grabbed his briefcase, which he'd left on the floor by the nightstand earlier, riffled through it, and brought out an unread prospectus. Even though his love life was in shambles, he could always find a way to make more money. The realization held little comfort. He took a sip of wine and settled in for an hour or so of reading.

~

Secure in the guesthouse for the night, Kate paced, wishing she had a glass of wine. She needed something to numb thoughts of Paul, of the afternoon and evening she'd spent with him. She didn't like the fact that she was starting to see him as human—a very appealing, sexy human to boot. She didn't dare let on about this unwanted attraction. Wouldn't he have a field day then?

His polite gestures of paying for dinner and groceries bothered her. She didn't want to be beholden to him...didn't want to find him nice and considerate. These traits were so opposite to the guy she thought she knew. Nor did she want to compare him to James. James seldom opened her door for her; they'd been together too long for such little niceties. Though he paid on most of their dates, he never balked those times when she offered to go dutch. Besides, it wasn't as if she didn't have the hands to open her own door or the money, though in short supply, for her own food. It was the courtesy of Paul's acts that threw her.

Kate stuck her head out the guesthouse door and listened. A nightlight visible through the patio window revealed no movement. A positive sign, she thought, as she slunk toward the kitchen for some liquid distraction.

Once back in her room with a glass of wine, she fluffed the pillows behind her, hoping to immerse herself in a good book. But as she relaxed on the bed, images of Paul and their time together snuck back inside her brain and wouldn't budge.

He seemed so cocky and sure of himself. Confidence was definitely a Morrison trait. Paul had a way about him that made him much more attractive than James, which had become more evident in his demeanor during the evening. His quick sense of humor wasn't always used to enrage. Most of the time, he used it to win over and charm. Kate was one of the few who ever felt the harsh sting of his words. Heaven help her, if he ever turned that charm and humor to disarming her.

The idea of James not being her one and only finally took hold, as her discussion with Paul during the ride to Tahoe filled her mind. She was tired of dreaming for something that may never happen. She didn't want eight years to turn into ten. Dealing with James and his evasions for so long had nearly done her in, she certainly didn't want to become entangled with his brother. That would be too much, even for her.

The morning couldn't come too soon. Skiing would provide the means to keep Paul at arm's length. Her gaze flew to the big picture window. She grinned, excited to see the snow's accumulation. Tomorrow would be an awesome day. She could handle skiing fresh powder and she could handle her silly infatuation. James' presence—and hopefully Judith's—would provide a buffer, so after one day on the slopes, she'd no longer have to deal with Paul one on one.

Chapter 5

Paul woke the next morning and stretched. He glanced at the clock, noting it was just after six, sleeping in for him. His gaze moved to the window. Darkened shadows were highlighted in white. A grin took over his face at what that meant. A spectacular day of skiing. Fresh powder wasn't much of a consolation without Judith here to share it with him, but it was better than rain.

Once out of bed, he headed for the bathroom, wondering if Kate would be ready to go by eight. He wanted to be on the mountain before the lifts opened.

After showering, he veered toward the kitchen for a dose of caffeine. Having lived in the Bay Area his entire life, he was one of those who'd been raised on exceptionally strong coffee, the likes of which would grow hair on a turtle shell. His morning ritual always included a cup or two…or three. He rounded the hallway leading from the bedroom. Light poured out of the kitchen.

In seconds, the heavenly smell of freshly ground coffee filled his nostrils. Soon, other smells hit him. He stopped at the doorway and took in Kate standing over the stove cooking bacon. Beside the skillet was a bowl filled with eggs.

He couldn't help but notice how attractive she was, dressed in body-hugging jeans and a thick burgundy turtleneck. The sweater not only brought out the contrasts in her dark brown hair and fair complexion, it showcased a nice pair of breasts, drawing his gaze. She definitely got his pulse going better than the caffeine he was after. His gaze moved higher when she looked up and smiled.

"Good morning," she said in a cheerful voice. Eyes full of mischief, she met his questioning gaze, reminding him of what Tinker Bell might look like without wings. "I hope you're hungry, because I'm making enough for two and I'd like the company."

"My, aren't we in a good mood this morning." He reached past her to grab a mug from the counter and picked up the coffeepot. "I take it you slept well?"

"Yes, I did, and I find even your obnoxious company can't dampen my spirits."

He grunted, as he poured. "What's on the menu? It looks an awful lot like bacon and eggs, and I find I have quite an appetite this morning."

Her grin expanded. "Well, cool your jets, bucko, because food is all you're getting. Should be ready in a few minutes. Orange juice is in the fridge."

He stifled a laugh, amused that she caught his little jibe. "Can't hurt a guy for trying."

"You can always try, but I've got news for you. Keep it up and you may be hurting, because I'm not so easily led astray."

"Oh? Is that a dare?" His eyebrows shot up, and he snared her attention, hoping to rattle her, since he was already off-center at the sight of her.

"No. It's a fact."

For some reason he had a hard time ignoring her words, tossed out with such moxie. He didn't want to be attracted to her, nor did he want to find the idea of leading her astray intriguing.

Shaking his head at the very idea, he laughed.

"Touché, you win. It's too early to start the contest of wills this morning. At least wait until I've had some coffee." He took a sip of the hot brew. Eyebrows raised, he held up the cup and admitted, "This is good."

She grinned. "I told you you'd like it."

Her attention went back to cooking, while Paul tried not to notice her cute derrière. But his eyes wouldn't listen to his mental chiding and he kept stealing peeks. He sighed and took another sip of coffee. It was going to be a long day.

"It'll be ready soon." She nodded toward the silverware drawer. "Why don't you set the table?"

Thankful for the diversion, he jumped to do her bidding. He damned well didn't need thoughts of Kate's butt roaming through his brain.

~

In minutes, Kate had everything ready. She handed Paul a plate and they sat at the table he'd set.

"This is delicious," Paul said, after eating a few bites. "I appreciate the effort. Thanks. It's always nice to have a hearty meal before a day of skiing."

She felt a rush of heat spread from her neck to her hairline, pleased as much by his praise as by his appreciation. "I enjoy cooking." She shrugged, ignoring the hum of awareness that surrounded them all of a sudden. "It's just as easy to make enough for two as it is for one."

"I know, but thanks anyway."

Kate took a deep breath and chanced a glance at him. His words sounded so sincere. Why was he being so nice? She wished he'd revert to the old Paul. She'd learned how to deflect his snide, cutting remarks. This Paul, however, was all new to her and very appealing. She certainly didn't need the complications that came with finding him appealing. He was James' brother—the same man who'd tormented her for years. Thanks to her evening with Paul the night before, she'd spent too many hours sleeplessly reassessing her relationship with James, unable to dismiss the idea that he'd disappointed her once again. Her camel's back of patience was nearing its breaking point. She was tired of being disappointed.

Even if she and James broke up for good, the thought of anything happening between her and Paul was just too much for her brain to imagine. Thinking about it the irony of it, she smiled, thankful to find some humor in the situation.

Paul grinned. "What's so funny?"

"Nothing." The one word came out in a rush, after being caught with such a ridiculous notion. Paul belonged to her best friend. He loved her, for heaven's sake, and Judith loved him. She couldn't stop an expression of guilt from forming, as more heat crept up her face.

"It's more than nothing." He eyed her speculatively. "Daydreaming about James, are we?" When she didn't answer, he chuckled. "Okay, I won't pry."

The understanding look he shot her sent another wave of warmth spreading from her toes to her forehead. She glanced at her plate, which held her attention for the remainder of the meal. Somehow, she had to hold on to her resolve of getting through the day without embarrassing herself.

Finished eating, she stood and picked up her plate, relieved to finally escape. "I hope you mean to get an early start, because I'm almost ready."

"Yeah," Paul said, checking his watch. "I just need to grab my gear and load up the car. Looks like I'll need chains."

"Do you want help?" Kate asked him when he

headed toward the mudroom, as she cleared the table and put the dishes in the dishwasher.

"No, it's easier to do alone, but thanks for the offer."

"I'll get my stuff."

Chains were definitely a necessity. The roads to Squaw Valley, their resort of choice, were barely passable. When they pulled into the ski area's parking lot, it was still snowing. At that moment, Kate was thankful for the full-sized locker the Morrisons rented in one of the lodges.

Paul parked the BMW and jumped out to help her before unloading the skis and boots. Loaded down with equipment, they headed for the lodge.

Kate came out of the women's room wearing a red ski suit, a recent birthday splurge, and walked up behind Paul, who'd also changed and sat on a bench putting on boots.

Once ready, they gathered the rest of their gear from the locker and trudged toward the tram.

"Look at all the powder," she said, glancing around and seeing only snow as they waited in a short line. "It's almost a foot deep already."

Paul glanced to the west, where the storm systems came from, and shrugged. "Looks like we'll have an awesome day." He retrieved his cell phone from a hidden pocket and pulled up the weather page, then showed her the screen. "There's a little clearing on the radar, but the system isn't done dumping yet. We should ski as much as we can before it starts to get nasty."

"Sounds like a plan. I'm ready and willing to ski till I drop." She peered over at him and added, "I'm glad you're here. I like the company. I ski alone a lot, so this is a treat."

"Yeah, I hear you. I've experienced too many solitary

days myself," he said. "But you have to keep up, or you'll be left in my tracks."

She laughed. He was an expert skier, but then, so was she. "You seem pretty confident that I'm going to be following you." Oh, yeah. This was going to be fun. She'd definitely give him a run for his money. He'd be lucky not to be left in her tracks. Her smile turned smug. "You might rethink your opinion, Morrison. You'll be eating the snow from my turns."

Then, she hurried to reach the open doors on the tram, which had just landed. Seconds later, the doors closed, and the car carrying a throng of skiers started its ascent to the top of the mountain.

~

"Try to keep up, bucko," Kate goaded, waving a pole in the air and racing ahead of Paul when he bent to tighten his boots. "See ya at the bottom!"

She hit the rough terrain and she didn't dare slow, instead releasing her edges to increase her speed, knowing he'd have to work hard to catch up. It would be a battle of skills and wills, just like it had been most of the day. Her agility and size more than made up for his strength and endurance. On the straightaways, however, he was faster.

She sensed him behind her, narrowing her lead. Unable to risk glancing back, she let loose a little more. The path in front of her was visible enough and no one was around to impede her progress. She'd almost made it to the lift line when he edged ahead.

"I won."

"No fair," she said, laughing at his satisfied grin. The same grin he'd sported hours ago, after winning their first impromptu race. "You're bigger than me, so you pick up more speed near the end."

"You got a running start."

"So?"

"Concede, Kate." She followed when he skied to the lift and both waited for the next chair. Once seated, he turned to her and said, "I beat you fair and square."

Kate rolled her eyes and snorted. "I could've won, if I'd really wanted to."

"Not while I'm around."

She laughed. "I can't believe we both hate to lose." Her skill brought out his competitive nature, caused him to take on every challenge she threw his way. She understood his motives. She felt the same. She relished any chance to best him when behind and worked to hold on to any lead if he was the one in the rear.

"Yeah," he said. "But I don't cheat."

"I only gained a second or two advantage." At least he didn't have to wait for her, which definitely pleased him. They'd spent their morning hiking to pristine powder mountaintops perfect for carving figure eights, moving to other lifts when one run became boring because they ran out of fresh powder.

The chair reached the top of the lift. They exited and skied to the cliff's edge.

"Doesn't look good," Paul said, nodding at the darker clouds rolling in. The snowfall thickened, but they still had visibility. "We've been lucky so far, but judging by what's ahead, we only have a few more runs."

Kate pushed off, laughing. "Meet you at the bottom."

Three-quarters of the way down, Paul whizzed by her. Though breathing heavily and feeling the burn in her thighs, she pushed on, unwilling to give him the satisfaction of seeing her quit. He only had to shift that knowing blue gaze, so like James', in her direction and she'd respond. Why did it have to be Paul who brought this competitive drive to the surface, when no one else ever had? It rankled to admit she enjoyed skiing with him, but she couldn't deny the elation rushing through her.

As she neared the end of the run, Kate realized couldn't remember a more exhilarating day, one where she'd been challenged and taunted so much.

She hurried to catch up with Paul to repeat the process twice more. At the top of the third lift, he said, "Time to quit." The heavens had totally opened up, dumping pure white and hampering visibility. "Let's take this one easier. No sense killing ourselves in a burst of speed when we can't see a foot in front of us."

She nodded and followed him, barely able to see the dark outline of his coat and only too glad to have him in the lead. They'd put in a vigorous five hours and skipped lunch because the mountain beckoned. Her muscles ached. She was tired—a good tired only felt when one had exerted to the point of soreness without overdoing it.

At the bottom, they both stepped out of their bindings. When Paul hefted both pairs of skis onto his shoulders, she shook her head and reached for hers. "I can carry my own gear."

"I got 'em. You grab the poles," he said, turning and heading for the locker room.

She sighed. His resolute expression told her it was useless to argue. She picked up the poles and followed, wishing he'd stop being so nice and considerate. In all the times she and James had skied together, he'd never carried anything for her. Not that she expected it. Still, Paul was definitely more courteous in a thousand ways that James wasn't. Now she understood what Judith saw in him. Kate didn't want to like him, yet she realized the more time she spent in his company, the more she did.

This wasn't supposed to happen.

"Geez. Look at it," she said, noting the blizzard-like conditions, in an effort to push her attraction to the background of her mind. "I think tomorrow might be a better day than today, and it doesn't get much better."

Paul looked around and nodded.

Once they made it to the lodge, he held the door open and waited for her to go ahead of him. They'd leave the skis and poles in the locker overnight, although neither dared leave their boots there. Nothing short of sticking them next to a heater or the fire would dry them out. Putting on a damp boot tomorrow was a sure way of spending the entire day with cold feet on the slopes, so it was worth the inconvenience of carting them back and forth.

At the locker, she watched him work the combination lock. He unlatched the door, took out each of their bags, then placed both pairs of skis inside and turned back to her. She passed him the poles.

He closed the door and spun the dial. When his hand moved toward her, she leaned away.

"Hold still." He grinned as he gripped her shoulder with one hand and brushed her hair with the other. "You look like the abominable snowman."

She stood stock still, allowing him to sweep the snow off her bangs and hat, then shoulders. She hoped he couldn't feel her heartbeat pounding out of control as the heat of his fingers on her shoulder overwhelmed her with a warm sensation.

"Thanks," she murmured, risking a quick glance at him. His blond hair, darkened from all the melted snow, framed his handsome face. He looked so much like James, but he was nothing like him. The thought made her smile.

Paul caught it and his eyebrows shot up.

"What?"

"Nothing," she said, and turned to grab her street clothes to change. She rushed toward the ladies' room as fast as her legs would carry her, feeling her face flame, hoping he hadn't noticed how red it must be.

In the privacy of the restroom, Kate forced herself to breathe. She took her time dressing, and stewed the whole while.

Their hours together had all but wiped out her resolve to not interact with him. Who knew Paul Morrison's personality would draw her with the force of a magnet? His daring taunts and boyish grin were hard to resist. She wished she could ignore both. Being stuck with him no longer seemed like a chore, a notion that didn't bode well, especially since she couldn't see a way to make it through the rest of the afternoon without unwittingly revealing her attraction.

How had she gotten into this position? Why did Paul Morrison have to be the one to make her heart flutter now that she entertained the notion of moving on with her life? He'd have such a laugh if he knew. After enjoying the man and his challenges for a change, she never wanted to revert to being the butt of his jokes again.

~

Paul strode out of the men's room carrying his wet clothes. As he stuffed his ski suit into a bag and gathered their boots together, his thoughts centered on Kate, torturing him with unwanted desire. Every provocative smile she'd sent his way during their hours on the slopes had twisted his insides with an incomprehensible need. He was certain his attraction had nothing to do with his lack of sexual activity. This was different. He'd certainly never felt this way about Judith.

He turned when the ladies' room door opened. *Damn! How had this gotten so crazy?* He watched her saunter toward him with such attitude and grinned. Though tiny, she knew how to move to attract him, as he'd spent the morning discovering.

That wasn't all that attracted him. Every time she'd state an opinion, something in her voice infiltrated his brain, and his body responded. Like now, when he worked to ignore the hum of awareness that hung in the air, a tension that had been present during every lift ride they'd taken.

All day, he'd diligently worked to keep his eyes off her svelte form. Too often, thoughts of unzipping her ski suit, to see exactly what lay beneath had flashed inside his mind. Thoughts that wouldn't shut off, no matter how many times he'd flipped the mental switch.

He shook his head and snatched both pairs of boots, holding them with a firm grip. His internal switch was still on the fritz so he was glad to have something to keep his hands busy, preventing them from following that crazy impulse to explore underneath Kate's clothing.

"You ready?" he asked, surprised that the steadiness of his voice revealed nothing of his inner turmoil.

She nodded with a smile and reached for her bag.

Paul started for the door, refusing to be taken in with such a beguiling expression. Yet his mind continued paying no attention to his commands to ignore the way her hips swayed with each step as she walked toward him. He sighed, then averted his gaze as he held the door open, waiting until she was out before following, purposefully not looking at her butt.

Halfway to the car, he noticed the white-out conditions and wondered how long it would be until James arrived. It couldn't be too soon for his peace of mind. He had no idea how he'd survive the rest of the day trapped with her in a winter wonderland of snow, snow that continued to fall relentlessly.

By the time he and Kate reached his BMW, they were almost white again. He brushed as much as he could off her and opened the passenger door.

Once she was seated, Paul quickly put the boots and bags into the trunk. He shook snow from his body before he opened his door, then slid in next to her, and started the car. "I'm glad I put the chains on earlier."

"Yeah. There's only one thing worse than taking chains off a car in a parking lot, and that's putting them on in the same parking lot during a blizzard."

He nodded and shifted into gear. Both remained silent as he steered carefully out onto the road.

Forced to drive at a crawl because of the conditions, he chanced a couple of surreptitious peeks in her direction. On his last, several emotions played across her face and ended in a cheshire grin that drew his gaze to her lips. "What's so funny?" he asked.

"Nothing," she said too quickly, as her glance darted to the window.

"Nothing, huh?" His tone sounded skeptical. The experience was too similar to the other times he'd caught her smiling throughout the day. She was definitely hiding something. "That's what you said this morning. I think it's a secret."

She offered a half shrug. "Maybe."

He shook his head and grinned. "You know, I have ways of finding these things out."

"Oh, really?" She crossed her arms. "Good luck trying."

His focus landed on that self-satisfied smile again. "I bet I can get you to talk." He meant the words in jest, but they came out in a flirty, almost seductive tone. He stared at her lips a little too long, having a hard time remembering why he shouldn't have made the comment in the first place.

"I'm sure you could," she countered in an equally sultry manner that sent a signal south and brushed Judith and James further into the background of his thoughts. "Which is why I'm not willing to risk it."

"Spoilsport. I would've enjoyed trying to loosen your tongue," he murmured, wondering for a fleeting moment what it would be like to kiss her.

Kate didn't reply. She whipped her head around to stare out the passenger window as if fascinated with the snowy vista.

Just as well, he thought, sighing. Thinking about kissing her wasn't the best idea either. He concentrated more on driving, intent on ignoring this hum of attraction that continually overrode his good sense. Still, as much as he struggled to expel them, images—of the methods he'd use to loosen her tongue—clung to his mind.

Quit thinking about locking lips with her. His mental urgings did no good, as his gaze kept zeroing in on her mouth.

He blew out a silent expletive. *Not good, Morrison. Not good.*

His only recourse at this point? Put some distance between them. Thank God, she was staying in the guesthouse—well away from him and his crazy desires. He turned on the radio.

As Train's "Soul Sister" slowly faded, a news bulletin interrupted in a loud blare, informing drivers that the winter storm system had stalled. The forecast called for flooding in the lower elevations. Interstate 80 and Highway 50, the main thoroughfares from the mountains to Sacramento were a mess. The highway patrol required chains through Donner Pass, a common event. The storm had already produced twenty inches in the last twelve hours and the weather service predicted another twelve to twenty-four inches.

"Damn." The one word came out in an explosive rush of annoyance. Stilling the urge to hit the steering wheel, Paul gripped it tighter and glanced at Kate, frowning. "No way Judith will make the trip now." She'd check the news and would never attempt to drive in a snowstorm, let alone deal with putting on chains. He mentally snorted. Not that he believed she'd have made it before the storm hit harder than expected.

"I hope James is okay." Kate grimaced, then sighed and shook her head. "This weekend isn't going the way I planned."

"Don't worry. He should be fine with four-wheel drive," Paul said, not adding his other similar thoughts. This weekend wasn't even close to what he'd expected. Awareness was a bitch, he thought, unable to shake the thought that for years he'd given the woman sitting next to him grief over something he was equally guilty of—a humiliating realization, to say the least.

Though slow going, they eventually arrived at the house and he was only too grateful to see Kate veer toward her haven, mumbling about having things to take care of.

Paul got another fire going in his room, then started for the kitchen, glad he'd had the sense to load the wood bin before two feet of snow made it more difficult.

He found that he was starving, and rummaged through the cupboards and fridge. Thankful they'd stocked up the night before, he found plenty to work with. After fixing sandwiches, he poured himself a glass of wine, hoping to dull his out-of-control thoughts. To complete the feast, he added cookies and chips.

Plate in hand, he went to the guesthouse and knocked. "I fixed something to eat."

Kate opened the door and eyed the offered food. "Oh you sweet, sweet man. How'd you know I was ravenous?" Grinning, she quickly took the plate from him. "Thank you!"

Paul couldn't contain his smile at the animated joy in both her voice and her expression. She certainly had a zest for food. Then his thoughts shifted, as the notion of her looking at him with the same eagerness and hunger infiltrated his brain. Blood rushed south in a hurry.

He swore under his breath. No one had *ever* affected him this way. "It was only fair, since you made breakfast," he murmured, before swiftly retreating. All she had to do was smile at him and need turned his brain into mush, a feeling as unnerving as it was unwanted.

Back in the main house, he grabbed his lunch, along with the wine he'd poured earlier, went over to the table, and sat.

Damn! It felt as if he was caught in some kind of *Twilight Zone* episode. Though not funny, the irony of the situation did amuse him. He'd always had a twisted sense of humor. Maybe later—years from now—he'd be able to laugh.

As he ate and sipped his wine while looking out the window and seeing nothing but white, Paul contemplated his options for the evening. He could go to a movie, maybe even check out one of the many bars. Friday night meant Tahoe City would swell with weekend visitors. For some reason, the thought of spending time with someone other than the woman in the guesthouse just didn't seem as thrilling or as exciting.

He sighed. There was always work. No! His thoughts were too jumbled. No way would he be able to concentrate. He raked a hand through his hair and rubbed his neck. How had his life become even more messed up? How had he gone, in a matter of twenty-four hours, from pining after a woman who didn't love him like he wanted, to pining after another who belonged to his brother?

Well, just make the best of it and stay in your room as much as possible. Don't let her know she bothers you.

His breath came out in one loud groan. If his secret ever came out, she'd have the means to get even with his badgering over the years. Wouldn't that be some kind of poetic justice?

He walked over to the sink with his plate. After rinsing it, he stuck it in the dishwasher, then topped off his wineglass and retraced the steps to his room.

Warmth from the fire hit him. The room glowed. He loved fires and he loved the snow. He'd relax and enjoy the rest of the afternoon until dinner, absorbed with TV or a magazine. Paul grabbed the remote, hit the On button, and scrolled through channels until he spotted an animal show that caught his interest. But after staring at the screen for too long without paying attention to it, he shut off the TV and walked over to the huge window.

Snow continued falling, silently providing a sense of isolation in the view outside. His focus landed on the blue lake, barely visible with all the white in the foreground. Nothing disturbed the quiet, which added to his loneliness.

No longer willing to wait for something that would never happen, he sighed and finally accepted the truth. After spending such a wonderful day with Kate, he realized he wanted more than chasing a pipe dream with Judith. A heck of a lot more.

Chapter 6

Long after finishing her sandwich, Kate rested her shoulders against the bed's propped-up pillows and, for the umpteenth time, tried to focus on the same page in the latest suspense novel she'd brought. Disturbing thoughts insisted on annoying her, interfering with her concentration. Unable to continue pretending interest, she put the book down and stared at the ceiling.

In seconds, memories of the day consumed her—a day where Paul had always stayed a step ahead of her. It was exhilarating and frustrating at the same time, considering his competitive drive, as strong as hers, hadn't allowed her to gain any advantage. It was as if some instinctive male trait of his burst forth, shouting his supremacy over her and dominating her in some age-old battle between the sexes. Because he was stronger and more stubborn, he was winning.

She'd never felt this on edge because of a man—any man—not even James. Even worse, the day only increased her disillusionment with her current relationship. Too much time had slipped by since she and James had shared such a carefree day. In fact, she couldn't remember the last time, which only highlighted bigger problems—including having to endure a trip back to Chicago for her sister Chrissie's wedding to face her family without James, or the engagement ring she expected to be wearing.

Too agitated to keep gawking at the ceiling, she jumped up and started pacing. Why had she pushed for this weekend? Why did she find Paul attractive? Why, why, why?

She'd never been fickle, just the opposite in her pursuit of James. So how could her thoughts shift from the love of her life to Paul so readily? In less than a day?

Her relationship with James had been an experience—one she was beginning to determine had no happy ending. Actions spoke louder than words. She'd given him several months to make a decision that he shouldn't even have had to think twice about. As much as it hurt to realize the truth, giving him more time to commit would only be wasted, which in the end would be a mistake. She understood that now and certainly had no desire to make a bigger mistake by becoming involved with Paul when he still loved Judith. That could only bring on more heartache for everyone involved. Judith was her best friend. She had only to remember that!

Heavens, she needed a drink. Something. Anything. She needed to stop thinking of him. Most of all, she needed to keep him from discovering her unsettling attraction to him.

Like the night before, she stuck her head out the door to listen. The coast looked clear. She stole across the patio, stepping around the snowdrifts, and stopped at the patio door to peer inside. Still clear. She crept into the kitchen. A bottle of the Puligny-Montrachet chardonnay he'd bought the night before, per her request for their French dinner, sat on the counter, uncorked. She quickly poured a glass, then tiptoed out the way she'd come.

Back in her room, she sipped and paced, wishing her foolish thoughts would cease.

Maybe when James arrived, seeing him again and being able to compare him side by side with Paul would jar some sense into her. Maybe her attraction stemmed from the fact that the two brothers looked so much alike. The minute the thought came out, she rejected it. They were like night and day. No two people who looked so much alike could be any more different from each other.

Kate sat back on the bed and picked up the book again. After a long pretense of absorption, she glanced at the clock on the nightstand. Almost 6:00 p.m.! Breathing a sigh of relief, she rose, grabbed her half-full glass and headed for the kitchen. The door to Paul's room was closed.

Thank the stars above, she'd be able to cook in peace.

She topped off her wine, took a small sip, and set the glass on the counter, feeling somewhat better. *I can deal with my attraction.* Smiling, she gathered the necessary ingredients—ham, eggs, three kinds of white cheeses, garlic, butter, half-and-half, onions, mushrooms, fresh marjoram and basil—then got to work chopping, grating, and mincing.

Finally, everything was ready for the oven, but the temperature wasn't high enough yet.

Her cell phone rang. She wiped off her wet hands, reached into her pocket, and dug it out. James' name flashed on the screen.

It's about time she heard from him. "Hey, James. How far are you? I'm cooking dinner now." He cleared his throat, and the sound alerted her. "Is something wrong?"

His hesitation before another throat clearing were sure signs that her intuition was dead on.

"I'm still in the Bay Area."

"What?" She'd expected his delay, but this news

85

caught her off guard. Anger slid its way up her spine as it straightened one vertebra at a time. She took a deep breath and counted to ten before saying, "I thought you'd be here hours ago and now you're telling me you haven't even left?"

"I'm sorry, Kate. I got caught up with a problem that took longer than I thought it would."

Of course he did. There was always a problem that was more important than spending time with her.

"Unfortunately, I doubt I'll make it up tonight."

"You're not serious?" At this point, holding in her anger took too much effort. "Tell me this is a joke," she said more harshly than intended.

"Have you looked at the weather?"

"Yeah, duh," she said, glancing out the window. "It's snowing." White stuff was still coming down and drifted halfway up the porch rail. Even so, she went over to the television, clicked the remote, and switched to the weather channel. Across the bottom of the screen flashed a winter storm warning for the Northern California/Northern Nevada area. *Old news!* If he'd left on time, *as promised*, he'd have missed the worst part and have made it to Tahoe hours ago.

"The highway patrol just closed I-80," James said. "Highway 50 was closed hours ago."

"You're kidding." Still praying that somehow he was teasing her, she read the scrolling banner on the TV that confirmed what he'd said and her mood took a nosedive.

"I wish I were," he said. "But it doesn't look good. The storm's producing so much snow, the plows can't keep up." She wanted to cry when he added, "They're also saying that when they reopen, people should stay off the roads since they're predicting another twenty inches tonight and maybe more if the system doesn't move."

"Great!" She scrunched her nose while rubbing her temple. Could anything else happen to make this the worst weekend of her life? "You missed an awesome day of skiing."

"I know. I wish I could've broken away earlier. At least you and Paul are making the best of it."

"Yeah, me and Paul." If only James hadn't let her down again. But he had. Big-time. She now understood what Paul meant when he'd accused her of putting up with too much shit from James. Hell, the Paul she'd come to know would never renege on a promise. Kate blinked back the moisture filling her eyes as the truth hit her head-on. She was worth more. And Paul, using his biting wit, had tried to tell her that for years.

"I was thinking we could drive up next weekend," James said. "The powder should last a few days, don't you think?"

"Probably." There was no way could she count on him. He'd disappointed her one time too many. Whether expected or not, it still hurt to know it was time to say good-bye to him and this one-sided relationship. What made the pain worse was the realization that she should have let go sooner. A few tears trickled down her face. She wiped them off and swallowed hard. "We skied in knee-deep powder today," she said, hoping to rub it in a bit to make him regret not coming up earlier, despite the futility of the wish.

She switched off the TV and turned back to the kitchen. "It was one of the best days I've ever had, and tomorrow looks to be even better."

"Sounds like I missed out. I'll make it up to you next weekend. Will you be okay with Paul by yourself?"

"Sure." Her lips curled into a semblance of a smile. "We're having loads of fun."

"I hate to leave you hanging like this, especially since you don't like being with him."

"Judith didn't make it either, so Paul and I are on our own."

"Ooooh. Now I'm doubly sorry."

"Don't worry about it. I'll survive." Just like she'd survived all those other instances he'd canceled.

"We'll get together during the week for dinner to make plans, okay?" he said, like it was some kind of consolation prize.

Strangely enough, the idea of spending a weekend together no longer appealed to her. Forgiving and forgetting simply weren't in her this time. "I don't think so." Despite saying the hardest words she'd ever spoken, a surge of confidence kept her on track. "There's no reason."

"Huh? What do you mean?" He truly sounded puzzled.

She smiled through her tears. "I mean, I don't want to go out to dinner with you or go skiing with you next weekend."

There was dead silence on the phone, until Kate ended the conversation with, "I'll give you a call when I feel more up to it." Then, she disconnected.

Suddenly, the burdensome weight of self-doubt lifted off her shoulders—which seemed odd, considering the invisible fist squeezing her heart. Despite the pain, she felt freer.

She stared at the phone, wondering why she'd settled for less for far too long, and why had it taken so much time to recognize the fact. Thank God, Chrissie's engagement jarred her into thinking clearly.

The ding on the gas oven indicating it had reached the right temperature drew her attention. Her dinner!

She'd almost forgotten about it. Thankful for the task of cooking to keep her from dwelling over her situation, she dashed back to the kitchen.

She opened the oven door and placed her soufflé inside. She set the timer, then started on the chocolate melting cake she'd planned for dessert.

Moments later, her cake in the oven, she glanced up to see Paul sauntering, barefoot, toward the kitchen, stretching and looking mighty hunky in jeans and a navy turtleneck that highlighted his blond good looks.

"Man, I think I've died and gone to heaven," he teased with an approving expression.

As he walked across the room, her focus remained on him. *Too bad James wasn't more like his brother.* Heat rose up her face when the thought registered.

"I've never smelled anything like it," he murmured, sniffing and indicating the oven. He reached for the handle, but her hand on his wrist stopped him.

"You'll ruin it if you open the door now."

"Wouldn't want to do that. But..." He pierced her with a stare. "I'm dying to see if it tastes as good as it smells."

Her breath caught in her throat and her heartbeat quickened. "It will."

"Promise?" His grin tightened the pretzel in her stomach, changing the knot from hurt to tension in seconds, as her mind went blank.

"Promise what?"

"Promise me that it will taste as good as it smells?"

She cleared her throat, struggling for normalcy, and ignored the way his eyes crinkled at the edges, which only added to his appeal. "Of course it will."

"Then I can wait." His tone and look made her feel as if he was talking about something other than chocolate melting cake or her soufflé.

Oh, for heaven's sake. Stop gawking at him!

Her gaze shifted lower. "Well, I'm glad you approve," she said, mentally shaking the effects of his nearness and finally remembering her phone call. "By the way, it's just going to be us tonight."

"Really?" His brow wrinkled with concern. "I thought James would be here by now."

"No, I-80 and Highway 50 are closed and there's no relief from the storm in sight, so he's not coming at all." She went back to fixing an endive salad and had to swat his hand again when he tried to steal a bite. "Here, do something useful while I finish dinner." She opened the silverware drawer, using it as a buffer to get her mind off the idea of him putting those hands on her. "Go set the table." *Whoa. I need to quit thinking such thoughts!*

Grinning, Paul snapped to attention and saluted. "Yes, ma'am."

Don't look at him. Ignore him. Remember Judith…he belongs to her.

Paul got busy and soon the meal was ready.

When she picked up the salads, he pulled them from her hands. "You go and sit." His nod indicated the table. "Since you cooked, the least I can do is serve you."

"Okay. But I should warn you. I could get used to being served," she said, following him and trying to extinguish the flames in her belly that his nearness recently started igniting.

He laughed as he set a bowl at the tip of each fork, then rushed to pull out her chair. "I'll keep that in mind."

More heat streaked up her face as his intense gaze met hers. Glancing down, she sat, hiding her reaction in the act of putting her napkin on her lap. He left and returned with the soufflé and garlic bread, without giving her heartbeat enough time to slow to normal.

Damn. If only he didn't love her best friend. If only Judith didn't love him. If only he'd stop being so nice. A lot of good 'if onlys' did when not one of them helped keep her attraction in check.

"Say when." Now standing beside her, he added a spoonful of the egg and ham mixture onto her plate.

"That's good," she said. His acting as if her desires were the most important thing to focus on was heady stuff and hard to ignore. Despite knowing it would never go anywhere, she couldn't help but enjoy his attention.

He eventually sat and served himself.

They'd barely started to eat when the lights flickered out. The room was completely dark except for the softly flickering candles Paul had placed on the table earlier.

Double damn, Kate thought, glancing at him. Shadows fluttered over his face, lending it a roguish appearance that any woman would find hard to resist, her included.

She averted her eyes, reminding herself that eating this close to him with the lights on was difficult enough. In candlelight, it was near impossible to stave off her errant thoughts of being completely alone with him. How would she make it through the meal without slipping?

Chapter 7

Kate picked up her wine and downed a healthy swallow. Once she could speak without giving herself away, she asked nonchalantly, "I wonder how long the electricity will be out."

"I don't know." Paul shrugged. "I can't remember it ever happening here before."

She nodded. Neither could she. It wasn't a common occurrence.

"We should be okay, though you may want to move into the house, just in case."

"Why?" Her concerned gaze sought his.

"No heat out there without electricity."

"But I thought the entire house was heated with gas?" She had to glance away again. He was just too appealing in candlelight and that did not bode well for the rest of the night.

"It is." He broke off long enough to finish another bite. "Unfortunately, the units work off an electric blower and starter. Both use electricity."

"Oh?" The one word held none of the panic storming over her senses at what moving closer to his room meant. How could she sleep with him so near?

"Could be worse. At least the fireplace is gas." He eyed her for an extended moment and obviously mistaking her concern, said, "Even without a fan, it'll put out heat. And the heat from the fire in my room will add to it if I keep the door open. But we should close off the rest of the house to try to prevent heat loss, since it's in the high twenties outside."

More warmth stole up her face at the idea of him leaving his door open. Did he ever have it wrong. She wouldn't have trouble keeping warm. Not with the heat sizzling through her body whenever his intent gaze landed her way. Thank the stars above for candlelight, she thought, as Paul got up from the table.

On his way to the kitchen, he asked, "Do you want more wine?"

Heavens no! Too much wine too fast would just make the situation crazier. "No, thank you. I'm fine right now." Reaching for calm, she cleared her throat and pushed her short hair behind her ears. "Do you think the power will be out all night?"

"Don't know. But, look on the bright side. At least we have plenty to drink!" he said holding up the second bottle, still unopened. He came up behind her carrying the other half-full bottle. "Are you sure you don't want any? This French chardonnay is really good."

"Okay. But only half a glass." She held her breath, totally aware of his nearness while he poured, and wasn't able to inhale or exhale until he sat down.

Paul took a sip before picking up his fork.

"How can you be so calm?" she asked, watching him eat.

He ate a couple of bites and paused. "It's very simple. I have no choice." Then he grinned. Light from the candle's flame captured his expressive eyes and cast his amused gleam quite well, adding to the affectionate, teasing quality in his voice when he added, "Why worry when we have all we need? Excellent wine and great company. Plus, the food is incredible. I didn't know you were a gourmet cook."

His words encompassed her like a warm blanket, filling her with well-being. She smiled. It felt like her whole body wanted to smile, even her toes. He liked her cooking. "It's a hobby," she said, pleased to have something else to focus on other than how sexy he looked in candlelight. "This soufflé is my creation. I like experimenting with different spices and seasonings."

Kate resumed eating, but couldn't relax. All too soon, the current of awareness that had permeated the shadowy room earlier returned in full force. She had to fight doubly hard to ignore him, purposefully keeping her attention on her food, too afraid that if she glanced his way, he'd see the spark of attraction she couldn't hide.

Wouldn't he have a good laugh over that? Heaven help her! This attraction wasn't real. It couldn't be. It was a fluke…a rebound…a coincidence of circumstance due to suddenly finding herself free to look around again for the first time in years. Of course, it was just her luck that Paul—Judith's Paul—just happened to be the best man in front of her now that her eyes were open.

Why did he have to be so attractive? Why was he being so nice? When she did chance to glance up at some comment he'd make and her focus would land on his engaging smile, she wondered about the biggest question of all: What would it be like to kiss him? She closed her eyes and almost groaned aloud in disgust. What kind of person lusted after her best friend's boyfriend? Judith deserved better than a friend like her for even entertaining the thought.

He stood. "I should get the fire started out here and check on the one in my bedroom."

Thankful for the disruption, she jumped up. "I'll help."

"Why don't you close all the bedroom doors and grab your stuff from the guesthouse?"

"Sure," she murmured, rushing to get away from him.

~

Paul watched her go wondering what went on in that sharp mind of hers, especially during dinner when she never stopped fidgeting. Her hands had constantly moved. Whether twisting her napkin or fingering her wineglass, she appeared nervous. As nervous as she'd been the day before when they first arrived, and so unlike the woman he thought he knew. Kate Winters was always as bold as brass and twice as nervy, almost to the point of being pushy. Instead of irritating him as she'd once done, now she intrigued him...made him want to see what would happen if he pushed back.

Interesting and definitely surprising.

He lit the fireplace in the living room. The flames roared to life when he adjusted the setting to the highest level.

He then went around the house searching for candles. The two on the table simply weren't enough. The shadows they cast added a romantic element to the room. No freaking way he could sit with her in such a romantic environment and act as if he wasn't dying to kiss her.

"Help me light these," he said, nodding to the half dozen he'd found when she walked back inside. They placed a few in strategic spots. While they added more light, it wasn't nearly enough and did little to ease his torment.

"How about a game of Monopoly?"

She nodded. "Sure."

He knew damn well he shouldn't be suggesting any game, but it was too early to retire. Besides, if he eased up on the wine, he should be okay. But Kate might like another glass. "There's more wine if you want it."

"No thanks. I'll have some later, after dessert."

He headed to the kitchen and placed his glass on the

counter. "How 'bout water?" he shouted while rummaging through the refrigerator and bending to reach the bottles in the back.

"Actually, hot chocolate would be great on a night like tonight." Startled to realize she'd followed him, he almost jumped when she added from just inches behind him, "Do you have any?"

"Hot chocolate, huh?" He straightened and threw her a quick smile. "I think I can find some. Funny, but I never pegged you as the type." In his mind, she was more the hot toddy, heavy on the bourbon type.

"There are a lot of things you don't know about me." She scooted him out of the way and grabbed the milk from the still-open refrigerator.

"So I'm finding out." His smiled deepened. "Since I'm so far off—you know—regarding what I know about you—care to enlighten me?" Though he knew he shouldn't, he couldn't help raising his eyebrows and taunting, "We've got nothing better to do." He paused, then added, "Considering our situation."

"Oh, no, bucko. You may have a need for a tell-all, 'Kumbaya' experience tonight, but I prefer to remain a mystery."

Of course she did, he mused, as he pulled out a container of Nestlé Quik from the cupboard and handed it to her. "Just for the record, I don't even know what 'Kumbaya' means, but I'm a pushover for hot chocolate. Especially during a snowfall." He'd get her to talk about herself. People didn't call him personable for no reason.

"Oh, that's right." Kate tsked, shaking her head. "You've probably never experienced singing around a campfire, since your family never drove anywhere."

"Neither did James," he answered, holding back a laugh at the impertinence in her voice. "You don't seem to hold it against him." He nodded to the stove and the chocolate melting cake they had yet to eat. "Just work your magic and I'll set up the board. Then, you can tell me all about singing around campfires."

She laughed.

Minutes later, she carried in a tray. "What happened to Monopoly?" she asked, indicating the Trivial Pursuit board he'd set up.

"It's the only game I could find. Figured we play this or sit and stare out at the snow all night." Or her, in which case, playing an outdated game was definitely much safer.

She nodded. The scent from her delicious melting cakes drifted under his nose as she placed the dishes on the coffee table next to the game board and sat, Indian style, beside him. "Too bad we can't roast marshmallows over the flames. Then it would be just like camping."

He helped himself to the dessert. "I've never been camping, but I know this. If camping involved pure decadence like this and you added roasted marshmallows, it doesn't sound all that enjoyable." When she shot a confused glance his way, he explained, "I'd be sporting a sugar headache right about now."

She giggled and the sound zinged through his ears, the ring of it penetrating all the way to his gut.

In an effort to ignore her allure, he took another bite and closed his eyes, savoring the rich taste. "This is like eating a piece of heaven." Only one thing was better...he pushed the image of her naked in front of the fire out of his mind. He doubted she'd appreciate the direction his thoughts had wandered.

"I haven't played this game since college when we played for drinks rather than wedges."

"Wedgies?" he blurted out on a laugh. "Now that's a

round I wouldn't want to lose."

She gave him a look that could freeze fire and held up the little plastic piece. "I said wedges." She then pulled the green wheel out of the box, and placed it on the board. "I'll admit I wasn't very good at it."

"I doubt I'm any better, so we'll be evenly matched," he said, digging out the yellow wheel and setting it next to her green one. As she grabbed the die and tossed it, he asked, "So where'd you go to college?"

"San Jose State. With Judith." The look she threw at him this time was even more priceless. Any moment he expected her to knock on his head and say, "Hello, is anybody in there?"

"Sorry." He shrugged, as a bit of warmth hit his ears. "I guess I should've known that."

She rolled her eyes and an unladylike sound erupted from her throat. "Ya think?"

He reached for the die. "Oh, c'mon. So I didn't pay attention back then. I'm paying attention now." He rolled. "And I'm more than curious about your past."

When she started to shake her head, he put up his hand and said in a more wheedling tone, "It's just to pass the time." He leaned in closer and lowered his voice to a whisper. "Unless you're afraid to talk for fear I might discover your deep, dark secret."

"Of course I'm not afraid of talking," she denied, scooting further away from him. "Besides, I have no secrets." But the blush pinking her cheeks said otherwise.

"Then I don't see a problem."

"Okay," she said, and picked up the die to take the first turn, since she'd rolled the high number. "To show you how wrong you are, I'll play along. But my life up to now is rather boring."

"You're exaggerating, I'm sure."

"Don't say I didn't warn you." Her quick laugh ended in a loud groan as she landed on purple. "I suck at entertainment. The questions are based on ancient stuff only my parents would know."

Paul smiled indulgently and read the question.

Kate snorted. "Who in the hell cares what occupation Clint Eastwood's character was on *Play Misty For Me*?" She shook her head. "I have no idea."

Still grinning, Paul glanced at the answer. "Take a wild guess."

"A disk jockey."

Wide-eyed and open jawed, Paul could only stare. "How in the world did you guess that?"

"So I'm right?" A giddy laugh escaped her lips. "Who knows? I might just win."

"And since you're so curious about me..." she added a purple wedge in her wheel and tossed him an almost gloating grin, "...I'll tell you the basics. I grew up in a suburb outside Chicago. In high school I got interested in art, which lead me to San Jose State and that's where I met Judith." Before she moved her piece, she asked, "How about you? Did you go to Woodside High School like James did?"

"Yeah."

Kate took another turn, earned a second wedge, and then was stumped on the next question. Handing him the die, she said offhandedly, "So, did you play football, too?"

He hesitated and his eyes narrowed, wondering about her question. "No. I was into swimming."

About to pick up a card, she halted and looked at him. "Wow, that's cool."

"When I was fifteen, I won two championship races for my summer swim team," Paul said, moving his piece to an orange square. "Breaststroke and butterfly in the fifteen- through eighteen-year-old age group."

"Really?"

"Yeah, really." He nodded and had to look away. The approval in her eyes did something to his insides and made him secretly glad for the wins to impart in the first place.

He then told her about making his high school swim team as a freshman. "I went to regionals that first year." He kept silent about the part his achievement played in helping him overcome his shyness.

He found himself opening up to her as they continued playing. Despite Kate earning two wedges to each one of his, he was totally enjoying the game and the conversation.

He'd shared more than of his past with her than any other woman, except Judith. What surprised him the most was that the words came out so naturally, probably a result of seeing admiration flash in her eyes after his revelations. Normally, he wasn't the type of guy who beat his chest, but that's exactly what he felt like doing.

Kate finally answered incorrectly, giving him a turn for a change.

"If I didn't know better, I'd think you were hustling me." Grinning, he reached for the die.

"You were the one who wanted to play," she said. Her easy laughter touched his heart and caused his breath to catch in his throat. "My skill comes from playing all those games on car rides answering all kinds of questions. And I love *Jeopardy*."

"Figures." He counted out the spaces. "Besides never traveling by car, I'm not a big *Jeopardy* fan."

The game had gone on for almost an hour when Paul stretched his legs toward the fire. He leaned on his elbow, not caring a bit that she only needed an orange wedge to win after landing on that color. He was having too much fun.

She'd been a cheerleader and homecoming queen in high school. Considering her bubbly personality, he could see her as both. Still, they had a lot in common. She grew up in a suburb of a big city and was the product of traditional upbringing. Her mom was a schoolteacher and her dad a businessman. Rather than having an older brother like him, she had a younger sister.

He took a card, read it, and then grinned. The game wasn't over yet. There was no way she'd answer this one correctly. Not in a million years.

"Where is Gasoline Alley?"

She didn't even have to think about it and said in a rush, "The Indianapolis Motor Speedway." She reached for the last wedge and stuck it into her pie. "I won."

"Now I know I've been hustled," he said, laughing at her all-too-smug expression. He'd finally come to the conclusion that his brother was a fool. She'd captivated him all evening. How had he been so wrong about her? Kate was nothing like the scheming, manipulating woman he'd pegged her to be. His skewed thinking made him feel shallow and cruel. Admiration for her swelled because she'd never backed down over the years, even when he'd really twisted the knife with his words.

"Ha!" she said. "You just don't like it that I won. Can I help it if my dad was a car nut who loved the Indy 500?" Her eyebrows rose in question. "You want to play another?"

"And have my ego smashed again? No thanks." Even now, he didn't want to accept the attraction between them. But the pull was too strong. The thought of kissing those soft lips, smiling at him now, overwhelmed him.

"Then, what should we do now?"

"We can keep talking." Maybe talking would get his mind off kissing her. "Your dad sounds like a great guy," he said nonchalantly, putting the game board and pieces away.

Her smile turned wistful. "He is. I miss him." She looked into the fake flames and sighed. "But I don't miss the Chicago winters."

"And that's why you ski so much?" He nodded knowingly. "Makes perfect sense."

"Tahoe winters are nothing like midwestern winters. The wind chill can be brutal; it isn't for the weak. I've seen blizzards caused by the lake effect that make this storm seem puny in comparison." She shrugged and kept her attention on the fire. "Still, I'm midwestern through and through." She broke off. It was several seconds before she spoke again and this time her voice sounded sad. "I feel as if I'm letting my family down somehow."

"What do you mean? How?"

"I'm the oldest. My parents can't understand why I'm not married yet. Now that Chrissie is getting married this summer, I'm starting to wonder the same thing."

"James'll come around." He'd be a flipping idiot not to, Paul thought, seeing the same sadness he heard now creep into her expression.

"Yeah, maybe." She offered a wan smile.

He cleared his throat, not liking the squeezing sensation in his chest as more anguish seeped into her eyes. "You want to talk about it? Sometimes talking helps." No one, not even James would be stupid enough to let her get away. *Once he realized what he had, that is.*

One thing he knew for certain. If Kate were his, he'd never cause her such sorrow. Images of laying her down in front of the fire and kissing away her pain flitted through his mind.

"If I'm going to talk about James, I need more wine." She stood.

Before he could stop himself and question the sanity of his actions, he reached out and grabbed her arm when she moved past him. Caught off guard, she toppled on top of him.

"What're you doing?" Laughter was present in her question, as he removed the empty glass from her hand and set it on the table.

"This," he whispered. He quickly captured her mouth without giving her a chance to withdraw. Having her right where he'd wanted her all evening, he wasn't about to lose his advantage. Her moan floated up and ignited his passion. He softened his lips and when her tongue darted tentatively inside his mouth, blood rushed past his ears, a freight train of desire hurling inside his brain.

At the same time, her scent rose up to fill his nostrils. More sensation raced to his core. Need and want slammed into him from all sides, swamping him in a sea of emotion. His hands, aching to reach underneath her sweater, found the sides of her breasts and stroked. All day he'd imagined what it would be like to taste her. Now that it was reality, he couldn't stop.

He immediately rolled over, pulling her underneath him in an effort to bring her closer. She couldn't miss the extent of his need as his erection settled into that perfect spot. He spent long minutes doing nothing but letting his mouth slowly savor hers, wanting to enflame her senses because his had already spread out of control.

Through his sensual haze, he registered her pushing on his chest. Reality hit him like a bucket of ice water to the head and he froze. Shit! He broke the kiss, released her, and rolled over on his back, even as untamed desire hummed throughout his entire system.

How in the hell had this happened? He brought his hands up to his face, rubbing it with his eyes closed in an effort to clear his mind and gain control. He opened them seconds later only to see her kneeling in front of him with a dismayed look on her face.

What have I done?

He never should have kissed her, but contrition wouldn't come. Not for something that felt so right.

Paul surged to his feet and shoved a shaky hand through his hair. "I wish I could apologize for my actions, but it wouldn't be heartfelt," he said. "So, I think it's time I said goodnight." He then pivoted and forced his unwilling feet to carry him to his room.

He didn't regret kissing her. But guilt weighed a ton more than remorse.

Chapter 8

Kate huddled under a thick blanket, shivering, having spent a miserable night on the lumpy sofa. No matter what she did, she couldn't seem to get warm or comfortable.

Worse, thoughts of Paul and that kiss, one that would give anyone insomnia, wouldn't budge. She pulled her blanket higher and turned. Her eyes felt gritty. Persistent jackhammers attacked her skull from the inside out. Any minute, they'd break through the surface and her head would explode.

Hours spent obsessing in the dark had only increased her agitation. If only she'd recognized the truth about James earlier, she wouldn't be in this mess, freezing her tush off and pining over Paul. She'd cursed everyone by this point—James for his lack of consideration, herself for letting him get away for it for so long, and Paul for being so attractive. She even blamed Judith for not caring about such a great guy, and for not making a better effort to please him. If Judith hadn't had to work, then last night wouldn't have happened.

Upon realizing how irrational it was to place any blame on her best friend, she swore and hit the pillow. *Morrisons! The fault rests on both their shoulders.*

As a sliver of light peeked through the window, she cursed the two brothers all over again—especially Paul for kissing her in the first place.

Damn! Why had he done it? From her vantage point, he and Judith were James and her. Only in reverse, with one exception. Time didn't mean as much to their situation as it did to Kate's. A few years younger than her, Judith still had to get her company off the ground. But a year from now when work took a backseat, her biological clock would hit the witching hour, and Judith would be ready for what Paul wanted. Then, they'd live happily ever after and Kate would dance at their wedding—*knowing that he'd kissed her*. And worse. Knowing she'd enjoyed it more than anything she'd ever experienced and hadn't wanted him to stop.

Groaning at the memory, she closed her eyes and covered them with her arm. She had no excuse other than how wonderful it felt to see warmth in the same gaze where she used to see only ridicule. Plus, he had seemed so into her last night. She couldn't remember a time when James showed the same type of interest. The idea that it was the setting and not Paul at all added guilt on top of guilt. He was just being himself and, in all truthfulness, she was angrier at herself for falling under his spell, which brought her jumbled thoughts full circle.

She stretched out and stared at the ceiling as more light filtered into the room. Sleep would be all but impossible now. All she wanted was a hot shower followed by a steaming cup of coffee, preferably strong.

Yeah! Fat chance of either happening today.

She glanced over at the wall of windows and saw a deep white wall had built sometime in the night. At least it had stopped snowing.

Kate closed her eyes and brought her knees to her chest in another attempt to warm up, wondering how she'd face the man this morning, much less spend any amount of time with him. She doubted they'd be able to drive to Squaw Valley. The roads had to be impassable. Even if they made it, she wasn't sure the resort had power.

No, more likely she'd be passing the day in this prison, housebound with Paul, faced with the imminent possibility of making a bigger fool of herself in the process.

How had an innocent weekend of skiing turned into a nightmare?

The only thing that could make the nightmare worse walked out of his room at that moment. Her temper flared when she saw him looking too damned attractive, despite bedhead and a morning beard. "What do you want?" she asked in a voice colder than ice, hoping to prod him into reverting to the jerk she could handle.

~

The accusatory tone drew Paul's attention. He halted and glanced at the sofa.

"What do you mean, what do I want?" he snapped back, catching Kate's annoyed frown and stiff posture as she sat up in a huff and crossed her arms. Even her hair looked stiff, adding to her unapproachable expression, which was okay by him. Being jovial this morning required too much effort.

"It was a simple question." Her chin angled higher. "What part don't you understand?"

Her snippy words only provoked him further so he tuned her out and continued walking toward the kitchen. He had no desire for a confrontation. Not when his head ached—more from lack of sleep than overindulging in wine. He'd lain awake most of the night wishing he hadn't kissed her because erasing the taste of her from his mind had been next to impossible. And it was all her fault. If she hadn't attracted him or acted so damned interested in him, it never would have happened.

"What? Ignoring me now?"

"This isn't a good time, Kate. I didn't sleep well."

When he had slept, he'd dreamed. Tormented dreams that had seemed so real. Dreams of Kate in which she beckoned him with her body, mocked him with her smile, and laughed at him when he tried to possess her and failed. They were so erotic and disturbing, he woke up several times in a cold sweat, rock hard, and burning with need. In fact, he was still aroused, and in this foul mood, he was itching for a fight. Not being a total fool, he realized this seemed a good time as any to follow his mother's advice about saying nothing at all if he couldn't say something nice.

"So that precludes you from common courtesy?" Judging by her stance, she wasn't about to back down, a suspicion confirmed when her scowl deepened and her tone became more combative. "You can't even answer a simple question?"

"To be honest, I don't even remember the question."

"Of course you don't, because you were ignoring me."

Was she serious? "I wasn't ignoring you." The vice on his head tightened. Closing his eyes, he stopped. "Just let me wake up and I'll answer any question you have," he said, when he could finally speak without blinding pain. "So, back off. At least until I've had coffee." He continued toward the kitchen, saying over his shoulder, "I can't deal with any shit right now, especially yours."

"How dare you!" She was off the sofa and after him in a flash. Coming up behind him and poking him in the back. "Don't you dare try and blame this on me. For your information, bucko, you started it."

"I'm warning you, Kate." He spun around and grabbed her hand. "Back off."

"And what are you going to do to get me to back off?" she taunted, stomping her foot and pulling out of his grasp. "I'm sick to death of you Morrisons having everything your way," she said, poking him again. "You're just as bad as James."

"Oh, yeah?" He hated being compared to his brother and doubly hated the fact she'd bring him up now. "Well, here's a news flash," he countered, leaning in closer and fighting his anger. "In case you haven't noticed, I'm not James."

"No, you're worse. You're certainly no gentleman." She hurled the words like a weapon and poked him again, this time harder, while adding, "In fact, I can't believe you're related. He'd never treat me like this."

His patience finally snapped. If she had such a low opinion of him, he'd show her just how low he could go. He caught her wrist, swung her into his arms and, before she knew what hit her, his lips crushed hers in a bruising, punishing kiss fraught with all the frustration, irritation, and desire now burning his insides. Her arms moved higher and, rather than push him away as he expected, she pulled him closer.

In seconds, he had her back against the wall, leaving her no doubt about his arousal.

After what felt like an eternity, he broke the kiss and asked in a ragged voice, "You want to play with fire, Kate? You just keep pushing." Taking her hand, he moved it lower. "Here—that's fire and it's burning for you."

Then, he moved against her hand, scorching them both with his heat as she moaned. He captured her lips once again, only this time his lips softened. Where they were bruising before, now they were sensual, moving over her mouth, trying to seduce her. Where they were demanding before, now they were begging, asking for completion. He used his tongue, plunging into her mouth, invading her, filling her, working to make her yearn for things neither of them should want.

All coherent thought flew out the window, along with any remaining restraint. His only thought? Subdue her...dominate her...possess her.

He forgot about Judith. He forgot that Kate loved his brother. He forgot that she was the woman he'd derided for years and disdained. He forgot that he shouldn't be doing this because he was encroaching on his brother's girl. All he could think about was finishing what he'd started last night. The aching need that began two days ago as a simmering attraction boiled over into a desperate act of desire.

When he tasted her tears, it stopped him cold and yanked him out of the erotic haze that had taken control of his decency and tossed him back to reality faster than a cold shower.

He lifted his mouth from hers, suddenly immersed in self-loathing. How had this happened? How had he lost control like that? All these questions burned in his mind. But the biggest problem? How could he make it up to her? "I'm sorry." He looked into her tear-rimmed eyes as regret filled his. "You didn't deserve that." He kissed the top of her head.

He gathered her up, carried her to the sofa, and sat with her still in his arms. He spotted the blanket she'd used the night before and grabbed it, before he tucked it gently around her shoulders. She cried as he rocked her slightly back and forth, comforting her as if she were a small child instead of a grown woman.

His heart ached as he continued rocking, staring at the flames that danced in the fireplace.

Not once in his twenty-eight years had Paul ever been jealous or envious of his brother. He'd taken great strides to carve out his own identity and be his own person. He never lived in James' shadow. He'd never wanted to be like him; had never wanted anything he had. Until now. Now, he wanted Kate. He wanted the love she gave to James. He'd give anything he owned to acquire it. This all-consuming, burning desire for it overwhelmed him so much that he wondered about his sanity. Judith had never made him feel this way. He couldn't possibly love Kate, not after so short a time. But what he did feel was strong enough to dwarf what he felt for Judith, making him question everything in his life.

Finally, he glanced at Kate. She'd stopped crying and was sitting in his lap wrapped like a baby, looking up at him with questioning eyes.

"Better?" he asked.

She nodded and smiled in a fragile way that ripped his heart more. She seemed to have no intention of moving, so he held her and stroked her in an effort to ease the hurt he'd caused.

"Am I forgiven?" he asked minutes later, breaking into the silence that had settled upon them.

"There's nothing to forgive," she said softly, as that spunky gleam made a reappearance in her eyes. "We both were uncivilized and mean. I, for one, am not telling Judith about your transgressions, if you don't breathe a word about mine."

Her teasing manner and words caused him to scrutinize her more thoughtfully. His admiration of her spirit climbed a notch. It seemed nothing got her down or kept her spirit from bouncing back. Like a ball in deep water, you could push it under but ultimately it rose back to the surface.

When quiet descended again, Paul noticed the chill. "How long has it been this cold in here?" The fireplace, never meant to act as a heater, couldn't keep up with the falling temperatures outside.

"I don't know. It seems as if it's never been warm."

"Kate, you should've come into my room. There's no sense in freezing."

"Oh, yeah, after what happened last night, I'm just supposed to go knock on your door and say, 'Hey, big fellow…how about keeping me warm?' What kind of fool do I look like?" Then offering another feeble smile, she said, "No! Don't answer that."

He chuckled. "I definitely understand your reluctance. I should've let you have the bedroom. I'm sorry—I wasn't thinking straight last night."

"It's okay. I was fine."

"Well, it doesn't make sense to be uncomfortable. Tonight we can share the room."

"Excuse me?" she countered. "It may make sense, but I'm not sure it's wise."

"What? You don't trust me?" He laughed. "Don't answer that. Really, Scout's honor, I'll be on my best behavior. Even better, I'll be happy to sleep on the floor in front of the fireplace."

"I'll think about it."

"Well, while you're thinking, I'm getting cold." He stood and headed for his room with her still in his arms.

When they got to the open door, the warmth hit him. He unceremoniously dropped her on the bed and turned to stoke the fire. The room was about twenty degrees warmer than the one they'd come from.

He felt her gaze on his back before she spoke. "I guess it does make sense. Are you sure you don't mind?"

He kneeled and tossed a couple more logs on the fire. "Why would I mind?" He gave the fire another poke, before twisting around to see her response.

"Yeah, but—" She hesitated for several long seconds before clearing her throat. "I…umm…mean…umm…only two days ago we were enemies and now I'm going to be sleeping in the same room with you. I…umm, just want to make sure you don't mind."

He laughed because the whole situation struck him as funny. She had no clue of the emotions raging through him.

Damn, it is the Twilight Zone *and I'm living it.*

He looked around the room, half expecting Rod Serling to come out of the woodwork saying, "Imagine if you will…" and he could go back to being normal. The thought of that happening made him laugh even harder.

"I fail to see what's so funny about all of this," Kate huffed, crossing her arms and glaring.

Paul straightened and pivoted, still laughing, holding on to his stomach. "I know and that's what makes it so funny."

She eyed him intently before breaking into laughter herself. "Well, when you put it like that, I guess it is pretty funny."

After the laughter died, Paul grabbed a thick sweatshirt from his bag, along with some slippers, and put them on. "I'll go and see about coffee now. Why don't you stay here and try to get warm."

"Sounds good," Kate murmured to his departing back. "I'm too tired to move."

Paul rummaged through the kitchen drawers, really craving his morning fix of caffeine. He glanced at the useless electric grinder in front of him and frowned. Whole beans needed grinding. Then, remembering his mom's love of antiques, he dashed back out to the dining room. Hanging over the hundred-year-old buffet was a shadow box containing a Victorian coffee grinder. Heaving a relieved sigh, he retrieved it.

Short of pounding the beans with a hammer if the old grinder didn't work, he prayed it was functional and not missing any parts. After figuring out how it worked, he cranked the handle and smiled. Voilà. He had fresh-ground coffee.

"Thank you, Lord," he said under his breath, as he placed a pan of water to heat over the burner's flames. He grabbed a filter, set it inside the coffeemaker's holder along with the ground beans, finally adding the near-boiling water minutes later. The glass pot caught the brewed coffee as it trickled out. Once the pot filled, he poured two large cups, leaving the rest on the burner to reheat later. Not perfect, but better than nothing.

After putting half-and-half in both, he picked up the cups and worked his way back to the bedroom. He opened the door and spied Kate fast asleep on the bed, wrapped in the blanket from the other room. She appeared so peaceful that he didn't have the heart to wake her. He placed both cups on the nightstand, sat down on the floor next to the bed, and reached for two pillows. He fluffed them behind him before reaching for his coffee. He leaned back and sipped the strong brew, relishing its warmth.

When Kate murmured something in her sleep, he glanced up at the bed to see her curled into a ball, shivering.

"Are you cold?" he asked when she opened her eyes.

"I can't seem to get warm," she replied, nodding.

"Get under the down comforter," he said. "It's good for keeping in body heat but it takes a while to warm up when you're chilled to the bone." Considering the temperature was already cooler than normal to begin with, he wondered if she'd ever get warm.

"Maybe it'll help," he said as he stood, yanking the pillows and tossing them on the bed, "if we share body heat for a few minutes. Until you warm up."

She nestled under the comforter, but immediately snuggled closer when he lay down beside her. Grinning, he situated her against his chest. When he wrapped his arm around her and pulled the comforter up to her chin, a relaxed sigh floated past his ear. He lingered long after she fell asleep, just holding Kate and drinking his coffee, content to do nothing else.

For the first time in as long as he could remember, his loneliness abated. The realization only made his life appear emptier because this feeling was no more real than what he had with Judith. Still, holding Kate close gave him a glimpse of what his life could be like. Hopefully that would be enough to keep him on track to begin a new search for someone who would chase away the loneliness for good.

Chapter 9

Kate moved to stretch and was hampered with not only the comforter, but with Paul's arm, which was around her waist. Turning gently so she wouldn't disturb him, she took in his slumbering form. He looked so innocent as he lay next to her, his upturned face relaxed in sleep, head supported on a mound of pillows. Considering the way he kissed, the man was anything but innocent. Heat climbed up her face at the memory. More of the same conflicted thoughts swirled around in her head, yet she watched him for a while longer, noting how attractive he was and marveling at how comfortable she felt in his arms.

She was in deep trouble. Though this felt so right, she knew it was all so wrong. Those few wild moments last night had been too hard to resist. If it had been anyone else, she'd have thrown caution to the wind and jumped in headfirst. But, she couldn't. Even if Judith weren't in the picture, it wouldn't matter. She didn't trust him. Worse, she didn't trust herself.

When she tried to untangle herself, her movement was enough to wake him. Sitting up and rubbing his eyes, he shook off the sleepiness. The second their gazes connected, he grinned. Time seemed to stand still. She couldn't look away.

"You look well rested."

She nodded, returning his smile and wishing things were different.

He broke the spell and glanced toward the fireplace. "Fire's down to embers. I need to add more logs."

Unable to speak, she nodded.

"Thanks for...everything," she finally said, once she found her voice. She felt heat on her cheeks for what she'd almost blurted out. Thanking him for keeping her warm didn't seem like the smartest thing to say right then. "I feel much better."

"My pleasure." Still sporting that engaging smile, he extricated his body from hers and rose off the bed. While he stretched and padded over to the fireplace, she escaped to the bathroom. Upon her return, the first thing she noticed was the added warmth to the room from the now roaring fire.

Still holding the poker, Paul faced her.

Both stopped—and stood staring at each other for another awkward moment. Neither spoke.

She cleared her throat, smoothing her jeans in a nervous gesture, then walked toward the window and peeked out. "Sun's up." The storm had passed, leaving behind a bright blue sky that contrasted sharply against a white background of deep snow. She offered a wan smile. "I guess skiing's out."

"Yeah, no way we can get out to the main road. A BMW isn't built for this much snow. Hopefully the electricity will come back on soon." Paul glanced at his watch. "I can't believe we slept over four hours." He placed the poker aside. "Thank God for natural gas. At least we have plenty of hot water and we're able to cook. We'll probably have to spend a good part of the day in here to stay warm."

He started for the door, asking along the way, "Would you like a cup of coffee?"

"I'd love one." Kate followed him out of the bedroom. She went over to her bags and pulled out her toothbrush, toothpaste, fresh clothes, and toiletries. "I'm taking a quick shower. I'll be out in a bit."

At Paul's grunt, she smiled.

Things will work out. She'd survive. She and Paul might even be good friends after this.

~

Paul watched Kate disappear and shook his head.

I can handle this. If he could just keep his hands to himself, he'd get through the next twenty-four hours. Then he'd go through the process of getting both women out of his system. Smiling to himself, he began the task of heating the coffee. Since Kate knew her way around the kitchen, he'd leave the cooking to her.

An hour later, he looked out the window and sighed, feeling slightly on edge. They'd finished a filling breakfast, thanks to Kate's skill, and were cleaning up. After washing the last plate and sticking it in the dishwasher to dry, he reached for the coffeepot, now warming on the burner, and poured. He sipped the hot brew and paced, still unable to relax. "I hate being cooped up like this."

Kate glanced around the room, hugging her sides. "It does feel a little cramped in here."

"Why don't we get into our ski clothes and snow boots and go out for a walk?" His nod indicated the window. "The fresh air will do us good."

Kate's gaze followed his. "Sure. Should be fun and give us something to do." She practically ran to her bag, searched through it and brought out snow gear, then started for the spare bathroom. "I'll be right back."

He grinned. "Okay. And I'll do the same," he said on the way to his room, thankful for a diversion. The space inside felt too confined, made more so with her unsettling presence.

A few minutes later, he emerged from the hallway to find Kate pacing, bundled from head to toe in a snowsuit. The picture of her moving back and forth in obvious impatience brought a smile to his lips. She looked like an oversized child, except for those noticeable curves. No one could mistake her for a kid.

When she noticed him, her eyebrows shot up. "It's about time."

Paul laughed, grabbed her hand, and made a quick retreat out the front door.

On the porch, he inhaled and blew out invigorating puffs of frigid air that stung his lungs.

"I should shovel a path," he said, still holding her gloved fingers, as they trudged through knee-deep snow.

"I'll help." Her laughter bubbled up and the sound floated past his ears as she plopped to the ground. "Let me know when you have the shovels."

He watched her play in the snow, acting as if she hadn't a care in the world. He stilled the urge to roll with her. Instead, he turned toward the garage and punched in the code to open the door. Having too much fun would only get him into trouble.

He grabbed two shovels and walked back outside. The sun's glare bounced off the white background, increasing the temperature to the mid-thirties. Without cloud cover, it would probably turn colder once the sun went down, Paul thought, as he handed her one of the shovels. Which didn't bode well for the chilly night ahead. It was bad enough in daylight, but in candlelight?

He started shoveling, using exertion to ease the aching need lurking just below the surface.

Together, they spent the next forty-five minutes clearing the driveway, shoveling all the way to the street. Next, they tackled the sidewalk.

Their task finished, they trudged up the street, picking their way through the deep, fluffy, white stuff. On their way back, Kate began frolicking in the snow again. When she dropped to the ground and made a snow angel, he laughed.

"Try it. It's fun." She flapped her arms and legs, creating another one.

He couldn't resist her teasing dare. That sense of fun drew him in...had him falling in the snow like a big kid. Following her directions, he waved his arms and spread his legs. "Nothing to it."

"That doesn't look like any angel I've ever seen," she said, mocking his attempt.

"Oh yeah?" Paul gave it one more try, which caused her to erupt into giggles again. He joined her, and they both fell into the snow laughing. He couldn't remember a time when he'd laughed so hard.

He was still smiling when a snowball hit him square in the jaw. It didn't hurt, but it surprised him. Not to be outdone, he quickly packed snow into the perfect sphere. He then aimed and fired it straight at her head. She ducked and the snowball fight ensued in earnest.

Eventually, Paul tired of the game and quit throwing, but Kate wouldn't let up. She kept bombarding him with snowballs, one right after the other.

"Stop," he said, walking toward her and dodging white missiles. "Game's over." He understood her nature to keep pushing, recognizing the trait as one of his.

She only laughed and hit him in the cheek instead. "What're you going to do about it, Morrison?"

He frowned. He'd had enough. He did an about-face and started for the house.

"Where are you going?" she yelled, still laughing.

"I'm going in. I told you the game's over."

"Why? Because I was winning?"

Halfway up the driveway, he turned back. "No. I quit because it wasn't fun anymore."

"You're just mad because I clobbered you." When he ignored her taunt and continued walking, she shouted, "I can't believe you're serious." She hurried up to him. "It was just a stupid snowball fight."

He stopped and glanced at her. His sigh bore infinite patience. "We both know this isn't about snowballs." He watched several emotions cross her face.

"All right," she finally said, backing down. "I'm sorry."

Knowing he'd won the skirmish and that it had cost her, he held out his hand. "Still friends?"

She shook her head. "No. I think we do better as enemies." She then turned.

He watched her storm back to the house and shouted when she was almost at the door, "So, does this means our truce is off?"

"Drop dead, bucko." Without looking back, she sent him an unladylike hand signal.

He burst out laughing, then shook his head and followed.

Damn, she's feisty. No wonder his brother had a hard time with her. She was definitely a challenge as he'd discovered this weekend. Kate Winters rode roughshod over anyone who'd let her.

He had no doubt that he'd handled her in exactly the right way. He was perfectly willing to be friends, but he had no intention of feeling her footprints on his back. Even if she hated him for not allowing her to tread all over him.

Chapter 10

Kate tensed when the mudroom door opened at the same time the sound of the garage door closing filled the air. Out of her peripheral vision, she saw Paul amble across the room. She didn't look up. Instead, she flipped the pages of one of James' *Architectural Digests*, presenting an appearance of total absorption.

Thankfully, Paul ignored her and kept walking toward the bedroom hallway.

As she mindlessly thumbed through the magazine, the gas flames blazed away. Sunlight filtered through the wall of windows, providing extra heat. While still on the cool side, the room had warmed up considerably. But what about later, when the sun went down and the temperature dropped?

Unsure of how to act around him after making a complete ass of herself, she exhaled a relieved sigh the second he disappeared from view, then set the magazine on her lap. Pictures of modern architecture interested her about as much as watching golf on TV. She glanced at the doorway, pushing out the thought that she much preferred the grace and beauty of older homes and buildings over the square and glass monstrosities that had replaced them.

She had bigger problems to focus on. Namely, how in the hell she'd maintain composure once they had to move to the master bedroom for warmth. The sofa might be a better alternative. The minute the notion was out, she discarded it, knowing that Paul wouldn't allow anyone but him to take the couch. Somehow the idea of him being gallant on her account didn't sit well. Aside from his actions this morning, he'd been a perfect gentleman and that made her feel like pond scum.

She sighed again. In all reality, that kiss would never have happened if she hadn't provoked him into it. Her face burned with embarrassment just recalling the incident. Deep down, she wasn't sure if she hadn't wanted it. If she were completely honest, she'd have to admit that the snowball fight was more of the same goading. *Look at me! Like me! Choose me over Judith!*

How twisted could a person be?

Paul chose that moment to emerge from the hallway, pulling a hoodie over his head. The navy blue only highlighted his blond good looks. Her gaze traveled down those broad shoulders, which narrowed to a lean waist, finally landing on jean-clad legs. The guy was way too attractive for his own good. Especially since his male beauty was more than skin-deep and went all the way to his heart and soul. That was infinitely more potent because it only added to his appeal.

She closed her eyes and swallowed hard, regretting her earlier behavior even more. His response had only garnered her respect. He was definitely worth having as a friend, which meant being completely civil. The only way to do that was to control that obnoxious, pushy facet of her personality. If he could handle the attraction without being a total jackass, then so could she.

Nevertheless, the realization chafed. Big-time. She didn't want to respect him or like him. Viewing him as an enemy had always been so much easier.

"So, what are we having for dinner?" Paul stood, warming his hands in front of the gas fireplace, and glanced over his shoulder to eye her as if the past few hours hadn't happened.

Men! Her stomach churned as she struggled to keep her jaw from dropping. Though he stood several feet away, he was still much too close for her comfort. How could he be so calm after all that had taken place? "How about the hot dogs you bought?" She glanced at him, hiding her anxiety behind a tight smile. Did he really not feel the tension?

"You're joking, right?"

"No." She went back to the magazine she wasn't reading and flipped the page. "Why do you think I'm joking?" She fought to mirror his nonchalance, but it took some effort when his smile could make old ladies swoon. It certainly had her heart pitter-pattering at an accelerated pace.

He remained silent.

Sensing that he was waiting for her to look up, she finally did.

His gaze snared hers and held on tight, as that thousand-watt smile doubled in intensity. "After the feast you made us last night, I wouldn't take you as someone who'd settle for hot dogs."

She cleared her throat, praying he couldn't hear her heart race. Pitter-pattering seemed too mild a description for something that was now thumping wildly. She broke the connection, trying to remember the gist of the conversation. Oh, yeah. Something about hot dogs. Nodding, she said, "You have a point. Most chefs cringe at the thought of all those nitrates and saturated fat. But not me. I love them." She turned another page, going for bored. "Besides, I don't feel like cooking."

"Hmm. Something else we have in common."

She felt his gaze but ignored him this time, preferring not to dwell on their commonalities.

"How 'bout I cook dinner? Hot dogs are my

specialty." When she only nodded, he sighed and started for the bedroom hallway. "I have work to do, so let me know when you're hungry."

Surreptitiously, she watched him round the corner. The moment he was out of sight, she dropped the magazine on the coffee table and hugged herself. If only she could leave. Her gaze then moved to the windows. The scene couldn't be more idyllic. Brilliant white against the sky and a forest of evergreens. She could barely make out the lake from her vantage point, but it appeared tranquil and turquoise blue.

The thoughts got lost when Paul reappeared carrying a briefcase. He strode toward her with purpose, placed the case on the coffee table, and sat down on the opposite end of the sofa, not three feet away.

Was he nuts? "Can't you work in the other room?" Did he not realize her discomfort?

"You don't mind, do you?" He took out what looked to be a business prospectus from the briefcase and then propped his feet on the table. "It's too lonely in there," he said.

Far be it from her to admit that she minded when his tone sounded so forlorn. She shook her head, deciding he must have forgiven her for the snowball pelting. Besides, he *was* damned good company. She firmed her resolve to ignore the attraction.

Pretend he's James.

It worked. At least for a while. Until her mind sifted through the years. Her teeth ground together as she grasped more consistencies in her relationship that she'd brushed away as insignificant. Hindsight really was twenty-twenty. James wasn't much different back then from how he was now. Just thinking how she'd settled for less for so long got her blood pressure rising. What was worse, she was able to see her own part in the mix. Her response to his ambivalent attitude only prolonged this moment. Oh God. Mrs. Pike was dead-on with her cow analogy. He had free milk, so why *would* he buy the cow? Actions spoke louder than words, only she hadn't listened. She'd twisted the relationship to work, ignoring his needs as well as her own.

"Are you okay?"

Paul's voice startled her.

"I'm fine." She sent him a guarded look. Did he suspect her apprehension toward him, or could he read her mind? "Why would you think I wasn't okay?"

His nod indicated the edge of the sofa, where her hand gripped the arm tighter than an alligator's jaws held prey.

As warmth spread from her neck to her face, Kate quickly released her fingers. Flexing them, she placed her hand in her lap. "I was thinking about James." It was better than admitting some of those thoughts had been about him.

"Ah yes—James. How could I forget about him?" He offered an apologetic half smile and refocused on his reading material. "I imagine I'm a lousy substitute for my brother."

A genuine smile broke free despite all the angst residing in her system. If only he knew her true thoughts on the subject—that she was a lousy substitute for Judith. She laughed outright. It was better than crying.

"What?" His gaze centered back on her face. "You think me being a lousy substitute is funny?" He shook his head. "That hurts my feelings."

Unsure of whether he was serious or not, she eyed him thoughtfully. "It's not that." She'd take his sensitivity over James' lack of attention any day, but no way could she disclose that fact.

His eyebrows quirked, clearly saying, *Then what?*

"I was just thinking how much fun he and Judith missed by not coming this weekend," she lied. "James is such a workaholic. It's too bad CHP closed the roads."

He nodded. "Yeah, Judith is working long hours too. They both missed out." He hesitated a moment then added, "So do you think James' workload will ever slow down?"

No, she thought, offering instead, "It has to eventually." She inhaled deeply and threw him a quick smile. "If you don't mind, I prefer not to dwell on James or Judith's work ethics. Hopefully, we can drive back to the city tomorrow and this weekend will go down in the annals as a bad weekend and we'll both move on with our lives."

"Yeah." With an agitated snap of his wrist, Paul flipped to the next page as his posture stiffened. "Just a bad weekend all around."

"I didn't mean it that way," Kate quickly interjected. "I just meant that my eyes have been opened to what I need to do."

"And what's that?"

"Break things off with James. I can't move forward until I do."

"Well, that should definitely get his attention and give him a good wake-up call. You'll probably get a ring."

"I don't want a ring. Not any longer."

His brows arched, and those blues eyes underneath them were full of skepticism.

"It's true." So what if he didn't believe her. It was more important that she believe it.

He eyed her for a long moment, before nodding. "Guess we're both on the same page, since I'm ready to throw in the towel with Judith."

"What?" Her eyes widened in horror. "Why in the hell would you give up now?" Though she asked the question, she had more than a sneaking suspicion that this weird attraction between them was the reason.

"I'd be stupid not to follow your sage example."

"My situation is entirely different from yours and you know it." She crossed her arms and glared at him, daring him to dispute the fact. Heaven help her—she did not want to be the cause of their breakup. "Judith just needs more time to get her business up and running."

"Maybe." He shrugged and refocusing on his work in an obvious dismissal.

I know so, she thought, sighing and retrieving her book lying beside the discarded magazine. For the next few hours, the three worst of her life, she pretended to read…all the while acting as if the man working little more than an arm's length away didn't bother her.

When he finally reached for his briefcase, stuffed his reading material inside and stood, she sent up a prayer of thanks.

"Would you like a glass of wine? We're out of the French stuff, but red goes better with hot dogs anyway."

"I'm a beer and hot dogs kind of gal," she said in an effort to lighten the mood. "But I've been known to sacrifice my standards for whatever's available." So what if red wine gave her headaches. It would definitely help calm her frazzled nerves. Still, she'd limit herself to one glass now and one at dinner. No sense losing her inhibitions by overindulging, even though she'd love to drown her misery in something, headache producing or not.

Carrying two goblets by the stems in one hand, the wine and opener in the other, Paul strode toward her, still appearing all too composed for her peace of mind. "Just be thankful it's a decent cab and not Boone's Farm, which is what I used to drink in college when we were out of beer." He set the glasses down, then sat back at his end of the sofa to uncork the bottle.

After pouring, he caught her eye and handed her a glass before picking up the other. "The wine may have been cheap back then, but the company was always rich. Just as it is tonight," he said, offering a toast and giving her a smoldering look that could melt the polar ice caps. Then the look disappeared so fast, Kate wasn't sure if her imagination had gone into overdrive. She gulped down more than a sip, wondering if she was slowly going insane.

Please, just let me go just one more night without making a complete fool of myself.

Then, if she survived unscathed, she vowed to dump James and do everything in her power to find Mr. Right. Unfortunately, Paul owned Judith's heart, so he was no more Mr. Right than his brother. No amount of wishful thinking would change that fact.

~

"Want to keep me company while I cook?" Paul asked, pulling the trigger on the long lighter. Like the previous evening, he'd made his way around the room and now lit the last candle.

When Kate looked up, appearing startled by his question, he repeated it, adding with a shrug, "I just figured you needed a break from reading." Did he sound like a sap or what? *Why not just put a sign on my back that says, 'LONELY.'* "Never mind. It was a stupid suggestion."

"No, it wasn't." Kate set her book aside and stood. "And you're absolutely right. I do need a break. Besides, it's getting too dark to read."

He started for the kitchen.

She followed and leaned against the counter while he gathered the hot dogs, mustard, ketchup, and relish from the fridge.

As Paul glanced over at her while shutting the door with his rear end, he was glad for the groceries in his hands that prevented him from acting on a sudden, overwhelming urge to hug Kate. He never should have begged for her company, he now realized. Especially when dusk's shadows and the candlelight only softened her features and gave her a vulnerable appearance. He fought to ignore the glimpse of sadness he also caught in her expression—one that was much too solitary— reminding him of himself. He discarded the idea. Kate Winters was the least solitary person he knew. While he preferred his private lifestyle, her animated personality always drew a crowd.

He dropped the items on the counter and bent to search through the cabinets for a pan. After adding water, he set the pan on the burner, then turned to face her. "How about another glass of wine?"

She shook her head. "Not until dinner is served. But I'd love some water." She proceeded to get it herself, then moved to her previous spot against the counter and downed half the bottle. Crossing her legs at the ankles, she smiled. "I could get used to having a man wait on me."

She'd obviously meant the words as a joke, but there was still a hint of something akin to painful realization in her tone that grabbed his heart and squeezed. Hard. What the hell was wrong with James?

Don't look at her. Otherwise, you'll do something totally crazy, like try to comfort her. And that would be a big mistake. Touching her would lead to kissing, and kissing…well, it was just better if he didn't touch her.

He switched on the burner, then poured himself another glass of wine and took a sip, purposefully keeping his gaze on anything but Kate.

She was probably thinking about breaking things off with James. Paul had a good idea of what made his brother tick. Everything had always come easy to him. Kate, in his opinion, was one of those things. Mainly because she'd always been too available, which happened to be exactly the reason Paul had always given her so much grief. But James was no idiot. Once she quit being the aggressor and walked away, his brother would then realize what he was losing and take decisive action.

Was he a little envious of his brother? He groaned inwardly at the thought, unsettled by what that meant. Maybe it had always bothered him—on a subconscious level—that James never had to work at sustaining his relationship, while he'd worked tenaciously to merely gain Judith's friendship.

Staring into the burner's flames, Paul prayed for the water to boil faster.

He picked up his wine and sipped, wondering why he enjoyed having Kate nearby observing his cooking. The scene seemed so cozy...almost intimate. A brief glimpse of them spending more time in similar situations shot through his brain, and a longing for what would never be tightened the knot of regret forming in his gut.

First Judith and now Kate. What quirk of nature made him ignore those women he'd dated over the years and desire the only two he could never have? Was it because they were unattainable? Was that the draw?

To harbor a craving for what James had only added to his misery, especially when the desire for more than friendship with Kate was a hundred times stronger than what he felt for Judith. Even worse, he could never reveal his feelings because he doubted he could deal with seeing the truth in Kate's eyes. Being considered just friends with Judith was a cakewalk compared to taking second place in Kate's life behind James.

Paul took another large sip, hoping to dull the yearning.

If only one of them could be happy, he was glad it was her.

~

Kate sighed, content to watch Paul cook.

The object of her silent perusal finished dumping four hot dogs into the steaming pan, then turned around and winked. "Wait until you taste these. You'll think you've died and gone to heaven."

She laughed, trying to ignore that grin that never failed to steal her breath. She certainly didn't want to think about the way his crinkling, blue eyes tugged on heartstrings that were near their breaking point. "I'm sure it will be delicious. Besides, it's hard to ruin hot dogs."

She could stand here for hours, she realized, as the same sense of well-being that encompassed her last night while sharing space with him returned full force. She seldom felt this comfortable around James and the realization disturbed her more than a little, reinforcing her decision to break things off. There were so many differences in the brothers' actions—one in particular. Last night, Paul had clearly appreciated her meal, throwing out compliments right and left. James had always taken her cooking for granted, in fact almost expected it without ever complimenting her on a job well done. Of course, she enjoyed cooking and didn't do it for the praise, but to have her efforts recognized was more than a nice surprise. A courtesy that Paul extended and

James didn't. Just like offering to cook. In eight years, James had never once offered.

One thing led to another, and she found herself making other comparisons. Why did Paul seem so much more perceptive of her feelings than James? James wasn't rude by any means, was always generous and giving. But he was clueless about the things she found important.

She could be herself around Paul and he acted as if he enjoyed her that way. She never felt totally at ease with James. How sad to realize that by continually trying to get him to commit, she'd molded herself into what she thought *he* needed instead of who she was. The realization stopped her cold. How in the hell had she deceived herself for so long?

Thank God, she'd finally figured it out. *With a little help from a friend.* She smiled at Paul's back as he pulled buns out of the package.

"I guess it's time to set the table." She stowed her thoughts away and hurried to do the chore.

"All ready," he said a few minutes later, walking past her with two platters. He set them down. "While my skill is nowhere near your level, I hope you enjoy my one and only cooking talent."

"I can't wait to dig in." She followed him and pulled out a chair to sit. "Hot dogs are my idea of a feast and they look delicious."

"Oh, wait. I almost forgot." He jumped up, rushed to the kitchen, then brought back a full glass of wine and bowed. "For one beautiful lady," he said, holding it out.

The hand tracing the condensation on her water glass stilled and her wary gaze moved to his eyes. When nothing but sincerity shone in those blue depths, her eyes watered. It just wasn't fair, she thought, blinking back tears as she took the glass. "Quit being so nice. It's better if I hate you."

He sat back down without answering. In her peripheral vision, she noticed him picking up his wineglass. Instead of taking a drink, he hesitated, holding the glass inches from his mouth.

"Do you honestly believe after all we've been through, that either of us can hate the other?" His voice was hushed, drawing her gaze.

His intense stare held hers. For endless seconds she couldn't look away. Finally, she did, more confused than ever. It was as if she could see all the way to his soul. As beautiful as it was, it was also lonely, which didn't make sense. He couldn't feel alone. Not when he had Judith.

Shaking the unsettling notion, she refocused on the hot dog. Yet, she couldn't dismiss as easily the sense of connection that touched everything inside her being.

She took a bite, chewed, and eventually swallowed even as dissatisfaction over her failed relationship slammed into her from every angle. Now she was positive she and James were never meant to be.

After that, neither spoke.

The temperature dropped as they ate; a definite chill began seeping into the room.

Shivering, Kate took her last sip of wine, then set her glass on the table and rubbed her arms. Despite the heavy sweater she wore, her hands and feet were already freezing.

She hated being cold, which meant moving to the warmer room sooner rather than later.

Paul stood, grabbing both empty plates. On his way to the kitchen, he said, "It's getting pretty cold out here. Why don't you go and get comfortable in the other room, while I do dishes?" He added, almost as an afterthought, "I'll take my time."

"Okay." She smiled and nodded. *What a sweetheart. He's giving me space.*

"But first, I'll get the fire going again in there." After putting the plates in the sink, he quickly headed for the bedroom.

Kate followed and stood at the door to observe his capable movements, briskly rubbing her arms as he removed the grate and kneeled in front of the fireplace.

He added more wood to the embers, then stoked the logs. Kate's breath hitched in the back of her throat. In seconds, heat from the blazing fire enveloped her like a warm blanket and finally she was able to take in air.

She glanced at her hands and stepped toward the bed, unwilling to dwell on how attractive he looked, kneeling with poker in hand, and a lock of blond hair falling over his face. He possessed a boyish quality that made her want to go over and wrap her arms around him. What would his reaction be if she threw her scruples aside and just did it? Hugging herself, she grinned.

He chose that moment to turn and look up at her.

She laughed. *Heavens! This is becoming a habit.*

"What's so funny?" he asked, now eying her intently.

"You really don't want to know."

"Ah, another secret!" A small smile crept across his face. "How I wish things were different and I could pry your secrets out of you." He moved to poke the fire one more time before reluctantly rising. He placed the tool with the others. "I'll be in later." Then he was gone, having shut the door on his way out.

Standing as still as stone, Kate eyed the closed door for a long moment before sighing.

She rushed to wash her face and brush her teeth. After exchanging jeans for sweats, she quickly got under the covers. Several relaxing breaths later, she let her body go limp. She intended to be fast asleep before he finished in the other room.

Chapter 11

Paul worked slowly, using the mindless chore of washing and rinsing dishes to keep his thoughts off the woman in the other room.

The countertops and stove wiped down, he then topped off his wine, picked up his glass, and started for the living room sofa, blowing out candles along his way. He decided to give Kate more time, mainly because he needed it too. So he plopped himself down on the sofa and rested his feet on the coffee table.

He gazed into the flames, taking the occasional sip of wine, and a sense of peace settled over him. Despite the mess his love life was in, he couldn't help believing things would improve. He swallowed the last of the cabernet, yet made no effort to move. He was too relaxed.

A noise disturbed the quiet, and Paul glanced up. His eyes narrowed in confusion at the vision of Kate standing before him. It took a moment to find his bearings. He was still at the house in Tahoe, so he must have awakened from a deep sleep.

Kate leaned closer, then smiled and whispered his name. The yearning in her eyes matched the longing in his heart. He patted the spot next to him on the sofa. She quickly obeyed his silent request and sat beside him. Then she did the unexpected, turning his way and sliding her fingers around his neck, and with beckoning eyes, pulled him closer.

He didn't waste precious time trying to figure it out. He simply acquiesced to her invitation and lowered his mouth to hers. The moment their lips connected, if was if he was tasting manna from heaven, which eased some of the hunger in his heart.

Her contented sigh floated somewhere above him at the same time her hands began moving down his back.

She was so warm...so tempting...so responsive.

The longing to possess her increased exponentially in those few seconds, but he didn't dare overstep his boundaries. Suddenly, his worst fears came to fruition when he realized he no longer held her. Her laughter filled his head while disappointment and heartache filled his soul.

"Paul?"

His name drifted from afar.

"Wake up, Paul. The power's on."

He slowly emerged from a sleep-induced fog into reality. Opening his eyes, he saw Kate leaning over him so near he felt the warmth of her breath, only this time it wasn't a dream.

Their stares locked. Something indefinable passed between them, then grew. He planted his feet on the ground and sat up straighter to break the connection. Several questions played in his mind—his biggest? What would she do if he kissed her as he was dying to do?

When he risked another glance, her expression wielded the same passion that swamped him, and he couldn't resist reaching for her. She didn't hesitate to close the distance between them, planting a soft kiss— one full of promise—upon his lips. He'd kissed her twice before but nothing prepared him for the jolt of longing that suddenly overwhelmed him.

The kiss grew hotter, more intense, and he waited for his remorse to surface. He felt none. What emerged instead was jealousy, and an all-consuming desire to erase James from Kate's memory.

As irrational as the thought was, he couldn't stop himself from gently nipping his way across her chin and up to her ear. "Do you have any idea how much I want you?"

A soft moan that traveled straight to his gut was her only response, one that drove him further over the edge of sanity. "Does he make you burn like this? Does he make you feel on fire like this?" he whispered, unable to contain the jagged torment from slipping out in his questions. He shouldn't want her, but he was tired of fighting the attraction that went so much deeper than simple lust. Kissing her soothed his soul and took away the loneliness.

"No." She pulled away and pushed on his chest. "We can't do this."

The sudden movement and words jarred him fully awake. He leaned back against the sofa, bringing her with him. He closed his eyes, reaching for normalcy.

After gaining full control, he faced her. "Why can't we do this?"

"Because…" Her voice trailed off. She fixed her gaze on her sweats and picked at a piece of nonexistent lint.

"That's not a good enough reason."

She cleared her throat and smoothed the cotton fabric of her sweatpants. "We're both in other relationships."

"Didn't we both decide to end those relationships?"

"Yes, but…you don't understand," she murmured, not meeting his gaze, as a guilt-ridden flush spread across her features. "There's Judith." She hesitated. "And James. They deserve more."

He barely heard the last two sentences. Watching the emotions run their gamut, Paul assumed the worst. She regretted her actions because of James. Maybe he should regret his actions because of Judith, too, and he might have, if Judith had ever responded to his kisses like Kate had. Surprisingly, the jealousy he felt toward James ebbed as another realization set in. Their shared kiss proved his brother and Kate weren't meant to be, any more than he and Judith. He felt it in every fiber of his being. She'd never respond to him so naturally and wholly if she truly loved his brother. Somehow, he had to make her realize that fact.

He hugged her fiercely. "It's okay. We'll work it out," he said, before kissing her forehead. Because he believed his own words, a bud of hope sprung up inside his soul.

~

What have I done? Kate's shame mushroomed. Too horrified to move, she felt Paul's hands slide up and down her back in a soothing motion she didn't deserve. There was no excuse for her rash behavior, except he'd looked so lonely sleeping on the sofa. When he'd woken up and looked into her eyes, a sense of loneliness called to her. She'd felt compelled to kiss him to try to take the isolation away. Whether his or hers, she wasn't sure, and that only added to her guilt.

Unwilling to acknowledge the feelings he evoked, she extricated herself from his hold and stood. Still too embarrassed to face him, she pivoted and headed toward the guesthouse as fast as her legs could carry her.

In the privacy of the outside room, she rushed to the bed and climbed under the covers, remaining stiff as stone with her eyes closed. How could she have foolishly given into the urge to kiss him like some brazen hussy? Worse still…this time she couldn't blame Paul. No! She'd taken advantage of his relaxed state, had wanted to feel her lips on his more than anything. So much so, that betraying Judith hadn't seemed to matter. What kind of friend did that?

And what about James? She groaned and placed her hands over her eyes as more shame engulfed her. Only two days ago, he'd been her world and marriage to him had been her life's goal. Yet, instigating a kiss with his brother, then desiring more than just a kiss belied everything she thought she knew about herself. Thank God, she'd put on the brakes when she had. Otherwise, they'd have surely ended up in bed. Talk about giving the milk away for free.

Tomorrow. She'd deal with this tomorrow.

~

Pristine white snowdrifts reflected morning sunlight that poured in through the windows when Paul emerged from the bedroom feeling one hundred percent better than he had the day before. Using the towel around his neck to dry his hair, he headed for the kitchen, thankful for electricity. The house was finally warm and he'd been able to shave in front of the bathroom mirror, which meant fewer nicks. Best of all, putting on a pot of coffee wouldn't be the same ordeal as yesterday.

Today, the bean grinding took only seconds. He poured them into the filter and added water before turning on the machine. Listening to the slurping noise and watching coffee drip while the Krups worked its magic, he leaned against the counter. His thoughts centered on Kate and how he should best proceed with her. Nothing would sway him from the belief that she'd run away last night, too afraid to face what was between them.

As the brewing process neared completion, he took two cups from the cupboard and grabbed the half-and-half out of the fridge.

Thoughts of Kate, and the memory of the warmth of her lips pressed against his, made him want to bay at the moon. A sense of joy permeated his heart. Never before had a memory elicited such an intense reaction. He'd never responded with that much emotion or physical attraction toward anyone, not even Judith. With Judith, it'd never been about sex. If he were honest with himself, he'd have to admit that he wasn't that sexually attracted to her. She certainly didn't inspire the same soul-searing need that Kate did. In fact, no one he'd ever dated attracted him in that way. Why had he been willing to accept any less for so long?

Whatever the reason, he didn't want to dwell on it. Nor did he want to dwell on all those wasted years spent chasing Judith. She'd always hold a special place in his heart. If she'd ever given them a chance to be a real couple, things might have turned out differently, as his love and devotion for her had been total. He was convinced more now than ever that he was making the right decision to move on. Having experienced a taste of Kate's passion, he now wanted someone—namely her—who could keep that passion alive.

He finished pouring two cups of coffee, then turned at the noise of the patio door sliding open. A moment later, Kate walked into the kitchen, then hesitated when she spotted him.

"Good morning." He smiled as he handed her a hot mug and nodded at the counter. "Cream's over there."

"Thank you," she murmured. She eyed him with a guarded expression, before concentrating on pouring cream into her coffee.

Paul leaned against the stove and crossed his legs at the ankles. He sipped, keeping his gaze on her backside. She wore jeans and a sweater that did little to hide her curves. Her complexion had a rosy hue to it this morning. Her hair, swept off a face devoid of makeup, accentuated delicate features and he was again reminded of a nymph from a fairy tale. They were roughly the same age, but everything about her made her appear years younger.

He didn't believe he loved Kate. How could he? Not after such a short time. He'd spent too many years taunting her, landing and fielding verbal jabs, for him to be comfortable with the thought of loving her so readily. His original view of her was shattered this weekend, and now he wanted to dig down through all of her layers and uncover them one at a time. He had every intention of pursuing her until he had it all figured out.

~

The bright morning light was a stark contrast to the dark commotion churning inside her. Kate was no less conflicted than hours ago; she hadn't slept a minute. Lord help her, she hadn't wanted to face Paul, but hiding was never her style. Neither was evasion. She always met challenges head-on, so why change now?

Ignoring him, she put the carton back in the fridge. Mirroring his stance, she perched her rear against the opposite counter and warily watched him while she took a drink. He was dressed in faded jeans and a t-shirt that looked as if they were molded to his frame. Observing his nonchalant pose, she couldn't help but find him sexy, which didn't sit well beside her guilt. Nor was she happy about what his presence did to her senses. He simply took her breath away, made her heart beat faster. As cliché as that sounded, there was no other way to describe her feelings. Her gaze zeroed in on his lips, and memories of that kiss and her aggressive behavior flooded her. Something else she wasn't happy about. If only she could forget...everything.

"Would you like some eggs for breakfast?" Kate finally asked, deciding anything was better than standing there looking at each other.

Paul shrugged. "You don't have to bother. I can eat the Honey Nut Cheerios I bought."

"Don't be ridiculous. We have plenty of time before we hit the slopes." Then, her eyes narrowed. "You are planning on going, right?"

"Yeah, I'd originally planned on it. And I guess there's no reason not to now."

"Well, you don't have to go. Just drop me off and I can find a ride home on my own."

Her offhanded comment must have hit a nerve because he stiffened. "What? Afraid to spend the day with me?" he asked, piercing her with an icy blue stare.

"Come on, Paul. You can't think last night changes anything."

"Excuse me." An incredulous expression crossed his face. "I must be a little dense, so you need to spell it out."

"Hello—this is Kate—remember?" she replied in an exaggerated tone. "Butt of your jokes. Last night was a mistake."

"How can you say that after what went on between us?" Paul set his cup down so hard on the counter, coffee sloshed over the rim. He snatched up a dishcloth and attacked the mess with short, jerky motions, before throwing it in the sink.

"What about Judith? What about James?" Closing her eyes for patience, she sighed and counted to ten. "We can't pretend they don't exist for us."

"What about them? Yesterday you said you were done with James. Then you kissed me. You can't pretend it never happened." Paul's voice rose with his annoyance.

Raw emotion rose up like bile in the back of Kate's throat, emotion that shouldn't be there. Not toward Paul. They'd only spent three days together. Still, the thought of Judith and Paul together hurt and she snapped, "Look, I can't deny that I'm attracted to you, but neither of us is free." And knowing about Judith and his love for her, she added, "Even if we weren't, I can't see a future between us. So maybe pretending nothing happened *is* better. For both of us."

Paul shook his head, clearly not buying her reasonable suggestion. "How can you give James any consideration after the way he's treated you? He doesn't deserve you."

And Judith doesn't deserve you, she wanted to shout back, but didn't. There was no way she could let this continue. She'd already done enough to screw things up.

"Whether you admit it or not, something did happen and we have started something," he whispered savagely, stalking toward her with determination in his eyes. He took her cup from her hand and placed it on the counter. She was too stunned to do anything but gape at him as he pulled her into his arms and bent to kiss her.

The moment their lips touched, jubilation swirled inside Kate. Sensation rolled over her in heated waves. Too caught up in a building inferno, she responded without thinking of the consequences. Kissing James had never been like this.

She moaned into his mouth. When the sensual sound reverberated into her thoughts, she froze. Distress and emotional overload swamped Kate and she burst into tears. In seconds, they were free flowing.

Like the day before, Paul pulled away, shushing her, holding the sides of her face and kissing her tear-stained cheeks.

"I'm sorry. But you have to see what we have."

His voice held torment, which she ignored, too overcome with her own. "This changes nothing," she whispered. "It only proves we turn each other on." She pulled out of his arms, causing him to take a step back. She longed to hear words of love from him. Knowing she wouldn't, or shouldn't even want them, she had to get away. Using all of her strength of will, she spun around, and with as much dignity as she could muster, slowly walked out of the room.

The entire time her heart ached. She didn't want to love him, but she did. Somehow, she hadn't been able to stop it from happening and she knew she was in big trouble. What really concerned her was that her feelings for James were minor compared to what Paul made her feel.

~

Paul watched Kate walk off in the direction of the guesthouse, a whirlwind of chaotic thoughts swirling through his mind. To be fair, he had to admit that Kate was right. They did need to close the past. Still, why couldn't she acknowledge that what flared between them was more than physical attraction? For him, it only heightened their potential relationship because they shared so much in common.

He wiped his face in frustration.

How had things gotten so crazy? The whole weekend had seemed surreal. *Maybe it would be better if she did find another ride back to the city.* Once out, he dismissed the thought. He found the idea of not spending the day with her too disturbing.

He snorted. Damn! He had it bad.

He grabbed his coffee and headed for the bedroom. He stripped the bed of its sheets and worked his way to the laundry room off the kitchen, picking up as he went. He filled the washer, but didn't start it, waiting for Kate's sheets. Chores finished, he retraced his steps to the kitchen for a bowl of cereal.

Minutes later, Kate emerged with her sheets and a packed bag. She dropped the bag near the front door then turned toward the laundry room.

"I already added soap," he called. "Just add your sheets and start the machine."

He heard her follow his directions. After returning to the kitchen, she reached for the cereal on the counter where he left it and poured herself a bowl.

Warily keeping each other in view, they stood in silence while eating.

Paul was amazed at how composed she appeared, as if nothing had taken place between them. Unwilling to give her the satisfaction of seeing how she affected him and having had years of practice at covering up his feelings with Judith, he tamped down the surge of emotion bursting to break free. He'd let her take the reins for now.

Finally, he set his bowl in the sink. "I guess we can get in a couple of hours' skiing before heading home." Then, looking at his watch, he added, "It shouldn't take too long to clean up here and pack. We can be on the slopes a little after they open."

Kate shrugged. "Great. I'll help. Just tell me what you need done."

"If you vacuum and do the baths, I'll clean the kitchen and straighten up the living room."

"Okay." She rinsed her bowl and left him.

Chapter 12

Kate vigorously scrubbed invisible fingerprints off the mirror, thankful for an outlet to vent her frustration. She quickly polished the faucet, then wiped her hands on a towel and went to retrieve the vacuum. While working on autopilot, she considered her options.

Paul belonged to Judith. She had to remember that. She had no intention of becoming the other woman, so skiing with him was out. Otherwise, she'd do or say something she'd regret.

Even if the two weren't involved and Kate could reveal her feelings, she wouldn't. Their past prevented her from confiding in him. How could she when he'd mocked her for years? She doubted she could withstand his verbal blows now.

How ironic he was the same man whose derisive comments made her feel so low for caring so much for James. Especially when her current feelings dwarfed those in comparison. No! Even if Judith wasn't in the picture, there was no way she'd trust Paul with her heart.

She had to get away. Go home and lick her wounds. Break things off with James.

With luck, she could then forget this weekend—pretend it never happened.

Kate finished her chores, praying for the strength to follow through on her plans to find another ride home. Before grabbing her bag, she quickly wrote out a note explaining her decision. It seemed the best way to avoid more confrontation.

She rounded the patio door and saw Paul coming out

of the bedroom hallway.

"You about ready?" he asked.

She nodded and helped him pack the car.

Moments later they drove through freshly plowed roads on their way to the resort. Kate kept her focus on the beauty outside the passenger window. A pristine blanket of snow covered the grays and browns of winter. The cloudless blue sky contrasted with the stark white that reflected the sun so dramatically, she was glad she'd worn her sunglasses.

Paul glanced her way. "How long do you want to ski?"

Keeping her gaze out the window, she murmured, "I don't care." Her shoulders lifted in a careless shrug. "You decide." It didn't matter to her when her day depended on whether she could find a ride back to the city.

"Since we're making the attempt, I guess we should get in a couple of hours." He hesitated, clearly waiting for a response. When she remained silent, he said, "How does that sound?"

"Fine." She felt his gaze and wished she could meet it. But doing so would only get her into trouble.

He sighed. "Look, Kate, it's not the end of the world. Things'll work out."

His words, so softly spoken, were almost her undoing. Tears suddenly threatened to spill. Blinking them back, she had the strongest desire to blurt out how much it hurt to love him while he still cared about someone else.

"There's nothing to work out," she said instead, firming her resolve. She closed her eyes and fought her jealousy. No guy was worth destroying a friendship.

Thankfully, he didn't say more, just continued driving. This whole trip had been the weekend from hell, except for the times she had been in Paul's arms—that had been heaven. How could she maintain her distance when all she wanted was to be back in his arms? And that could never happen again.

How had she gotten into this position? Wasn't it bad enough that she had to deal with James? Now she had to look her best friend in the eye and basically lie.

When the ski resort parking lot came into view, she heaved a relieved sigh.

In the lodge, they headed toward the Morrison locker. Giving him a sideways glance now as he walked beside her, she had to admit he was gorgeous. The more she was with him, the more she wanted to be with him. The urge to dump her plans was tempting. She shook it off. *No! Keep to your plan. You can't get more involved with him.* He wasn't hers, despite their attraction for each other.

"Be right back." Paul pulled out his ski suit and turned in the direction of the men's room.

The minute he was out of sight, Kate sprang into action. She pulled out the prewritten note and set it inside the locker. Paul wouldn't leave the resort if he thought she was still around somewhere waiting, and she didn't want him to be inconvenienced.

Grabbing her skis and boots, along with her clothes, she bolted out the door toward the other building.

~

As he stepped into his ski suit, Paul's thoughts centered on Kate. If only they could revert to the irreverent couple of the other night when their relationship had been easy and open, he'd be the happiest man alive. But Kate had a guard up—one worthy of a prizefighter. Until he dealt with his unfinished business with Judith, he didn't think he should try to get around it just yet. Even though he and Judith were no longer a couple—in fact, had never been one in the true sense of the word—he still had to talk to her and set the record straight.

He straightened up, pulling at his zipper as a bigger question ate at him.

Would Kate end things with James? Or would she cave when his brother tried to smooth things over? Paul worried that her breaking up would represent a new challenge for his brother.

After sorting it all out, Paul decided those two just weren't meant to be. Eight years of chasing and dodging certainly wasn't the best foundation on which to start a life together. Maybe that's why he'd always given her a hard time...because it bugged him so much. He could always see their dance so clearly.

Paul pressed the last snap together and snorted. He grabbed his clothes and hurried out the restroom door.

"Kate?" He looked around and didn't see her. He glanced toward the restroom door, as Cameron Riley, another skier from the Bay Area, opened the locker adjacent to his.

"Hey, man!" he said. "How's it going?"

"Good." Paul nodded and twirled the wheel on the combination lock. Kate must have closed it when she went to change.

"Skiing should be great today." Cam reached for his skis and poles. "I'm heading up the tram with Thomas and Jansen. Wanna join us?"

"I'm not ready yet. I'm waiting for Kate."

"I just saw her carrying her equipment on my way in. Looked like she was in a hurry," he said. "You're welcome to ski with us till you hook up with her again."

"Sure," Paul said, spying the note as realization set in. He quickly read Kate's note as his stomach lurched, then forced a tight smile for Cam's benefit. "Just let me stow my stuff." How could she? She actually ditched him like some creep she was trying to get rid of.

He slammed the locker, grabbed his gear, and followed Cam out the door. He'd had it with chasing after women who didn't want his attention.

The kiss changes nothing, Paul. It only proves we turn each other on. Kate's words, and the look on her face as she said them, played in his brain. Her disappearance said it all. She wasn't interested in being with him. No matter that it felt so right and he wanted her more than he'd ever wanted anyone else in his life, he knew he had nothing if it was all one-sided. Eight years of chasing after Judith taught him that. He'd learned his lesson well.

It was her loss. He'd just go skiing and forget she existed. Why waste of all this fresh powder? His heart wasn't in it, however, and he had to push himself onto the tram.

The gorgeous day and the awesome conditions did little to make him feel better. He skied several runs, trying not to dwell on Kate or her actions. Around one o'clock, they took a break for lunch, but Paul wasn't hungry.

"I'm done," he said to Cameron, as he stepped out of his bindings. He lifted his skis on his shoulder and nodded. "I'll catch you guys later."

"Oh, come on, man. You can't desert us. Not with all this powder. We're just getting started."

Paul smiled good-naturedly and shook his head. "I know, but I want to get on the road before traffic hits."

He walked away amidst more razzing about leaving early, not caring how they jeered. He just wanted to get home.

Then what? What's there to rush off to? The questions stopped him for a second but, without a decent answer, he continued with purpose. He only knew he didn't want to be here skiing any more. Every run he'd taken in the past hour brought back memories of the last time he'd been there with Kate.

When Paul reached the locker room, he couldn't resist doing one last quick search for her. Just in case she'd come to her senses or couldn't find a ride home. But it was a wasted effort.

After changing, he gathered his gear and walked to his car.

The entire drive home was filled with thoughts of Kate and their time together.

When he finally arrived at his apartment, he unloaded everything, including Kate's bag. Possessing her bag gave him an excuse to see her in the near future. Maybe by then, he'd cool off enough to hear her explanation as to why she deserted him. But not tonight—tonight he'd do what he did every night when he had nothing to do—immerse himself in work.

~

In the lift line to Red Dog, Kate caught a glimpse of Paul walking toward his car carrying his skis and boots. He was obviously leaving. She expelled a sigh of relief. Earlier, she'd waited until he'd gone skiing with several guys before meeting up with Andrea Delano, a fellow skier.

As luck would have it, Kate had provided Andrea a ride back to the city several times this season, so asking had been no big deal. The only drawback was she'd be sharing the SUV with three friends. One of them, Mike Smith, was someone she'd met briefly two years earlier.

After ending up on the lift with him several times, she was pretty sure they were orchestrated opportunities rather than pure happenstances. He was a decent skier and she found his company fun, which kept her mind off Paul, except when she was comparing the two.

The day still dragged. Kate was never so glad to finally pile into the Lexus four-by-four. Unfortunately, Mike maneuvered his way into the spot next to her.

For the next three and a half hours, she worked at being cordial and friendly when all she wanted to do was bury her head in a pillow and cry.

A lifetime later, the Lexus pulled up in front of her building.

"Thanks for the ride," Kate said to Andrea before climbing out. "You're a lifesaver."

Mike followed and helped her undo her skis. "I'll help you carry your equipment upstairs," he said, sporting a smile that most women would swoon over.

But not her. Great smile or not, he wasn't Paul. She shook off the thought and offered a smile, going for cheerful. "Thanks. I appreciate the help."

At her door, he leaned the skis against the wall while she reached for her keys.

"There you go, all safe and sound."

"Thanks for the company." She tried to sound upbeat. He really was nice, but he wasn't Paul. "I enjoyed skiing with you." She forced a quick laugh, then inserted the key into the door and glanced over her shoulder.

"It was my pleasure." Mike winked. "Besides, you're the one who put up with me trying to keep up with you all day. It was like taking advanced lessons." The width of his smile increased, if that were possible. "Any time you want a repeat performance, let me know. I'm game even if my body won't forget the beating for weeks."

A bit of remorse filled her remembering the advanced terrain they'd skied. None of the others wanted to stay on the intermediate runs, preferring fresh powder. Mike had eagerly gone along with the group, but had admitted to a few reservations on the lift. At that point, she'd taken pity on him and had given him some pointers. He had a few problems keeping up, but he stuck with them and improved, never quitting, which made him a winner in her book.

While standing there, she realized something else. Mike was good for her ego, and looking into his amused eyes, her smile felt more natural. He really was a nice guy and attractive, too.

But he wasn't Paul. *No! You're not going to start doing that.*

She'd always compared every guy she had ever met with James and now she was doing it with Paul. It was time to make some changes.

"Well, thanks again." He placed his hands on her shoulders. When Kate looked at him with a question in her eyes, he gave her a quick kiss on the cheek and added, "Mind if I give you a call sometime?"

"I'd like that," she said honestly. She opened her door and turned back. "You have my number."

She headed inside, thinking for the first time in weeks that Paul was right.

Everything would work out.

Chapter 13

Kate walked the length of her apartment in long strides, dreading James' arrival. She stopped at the window to look out. Noting an empty driveway below, she continued pacing.

They'd only spoken briefly after her return from Tahoe. So much had happened since then that her entire mindset had taken a one-eighty. How much easier it would have been, if she could just ignore James, like he'd always ignored her, and hope he'd quit calling. Even as the thought registered, she knew closing the door properly was the only way to end this episode in her life.

The doorbell's shrill buzzer jerked her out of her thoughts.

She hit the intercom button. "I'll be right down."

"Okay."

As she grabbed her jacket, she wished Paul waited below rather than James. She missed him. Tons. She'd gone back and forth a million times over whether she'd done the right thing by abandoning him at the ski resort when he'd been so nice.

It had taken every ounce of willpower she'd possessed to keep her from reaching for the phone to apologize. Part of her knew self-preservation was paramount, but the other part knew that deserting him was a coward's way out. What if she'd misread things between them?

She hurried down the stairs, hating the roller coaster of emotions she'd ridden ever since stepping foot in Paul's car.

At the door, James stood on the other side and

helped her open it. Finally out, she headed to the passenger door and hopped in the car at the same time he did, as was their habit. He hadn't given her a hug or a kiss. Kate also noticed his reticence at making eye contact. Instead of her usual annoyance, all she felt was relief.

He backed out of the driveway and onto the street. Kate snapped her seatbelt into place and glanced over, studying his capable movements.

What's changed? Why didn't she find him as attractive or as exciting as she once had?

He still has the same eye-catching looks. Blond hair, startling blue eyes, and a ready smile. So, what's different? She never thought in a million years she'd be anxiously working up the nerve to break up with him.

"I thought we could go over to Sausalito." He turned left on Marina Boulevard, driving toward the Presidio. "It's midweek and the Walter Street Grille shouldn't have a long wait."

"Sausalito and the Grille are fine," she said, sinking into her seat. He looked so much like Paul but he was nothing like Paul. He'd been her obsession for so long that it seemed weird to think of life without him. Curiously, the thought of life without him no longer bothered her, which led her to question every facet of their relationship. Had she really loved him all those years? Or had she been in love with the idea of being in love? She wrung her hands and closed her eyes, not wanting to believe either scenario.

"So, how was the weekend with my brother?" James asked after a long pause.

She chanced a quick glance in his direction. Did he suspect something? "I survived," she murmured evasively, returning her gaze to the window. Time spent with Paul was the last thing she wanted to discuss with James.

"That's exactly the answer I got from Paul." James laughed. "Good to see neither one of you killed the other."

"Yeah! Imagine that. I'm still alive and so is he," she said. Too bad hindsight was twenty-twenty. It was hard to admit that Paul had been right all those years. He must have seen something she couldn't. Of course, if she'd never had to defend herself from his barbs in the first place, she might have figured all of this out sooner.

She sighed. *Or maybe not.* She'd had her mind too set on James. It had taken three days of being with Paul and his hot kisses to do what nothing else could have—break the spell James had on her heart all those years. Now she found herself yearning for the impossible. She didn't know what was worse—thinking she loved someone who'd never come around, or knowing she loved someone who loved someone else.

"So the skiing was great, huh?"

Kate nodded. "Yeah, I don't think it gets much better, especially on Sunday. You really missed out."

"That's what Paul said. I wish I'd been there."

"Oh well. Wasn't meant to be." At his second mention of Paul, she couldn't contain her curiosity. "So you talked to Paul? When?"

"Earlier today. I called to razz him about the weekend with you, but he wasn't very talkative."

"Nothing unusual there," she said nonchalantly, unwilling to alert him to the excitement shooting through her system. "I've never found him to be very talkative except when he's throwing out insults."

"He's not that bad." James smiled. "He got especially quiet right after I told him I was seeing you tonight. I asked him if he wanted me to give you any messages."

She laughed and pretended her tummy wasn't doing backflips. "I'm sure he threw out a few snide comments when my name came up." She shouldn't care, but she did. A lot.

"Surprisingly, he didn't. He just told me to have a nice time." James hesitated. "He also said I should treat you right." He shook his head. "He sounded serious."

"You're kidding—he actually said that?" Kate asked, fighting to keep the amazement out of her voice.

"Yeah."

She felt his gaze and glanced over. The speculation in his expression had her wiping all emotion off her face.

"Did something happen this weekend I should know about?" His eyebrows shot up and he continued with his thoughtful stare.

Praying her face hadn't turned beet red as he refocused on driving, she slowly shook her head. "Nothing more than Paul being Paul." A few seconds later, she threw out her best effort to appear innocent. "Why do you ask?"

"I don't know." He snared her gaze again for a brief moment. "You two are sure acting funny."

Kate rolled her eyes. "Your imagination's working in overdrive." She snorted. "We had the kind of weekend you'd expect two enemies to have. We each got in a few barbs and tried to stay away from each other as much as possible."

"Hmm. Maybe. But something's different. I just can't put my finger on it," he said peering at the road ahead. "Are you sure nothing happened?"

"Yes. Quit trying to make a big deal out of it." She crossed her arms and looked straight ahead, hoping he'd get the hint.

"Okay, consider the subject dropped."

"Thank you," she said softly, keeping her attention on the cars in front of them.

Finally, the Sausalito exit came into view, just past the Golden Gate Bridge.

A mile down the road, he parked in a spot not too far from the restaurant. Both emerged from his Sequoia at the same time, and walked side by side toward the building. As before, neither touched the other. Somehow, the simple omitted act of hand-holding portrayed what was wrong with their relationship. She used to wish for more affection from him, but he seemed oblivious to her need. How sad to realize she just accepted it as the way it was. Now she was only too happy she didn't have to hold his hand. It would be too weird. Somehow, after so many years, that saddened her even more.

James opened the door for her at the restaurant's entrance, and waited until she was inside before following.

Since James had been right about the night being a slower one at the restaurant, they were seated right away near a window overlooking San Francisco Bay and the city as a backdrop.

A waitress bounced up to their table and asked in an overly chirpy voice, "What can I get you to drink?" Just what she needed. A waitress who acted as if she were at Disney World instead of Sausalito.

The waitress returned within minutes, still bouncing, and placed two glasses of wine in front of them before pulling out a notepad. "You ready?"

The atmosphere was entirely too cheerful for a breakup meal, Kate thought, watching the waitress sashay away after taking their order.

Kate fidgeted with her napkin and focused on her

hand, stalling to gain some courage.

"Is something wrong?"

She inhaled deeply and her offered smile felt fake. "You might say that."

"I know." James shook his head. "You're mad at me for working. I've thought about it and I owe you a big apology. You deserve better."

She gaped at him, unable to believe he'd actually try to smooth things over. On the other hand, that was his usual M.O. when he'd pushed her too far. And she always bought it. Until now.

"I'm really sorry about last weekend. In fact there's a lot I'm sorry for in our relationship."

"What?"

"I know you're angry and you have every right to be. I wish I could make it up to you."

"Oh really?" Irritation rose up her spine. "Well, you're off the hook. I'm not angry. Not anymore. But I have one question."

His nod indicated that she continue.

"How were you planning to make it up to me when we rarely spend any time together?" Now that she'd finally let loose a little, why hold back? "I'm tired of it." Straightening, she crossed her arms and frowned. "Look, James, there's no good way to say this, so I'll be blunt."

About to take a drink, he hesitated and eyed her warily.

"I'm calling it quits," she blurted out, just as he managed a sip.

He almost choked on his wine. His eyebrows shot up and his eyes got round. "You're what?"

"I'm breaking up with you.

"Breaking up?" he asked, as if trying to take it all in.

"My news obviously shocks you. I don't understand

why." Kate shook her head. "Isn't it what you want?"

When he continued to stare at her, dumbfounded, she said, "Come on, James. Don't act like you don't have a clue about why."

He stiffened. "That's hitting below the belt, don't you think?"

"Are you denying your actions don't mean anything?"

"Well...no," he said, still appearing slightly confused.

Her gaze narrowed. "So you choose to be an ass instead of talking."

He held up a hand. "Wait a min—"

She cut him off and said, "Am I wrong?" Under her scrutiny, he squirmed as an embarrassed flush colored his cheeks. "For the past six months, you've been a total jerk. I'm through putting up with it," she said, after taking a deep breath, thankful to have actually said her piece before chickening out.

"So, this is it?" His jaw dropped as realization set in. "You're actually pushing me out the door. After all we've been through?" He blinked. Then took another sip of wine. A moment later, he wiped his face. "I can't believe it."

"Well, believe it. This *is* serious." She gritted her teeth and clenched her fists, stilling the urge to smack him. "You know damn well you don't love me," she said, knowing without a doubt it was the truth.

He grimaced. Several emotions crossed his face, the biggest being regret.

"Don't look at me like that."

"Like what?"

"Like you care." She averted her gaze so she wouldn't be swayed by it. "I'm not changing my mind."

"I *do* care. Just not enough," he said, placing warm fingers over hers and squeezing. "I'm sorry."

She snatched her hand away and glared. "Apologizing isn't enough, either."

"Okay. I understand you want to break up." He took a deep breath and nodded. "But I can't help but wonder what started all this. Why give me my walking papers now?"

"I thought I already told you what started it," she huffed, totally annoyed with his hardheadedness. "You did by your actions."

"But I was working. You know how I am about my designs."

"Yeah, I know," she shot back. "Work is your first love. I finally got smart and realized what a jerk you've been. Did you think that I would bow and scrape for your attention forever?"

"Is that how you saw it? Begging for my attention?"

When she nodded, he sighed. "I can't deny being a jerk about the way I've treated you, but I do care about you." He eyed her carefully.

Again, she spotted something akin to remorse in that blue gaze and, rather than allow it to soften her stance, she decided to use it to firm her resolve.

"You have a funny way of showing it." Tears formed. She blinked them back, but a few escaped. She wiped her eyes.

"I wanted us to work out." His gaze focused on the rim of his wineglass as he traced a drop of condensation. "I really tried to commit. I just can't bring myself to that point, not yet. Which means neither one of us is happy."

Great. Now she was crying in front of him. But damn it all, saying good-bye to a dream wasn't easy, not when his expression held such sadness.

"And I bear the brunt of the blame. I'm sorry," he whispered, clearly choked up. "You're absolutely right.

You didn't deserve to be treated so callously. I never thought about how it affected you, but you have to know I honestly never wanted to hurt you." He brushed her tears away with the tips of his fingers and begged, "Please don't cry. I'm sorry my actions led us to this. I've never liked making you cry. It makes me feel like a jerk."

She snorted, trying to smile. "You are a jerk."

He flashed a self-deprecating smile. "I do care about you," he said, meeting her gaze, sincerity evident in his. "I truly wish things were different."

"I'm not crying over you," she said, not liking the fact that his words and actions were of the man she originally fell in love with. "I'm crying because of all the wasted years I've spent dreaming of how things could be between us."

"Something else to regret." He sighed wistfully and looked away. "I should have had the guts to be more vocal."

"You're right about one thing. We aren't meant to be. Paul figured it out. I guess that's why he always gave me such a hard time."

"Paul?" He sent her a questioning look.

She cleared her throat and pushed a strand of hair behind her ear. "He told me I take too much of your shit. And he was right."

"I see." James grunted. "But right or not, he sometimes overstepped his boundaries. There were times I wanted to bash his face in for his snide comments."

She smiled through dried tears. "That's the sweetest thing you've ever said to me."

"At least you're smiling about it now." He offered her a lopsided grin. "Am I forgiven for not wanting to give you up?"

"That's so lame." Her smile inched wider. Leave it to

James to say something like that.

"What's lame about it?" He grinned. "You have to admit, we're comfortable together most of the time."

She quirked a brow. "Most of the time? What do you mean? And why did you let it continue for so long if that was how you felt?"

"I'm going for honesty, okay?" He caught her gaze and waited. When she nodded, he took a deep breath and continued. "Kate, when there's something you want or some idea you get in your head, you're like a steamroller pushing through, flattening every objection in your path. At first, I thought it refreshing to be with such a take-charge woman. You were fun, accomplished, and we had a lot in common. I liked you and it was easy. Then when you told me you loved, I got more caught up in your exuberance. No one wanted us to work out more than me. But I wasn't at the same place you were, and rather than going along for the ride like I did, I should've been more up front about it."

He shrugged. "My only defense is that I do love you and I kept thinking I'd change. You're bright, gorgeous, fun to be around, and you are incredibly sexy. What's not to love? But when you started talking marriage, I knew for sure it wasn't the kind of love that lasts a lifetime. That's when I backed away. You deserve someone who's sure. And you're right to kick my butt to the curb."

A bubble of laughter formed, and she tried to contain it. The irony of the situation was too strong, however, and she gave up. Her laughter erupted.

James raised one eyebrow in question. She answered truthfully because the moment seemed to require honesty. "That's funny because I finally realized I don't love you enough either." Then, she smacked his upper arm with the back of her hand. "Maybe if you'd been more honest sooner, we wouldn't have wasted so much time on the wrong person."

"That insult hurts. Almost as much as being dumped." A pained expression moved over his face. "I don't care much for either one." He reached for his wine. "But I owe you, so I'll survive." Before he took a drink, he caught her gaze. "Since we can't be lovers anymore, can we at least be friends?"

She offered a genuine smile. "I'd like that."

Their perky waitress reappeared with their meals and began serving, talking a mile a minute in the process.

James waited until she was out of earshot. "So, now that we've established friendship and are being honest, I'm curious. What really happened to bring all this on? Why now?"

"I'm not really sure how it started." Kate shrugged and ate a few bites before continuing. "I guess when this weekend didn't turn out like I wanted it to, I started questioning everything."

"And nothing happened?" James asked, examining her face closely.

She had to avert her gaze. "Are we back to that?" She refocused on her seafood linguine.

"Yeah. It's hard to wrap my head around it all. A week ago, you were gung-ho to plan a wedding, and now you're breaking up. It's not logical. Something must have happened."

"What difference does it make?"

James thought about her question for a few minutes. Then, he shrugged. "I don't know. It seems like a puzzle to be solved."

Shaking her head, she smiled at his relentless pursuit. "Like a dog with a bone?"

He picked up his fork. "No, Kate. That's you," he

teased, as a slight smile formed. "In fact, that's why this seems so surreal."

She laughed. "Was I really so bad?"

"No. Not for the right person. You have to admit, you are one tenacious woman." He sighed and took a bite. After swallowing, he added, "That by itself was a turn-on. What guy doesn't want all that attention? It was flattering for a while." He shrugged. "But then, I guess I just took it for granted." He hesitated. "Maybe if you hadn't been so aggressive in your pursuit and forced things to happen, instead of waiting for things to develop naturally, things would be different between us. I don't know. But I do know I took a coward's way out and pushed you aside, which didn't help."

Honesty had a few drawbacks. Until that moment, it never dawned on her that by chasing him for so long, she bore the brunt of responsibility for their problems. She'd always thought that going after what she wanted was a good thing, but she never realized the impact it had on others around her. She had been pushy and aggressive. Recognizing this, she could finally view his actions through different eyes.

She smiled. "I can see us as friends." How could she not have him for a friend when he'd been such a huge part of her life? Besides, she did care about him and always would.

James returned her smile. "And friends should tell friends what really happened."

"Now look who's being tenacious." A quick laugh bubbled up when his expression said he wasn't about let it go. "Okay—you're right." She had to hand him something. Otherwise, he might keep digging until he unearthed her feelings for Paul. "I have a date tomorrow night with someone I met two years ago."

"You're kidding?" Total surprise lit his face. "I never would have guessed that." He was silent for several seconds before asking, "So, who is it? Someone I know?"

She groaned. "What is this, the Spanish Inquisition? Why is my love life suddenly so important?"

"You're already in love with him?" James asked in horror. His hand went to his chest. "Why don't you just go for the jugular?"

"It's not like that. Mike's not you, but he's a lot of fun."

"So his name's Mike and he's fun?" He shook his head. "My radar must be getting rusty. I thought for sure something happened between you and Paul."

"Oh?" She worked to keep her tone even. James couldn't know what went on and she wasn't about to enlighten him. "That's pretty far-fetched. We did become friends, but that's it." She stared off into space. "After spending time with Mike, I started to question things. He was nice and treated me like I was special. I gave him a few pointers on skiing powder, and we rode back to the city together with three other friends. He's taking me to dinner as a thank-you. That's it. I'm not sure I'm looking for anything more serious right now."

He nodded, then took a long sip, and sighed. "I wish you the best. I hope it works out with this new guy."

"Thanks, James." She heaved a sigh of relief and smiled. "I'm taking it one day at a time. I've definitely quit being the pursuer." Thinking of Paul, she added, "If he wants me, he knows where I am." She looked at James thoughtfully, and said, "What about you?"

"Me?" Taken aback, James shook his head. "I'm a lost cause."

"Oh, come on! You're not so bad."

"You need proof? Look at us! I rest my case," he

teased.

"Why do you say that? You have a lot to offer someone."

"What good is it when I can't commit." He grimaced. "I seem to recall hearing those exact words popping out of your mouth too many times to count."

"Just don't concentrate on work so much. You have to admit it makes you a little self-absorbed and even selfish." Looking back, he'd used work as a wall to buffer her tenacity. But someday he'd meet someone who'd breach his defenses. "You never know what's around the corner," she said, remembering how in less than one week her life had become topsy-turvy thanks to one man. Kate's grin spread. "Someday, when you least expect it, someone is going to knock you off your feet." When that happened, he'd commit. "You just haven't met the right person yet."

"Yeah, right!" he snorted. "And if you believe that, I've got a bridge to sell you." Clearly not wanting to dwell on her words, he changed the subject.

They talked several minutes about the powder and how much snow fell. He was hoping the snow would stay until the end of the week. He'd planned to surprise her with taking Friday off to make it up to her.

"What about you?" he asked. "Why don't you come up too?"

She cleared her throat, unable to think of how to answer. "I'll think about it," she said, evading his searching eyes. She had to avoid Paul, which created a major dilemma.

She'd always had free use of the Morrison Tahoe house.

"Since we're no longer an item, it's probably not a good idea to continue using your house," she said, hoping he'd buy that excuse because he'd wonder why she wouldn't be the first one on the slopes this Saturday.

"That's silly!" James shook his head. "You'll always be welcome."

She scrunched up her nose. "I'd just feel uncomfortable."

He shrugged. "Well, if you change your mind, it's available. Paul and I are the only ones who use it in the winter. I know my parents think of you as family, so they'll never mind." He paused, then frowned. "Come to think of it, they're going to take this breakup hard."

"So is my mom," Kate said with a sigh. "I so wanted to be engaged by Chrissie's wedding."

"I am sorry about that." His gaze zeroed in on hers again. "Tell me you'll think about coming up this weekend. Because if you go, I won't feel like such a jerk for your having to face your family in Chicago as a single person."

"What's this? Trying to buy me off with your house?" she said.

"Maybe. You have to admit, your presence this weekend will go a long way toward easing my conscience."

"Let me think about it." Apparently, James made a much better friend than he ever had a lover. She never thought things would turn out this way, but it felt right. Who knew the idea of going skiing with James would be a fitting end to their relationship? "I'll let you know."

Chapter 14

Paul glanced at his watch. He sat at the bar in RJ's on Chestnut Street, nursing a glass of chardonnay. Judith was due any moment. His thoughts, however, were on Kate, and James' phone call the day before. His brother's casual mention of Kate and their upcoming date ate a hole in his gut. She obviously hadn't broken things off. He didn't want to care that she hadn't, but he did. Plus, he didn't want to be envious of their relationship, but he was.

To make matters worse, he had to be careful about what he said and how he said it around James. All part of the competitive game of one-upping they played, sibling rivalry at its best, where neither missed an opportunity to goad the other.

James was sharp. Paul had already caught the speculation in his brother's voice over his reluctance to discuss the weekend. He could have kicked himself after telling James to have fun and to treat Kate right. He snorted and rolled his eyes.

Talk about giving him an invitation to dig in deeper!

Since returning from Tahoe, he'd immersed himself in work to keep from going crazy. Unfortunately, after his conversation with James, investing money and seeing it grow failed to provide the usual escape.

He wanted to storm over to Kate's apartment and shake some sense into her. His desire to force her to see that she and James were wrong for each other was driving him nuts. Jealousy over the fact that she'd gone out with his brother last night had also reared its ugly head, and Paul didn't much like the feeling. Not toward James. And to top it all off? He now had to deal with Judith, who'd arranged to meet him for dinner. That had been another gut-eating phone conversation, to be sure. Especially when he'd zoned in on her solemn tone, indicating their meal would include one of her 'talks' about 'friendship.'

He shook his head and frowned. He looked forward to seeing her, but also dreaded it, wishing she didn't feel the need to set things right one more time.

He'd done some soul-searching over the last few days, and had concluded that Judith had always been upfront and honest. In all the time he'd known her, other than those few weeks they'd discussed marriage, she'd never wavered about just being friends. He had simply never accepted her words at face value.

He looked up just as Judith stepped through the door.

"I need one of those," she said, nearing the bar and nodding at his drink.

"Bad day?" he asked, meeting her gaze. He then signaled the bartender and ordered a glass of BV cabernet—her favorite.

"You don't know the half of it." She huffed out a huge sigh and plopped down on the stool next to him.

"Our table should be ready soon." As her wine appeared, he added, "So, tell me what's put that frown on your face."

"Why do some men have to be such pigs?" Her grimace widened as she reached for her glass.

"Ah." Paul nodded. "I gather this *pig* has something to do with one of your jobs?" When she nodded, he gestured with his hand and said, "Let's hear it! Who is it and what did he do to earn such a low opinion?"

"One of the inspectors on my strip mall project is giving me a hard time and won't okay the permit on the electrical wiring. There's nothing wrong with the work.

But he keeps citing nonexistent infractions. I think he's retaliating because I wouldn't have drinks with him."

"You want me to beat him up for you?" Paul joked, in an effort to make her laugh.

"Would you?" Her lips curled into a smile and her shoulders relaxed. "I'd derive an enormous amount of pleasure at seeing him bowled over in pain."

"Let me check my schedule." He pulled out his cell phone and pretended to peruse his calendar. "I can fit in a beating on Friday. Will that be soon enough?"

She laughed. "I don't know. I'll have to get back to you on that." She sighed contentedly. "It's amazing what the thought of having someone beat to a pulp does for my mood."

"I aim to please." A frown replaced his smile. "This guy's really giving you a hard time?"

"No more than usual." She shrugged. "I can get around it because I'll just keep calling for an inspection. With three or four inspectors available on any given day, I have more than a seventy percent chance of not getting him. Since the odds are with me, it'll eventually pass. But it's a hassle, not to mention a lot of wasted time and effort."

"Just another day of being female in the city, right?" When she nodded, he added, "Hey, you could always marry me and then you'd have a better excuse to keep the jerks off your back."

Paul groaned inwardly at her sharp intake of air and slight stiffening. How had it come to this? Had he been so clueless to the signals she put out over time? Regret filled him. What distressed him even more about this situation was that he'd spoken totally in jest, but she obviously felt differently.

"I'm sorry. I guess it's too soon to joke about that

between us." He valued friendship, especially Judith's. He realized at that moment he wanted her to view him as a friend, like she'd done before they'd started talking about marriage. He vowed to take the necessary steps to make it right.

She cleared her throat and pursed her lips, then met his gaze and hesitated, as if reaching for the right words. "Paul, you know I'm never going to marry you, don't you?" she said with quiet finality.

Thankful to have the words out and in the open, he searched her sad eyes, his full of remorse.

"Yes, Judith, I know that." He never wanted her to feel that she had to keep up a barrier in order to deal with him again. When she was about to say something more, he placed a finger over her lips. "You don't need to say another word. Let's just leave it as it was—a thought of what might have been. I asked and you said no. End of discussion."

"Wow!" she said, with a strangled laugh. "What are you drinking?" She picked up his glass and sniffed. "Maybe I should have one of these, too."

She was obviously trying to put a lighter spin on the seriousness of the situation, but she couldn't disguise the relief in her voice.

"Same thing I always get." He held up his glass and changed the subject. "Now, finish telling me about this schmuck who is making your life a living hell. Maybe I can give you some advice on how to handle him."

"If he gets to be a bigger problem, I'll call you." She relaxed on the stool as the hostess walked up with two menus in her hand.

Thank God, their table was ready.

Both followed the woman through the crowded restaurant to a cozy table in the back.

Once seated, Judith flipped open her menu. "So…how was Tahoe?" she asked after a few minutes of silence.

"Fine." Paul shrugged, deciding on a seafood burrito.

"That's it?" Judith looked up at him with eyebrows lifted. "Fine?"

He schooled his face to show no emotion, irritated because it seemed all anyone wanted to discuss was his weekend. His time spent in Tahoe was the last thing he wished to rehash. Not willing to make a huge deal out of it, which would cause more interest, he said, "We actually had a great time."

"You and Kate?" Judith's expression could only be called incredulous.

Refocusing on the menu, he took a deep breath to curb his annoyance. "She's not so bad."

"Wow—that must have been some weekend," Judith teased. "What happened to change your stubborn mind about her? Especially since I've tried for years to get you to lighten up."

"What'd you expect?" He dug deeper for more patience to alleviate some of her suspicion. "You told me I couldn't be mean and you told Kate the same thing. So, we were nice to each other." Offering a wry smile, he shrugged. "Well, for the most part, we were. You'll be happy to know Judith the Good struck again. We survived the weekend, and Kate's hide remains intact." He held up his hands, he continued. "As you can tell, I have every finger and if I took off my shoes, you'd see I have all ten toes."

"Whoa!" She put up her forefingers in the shape of a cross and tossed out a nervous laugh. "I'm merely interested in your weekend. No need to get testy." She dropped her hands to her menu. "I appreciate your sacrifice. Thank you for taking my friend up there. I realize it was much more than you signed on for, especially since you got snowed in."

"Well, you owe me big-time for that," he said, only too happy over this second opportunity to lighten up the conversation. "In all honesty, Kate's a great skier and I enjoyed skiing with her on Friday."

"What about Sunday?"

He resisted the urge to squirm, despite feeling like he was on the witness stand. Judith was obviously just making conversation and had no idea that Kate's defection was a sore subject, so he answered as honestly as he could. "Kate decided to ski by herself and left me in the locker room. I assumed she made it home okay. She had a date with James last night."

Judith sighed. "She was so looking forward to their romantic weekend and he gets stuck here." Not realizing her words sliced into him like a knife, she set down her menu. "She mentioned in passing about maybe going up this weekend with him, so I guess they worked things out."

He swallowed hard, as the knife twisted. "She's driving to Tahoe with James this weekend?" Apparently, his instinct about Kate not ending things with James was right on, much to his dismay.

"Mmmm hmmm, it sounded like that."

Paul's mood went further south. Somehow, he got through the rest of the meal without making a fool of himself. He kept his comments on autopilot as he conversed with Judith, asking about her work and listening with only half his brain. The other half was busy trying to discern what had happened between Kate and his brother.

After Paul paid the check, he walked Judith out to the

street, heading in the direction of her parked car.

"I assume you walked. How about a ride?" she asked, as they approached her vehicle.

"I have a lot on my mind right now," he said, shaking his head. "I need the exercise to think things over. But thanks for the offer."

He'd refused rides many times because San Francisco was a walking city and his apartment was only a few blocks away. Still, his refusal clearly surprised her.

She pressed the keyless remote to unlock the car, then considered him with a sad expression as a nervous laugh bubbled up. "I guess I have to get used to that."

"What?"

"Letting you go." Her features softened. "I needed to set the record straight for your benefit, but it still hurts. It was kind of nice to know you were there."

His smile was quick. "Come here." He opened his arms and immediately she stepped into them. He kissed her lightly on the lips to seal their friendship. When he leaned back, his grin spread. "Just because things didn't work out between us, doesn't mean I'll stop caring for you. No matter what, you'll always have a special place in my heart. One of friendship." He couldn't resist one more heartfelt hug. "And you *are* a good friend, Judith."

Judith hugged him back. "I'm glad we worked things out. I think we should make our non-engagement official—put the word out, so to speak." She smiled warmly, and reached up to pat his face. "You need to get out there and find someone special."

Her words and sweet gesture told him he'd achieved what he set out to do, even as a sad thought flashed. He'd already found another someone special. Only she was no more available than Judith had been. He didn't think he could survive finding a third.

He kissed the top of her head and looked down at her, offering a sincere smile. "That's much easier said than done. You're a hard act to follow. But, yeah, go ahead and tweet it, so it's official."

He opened her car door and she settled herself inside. "Drive carefully," he said, shutting the door. "Call me if you need anything."

He stood with his hands in his pockets, wistfully watching the car drive away before sighing and setting off in the direction of his apartment.

~

Kate rounded the corner and recognized Judith's green Passat, sorry she'd agreed to walk off their meal when Mike suggested it. She tried not to spy, but couldn't help zeroing in on the couple talking across the street. It hadn't been easy to keep the conversation with Mike going, especially after seeing Paul wrap his arms around Judith and kiss her.

Jagged pain had ripped through Kate the entire time she'd spent viewing the intimate scene—one of lovers saying good-bye, rather than just good friends.

She watched Paul walk in the opposite direction, and her stomach clenched. How foolish of her to even consider the possibility that he would actually break up with Judith. Or that he'd be interested in a relationship with her, as she'd half convinced herself last night, figuring Paul's comments to James meant something. What she'd just witnessed belied the idea and left her feeling totally bereft. There was no mistaking the love between her best friend and Paul.

Kate mentally shook herself, forcing her attention back to her date. She was able to coherently answer Mike's questions as they walked, but most of her sentences consisted of one or two words. Thankfully, they neared her apartment building quickly and, less than a minute later, she was unlocking her door. Her only wish was to make it inside without falling apart.

Mike cleared his throat, drawing her out of her thoughts. "Is something wrong?" he asked, staring at her intently.

"No," she lied, suddenly realizing her mooning over Paul wasn't fair to Mike. He'd been amusing company all evening and she couldn't allow her mood to ruin things now. He may not be Paul, but he was fun and the first guy besides a Morrison who interested her.

"Are you sure?" Concern shone in his gaze. "Because, up until a few minutes ago, I thought things were going great. You were laughing at my jokes and telling your own. Then, suddenly it was as if a light bulb turned off. Your brightness stopped." He observed her for several long seconds. "Such a big change makes me wonder if I said something wrong."

"No. Nothing like that." Using a great deal of willpower, Kate forced a quick laugh, shoving the pain and Paul out of her mind, and concentrated on the guy in front of her. She exhaled a deep breath and offered a wry smile. "I'm sorry. You caught me daydreaming about work and one of my hard-to-please customers."

"Gee, thanks. And here I thought we were connecting and you found my conversation riveting." His eyes held a mischievous sparkle as he added, "Guess this means you're not inviting me in for a nightcap?"

"Sorry." She winced. "I'm a little old-fashioned. It's a little too soon for nightcaps." She shrugged. "And I do need to take care of a few business matters." Her smile turned more apologetic. "But thanks for a wonderful evening. I had fun."

He grinned, clearly taking her reply in stride. "Can't

say I'm not disappointed, but I'm not totally dissuaded, either." He picked up her hand and laced his fingers with hers. He brought their intertwined fingers to his lips and kissed the back of her hand. "The thanks is mine. I had a great time. Can we do it again sometime?"

Kate nodded and her smile spread into a wide grin. "I'd like that."

He released her hand and took her chin with his forefinger and thumb, tipping her head back. He bent forward and his lips met Kate's in a soft, gentle kiss that sent tingles up and down her spine. Though not the same as kissing Paul or James, it was nice and made her think there would be life after the Morrisons.

Mike broke the connection and stepped back. "How 'bout Saturday? Dinner and a movie?"

Kate was caught a little off guard by the invitation, but his offer was a perfect solution to her dilemma with James. She didn't want to risk bumping into Paul in Tahoe. "I think Saturday would be perfect."

"Great! I'll pick you up at seven, okay?"

"Seven's fine." She turned, unlocked her door, and added before going inside, "I'll see you then."

Chapter 15

Paul closed the file, disgusted because his attention span was shot. He reached for the remote. For an hour, he pretended to watch some thriller, yet stewed the entire time. He eventually gave up and went to bed only to toss and turn, while wondering what to do about Kate. Finally, around two he dozed, having found no solutions.

Wide awake at his usual five a.m., seconds before the alarm sounded, he shut it off and lay there, his thoughts still centered on Kate.

In a nanosecond, his past conversations with Judith flew through his mind, full of her overt messages that he'd ignored. He stared at the dark ceiling, and realized he'd missed her nonverbal cues, as well. Thinking back to Kate and their weekend together, he hadn't noticed any similar cues that told him to keep his distance. To the contrary, her personality and body language spoke to him, pulling him closer. Obviously, the attraction was mutual. Had he misunderstood Kate's messages, just as he had Judith's all those years? That thought had him reevaluating their last day together.

He rolled out of bed and headed for the shower as more questions arose.

Why had she left him in the locker room? Why the note? She'd obviously decided to leave him earlier, so why couldn't she tell him to his face? He never took her for a coward. If anything, she was too ballsy—demanding what she wanted instead of waiting for it to come to her—so why take the easy way out and run?

He turned on the water and waited until it warmed up

before stepping inside, his thoughts racing to find answers.

Unless she was also affected by what they'd shared. Had she used her words and actions as barriers to keep him from getting closer? Mulling over the idea, as the hot water ran over his body, he decided it made the most sense. Once he accepted she might have run from what she felt, he viewed her actions differently, more objectively, which led to another conclusion. Kate might have agreed to the trip to Tahoe this weekend with James out of misplaced guilt due to what happened between her and Paul. He grinned. That also made sense.

Kate didn't love James. If so, she never would have responded to his kisses like she had. That was the main nonverbal cue he couldn't dismiss.

Paul turned off the water and grabbed a towel. Elation spiked, giving his energy level a boost.

"I've been an idiot," he murmured, looking at his face in the mirror. He couldn't let things go, hoping they'd work out, without doing something.

Even though Kate's actions pierced his heart, he could understand her motives. They didn't excuse her behavior, but did make him feel as if he still had something to fight for.

He dressed quickly, grabbed his electric razor, and headed for the kitchen and breakfast as his mind churned, moving to his next problem...James.

Paul knew James might take exception to his brother taking away something he thought of as his—and Kate fit that description. But James didn't love Kate. Not enough for a lifetime. Of that, he was certain. So why would James ask her to go skiing with him? He'd have to find out, which meant confronting his brother and risking his irritation. Kate wanted commitment, something he could give. She was definitely worth fighting for, as was that something special they shared. He'd be a fool not to pursue her until he had her right where he wanted her, by his side. For a lifetime.

His mood soared higher. Since he'd gotten behind on work, he planned to accomplish as much as he could before driving to Tahoe this afternoon. He'd confront them together and see what was what. Of course, there was always the possibility that somehow his thought processes were still screwed up.

What if she really did love James?

"Nah," he said, shaking his head.

He grinned and focused on eating his breakfast, eager to begin the day.

~

"Maybe next time," James said, mildly disappointed that Kate was bailing on the trip to Tahoe. "Okay. Don't be a stranger." He hung up, leaned back in his chair, and swiveled to take in the view out the spacious wall of windows.

In the two days since she'd broken up with him, he'd waited for the pain to hit. Since all he'd felt was a sense of relief—once the shock had worn off and the bruise to his ego had eased somewhat—he couldn't dismiss her claims. True, Kate had her faults, but he should have made more of an attempt to talk things out rather than hide his head in the sand. No one deserved that, especially Kate. He *had* been a tad selfish and self-absorbed for not putting her needs in front of his own. The thought brought him pretty low, and suddenly he wanted to help. But how?

He focused on the busy street below and a few pedestrians who were waiting at the light.

Kate had been evasive when he'd asked a second time about last weekend with Paul, claiming to have met someone who changed her life. Somehow, he sensed that was a smoke screen. Was she not going because of this new guy or some other reason? Like Paul's presence? Maybe he was the *someone* who changed her life. As crazy as it sounded, the possibility did fit with Paul's actions.

He'd called earlier to inform James that he'd be joining them.

Interesting way of wording it...joining them. Paul had obviously known that Kate was invited. Of course, she was friends with Judith, who was friends with Paul, so he saw the connection. But there'd been something in his voice, a steely resolve that said he was gearing up for a fight.

Even more intriguing. Why is Paul gearing up for a fight?

No reason, unless there was more to their weekend than both let on. Yep! There was something up between his brother and Kate and he planned to find out exactly what.

Had they slept together? No! He couldn't see either doing that. But what if they'd wanted to sleep together? He shook his head at the absurdity of that thought. They were always at each other's throats. Still, it had to be something.

He stood and moved to his drafting table, shoving the problem aside for now. Designing the entrance to Kirkland's office building was a priority.

Twenty minutes later, James swore under his breath and tossed his pencil aside. He rubbed his eyes, giving up all pretense of work, as one thought that tenaciously kept creeping back into his consciousness wouldn't allow him to concentrate. Kate and Paul had feelings for each other.

He had to admit the idea explained a lot, mainly Kate's sudden decision to break up. A total reversal on her earlier stance. Since her sister's engagement, she'd been determined to receive a marriage proposal.

There was also Paul's attitude during those phone conversations over the past week, which piqued his curiosity in the first place. One thing he knew for sure. If those two were suddenly attracted to each other, something—or rather, someone—was keeping them apart.

Judith Reid—the ice queen—an apt nickname earned in college. She had a cool demeanor and more than one good man felt her chill while trying to melt some of the frost coating her heart.

They shared a family connection, yet he rarely came into contact with her. When he did, mutual dislike aided his avoidance. In other words, she'd always kept her distance, which had been fine by him.

Thinking of her brought back memories from college—one in particular. A party during his last week in grad school when Judith's icy glare had frozen Devon McAllister on the spot. His good friend and fraternity brother swore it was a forgettable incident, but James had always wondered what had happened that night. Mac was a man women flocked to and gushed over. Few ever turned him away. But Judith did, and he suspected Mac had never really forgotten it.

Paul had been after Judith, too, for years with no real success.

James never understood either man's attraction to her. Maybe the desire for something unattainable was the lure. It really didn't matter. Besides, how could he judge someone else's life, when his own was such a mess? He was no hypocrite, but he had always wondered if Paul really loved Judith. Perhaps he was in love with the idea of being in love, just as Kate had been.

How in the hell had all their love lives gotten so

messed up?

He shook his head and picked up his pencil. Well, he planned to do something about it. In the meantime, he could have a little fun with Paul.

Smiling at the thought, he was finally able to focus on work.

Chapter 16

Paul arrived at the house in Tahoe first, after stopping at the store along the way. He quickly turned on both the water and the heat, then went back to unload the car.

Done unpacking and emptying the groceries, he noted the clock on the stove.

Close to six.

He opened a bottle of water and downed half, wondering when Kate and James would be arriving.

He headed for the master bedroom, intending to light a fire. As he positioned the logs into place, memories of Kate and their shared time together sprang forth and in response, an intense longing engulfed him. Damn, he missed her.

A fire suddenly didn't seem such a great idea.

He wandered to the living room and sat on the sofa, then grabbed his laptop. Adjusting the Wicks portfolio would keep him occupied until he could confront his brother and Kate.

Absorbed in reading a stock report, Paul didn't realize anyone had arrived until the front door opened. He glanced up to see James saunter inside, carrying his bags. Alone.

"Hey, Paul." James slowed, a big grin settling over his face. "How long have you been here?"

He frowned, slightly confused. "About an hour."

Still grinning, James continued past him toward the hallway and the bedroom he usually used.

Before he was completely out of sight, Paul couldn't resist blurting out, "Where's Kate?"

"San Francisco, I presume." James slowed and looked over his shoulder. "Why do you ask?"

"No reason." Paul adopted a nonchalant tone and forced his attention back to his laptop. "When Judith mentioned you'd invited her, I just assumed you two would come up together."

"Obviously, she had a change of plans." James rounded the hallway and was soon out of his peripheral vision.

His eyes narrowed. Totally baffled, he tried to make sense of it all. What was going on? Why hadn't Kate driven up with James? Though curious, he had to tread lightly. James was sharp enough to latch on to the least little clue and figure out his interest in her.

His shoulders slumped forward as some of the adrenaline drained from him. Without Kate's presence, his original plan of confronting them was out. Oh well, he thought, refocusing on work. Maybe it was for the better. *Look on the bright side.* She wasn't here, which had to mean something. Kate was tenacious. If she'd still been interested in James, nothing would have kept her away this weekend.

Suddenly, Paul's confidence returned full force. He had all evening to glean some information about their date the other night.

His brother stepped into the room just then, drawing his attention. He looked up from his laptop, his nod indicating the kitchen. "There's wine on the counter."

"Thanks, but I think I'll have a beer."

"I stocked up on the way here."

James returned with a bottle of Samuel Adams and sat across from him, still wearing a canary-eating-cat's grin that told him something was up. "I see that's not all you stocked up on."

Nodding, he concentrated on the screen in front of him, trying to figure out what that something was.

James then muttered a comment that sounded suspiciously like, "This is going to be too easy."

"What?" Paul glanced up and met his brother's eyes.

"The drive was easy," he replied. With raised eyebrows, he held his gaze and took a swig, as if daring him to disagree.

Paul cleared his throat. "Glad to hear it." He studied James for long seconds before standing. "I think I'll have a beer too." He started for the kitchen, wondering the best way to broach the subject of that last date.

Finally, he opted to just ask a few leading questions. Considering their relationship, his curiosity wouldn't be out of line. "So why'd Kate decide to stay home, especially after Judith said you specifically invited her? And that brings up another interesting point. Why'd you invite her? I thought you were in your avoidance mode again, dodging the marriage bullet."

James sobered and shrugged his shoulders. "I'd rather not discuss it."

Paul blinked back his surprise. James was always complaining about Kate's aggressiveness. Intrigued, he asked, "Why, what's the problem?"

"Look, you have your screwed-up relationship with Judith, and I have mine with Kate," he snapped. "Why don't we drop the subject of relationships for tonight, okay?" Then he leaned back and took another sip. "You want to go out for dinner? I'm hungry."

"I bought food to cook here if you want," Paul said, as his curiosity flared brighter.

"No, I prefer to go out." After taking a long drink, he set the bottle on the table. "You joining me?"

Paul closed down his laptop and set it aside. "Sure,

why not," he said, praying more would slip out at dinner.

"You doing okay?" James stared closely at Paul's face. "How's work going? Those dark circles say you've been burning the midnight oil."

"Work's fine," he shot back, not wanting to talk about work or why he looked like he did. "I'm a little behind. I'll catch up this weekend when we're not skiing."

James nodded. "So last weekend must have been pretty miserable. I really feel for both of you. I know Kate was dreading it. She hates your guts, you know."

Paul's eyes narrowed and he mentally scoured his brother's choice of words, looking for a hidden meaning, while noting James' mildly amused expression. The thought of Kate hating his guts didn't sit well. Neither did the fact that she and James spent Tuesday night together. "We survived," he murmured. "But I don't think we hate each other quite so much."

"I'll bet."

Aside from that comment, something in his brother's voice alerted him. He scrutinized his expression, searching for some hint, but James only grinned and added, "And it's a good thing because your barbs were sure getting monotonous."

Paul remained silent, now completely certain something wasn't quite right. First, James said he didn't want to talk about her, and then he brought her back up again. *Time to withdraw.*

James chugged the last of his beer. "I'm ready to go. Are you? That way we can beat the crowd."

There usually wasn't a crowd on Thursdays, but Paul nodded. "Let me grab my coat. Where do you want to eat?"

"How about the Lakehouse?"

Two hours later, Paul pulled into the garage and

switched off the ignition. Dinner had been a total bust. He wasn't able to learn anything more about what happened between Kate and James because whenever he tried to steer the conversation in that direction, his brother deflected his attempts. Finally, he'd given up and enjoyed James' company for the rest of the night.

"I'm turning in," James said, as they got out of the car. "I plan on being up bright and early for skiing tomorrow."

Paul nodded. "I'll be ready." He headed for his bedroom. After slipping inside and closing the door, he glanced at the fireplace. Tamping down his frustration, he grabbed the Bic and lit the newspaper he was using as kindling. As the flames built, Paul thought back on his evening. Did his brother suspect that there was more to last weekend? He didn't see how.

No, something else must have happened. He only hoped for the patience to wait until James told him about it, because no amount of prodding or finagling was going to get James to open up sooner.

~

"The skiing is great," James said, coming up behind Paul in the lift line.

Paul glanced around. "Yeah, we're lucky." It was a beautiful, cloudless day where the sun was shining brightly, adding warmth to the brisk, clear air. As a bonus, it wasn't crowded. Weekdays were dead, so this was as good as it got without more snow. The multitude of skiers who took to the slopes after a storm usually caused the mountain conditions to deteriorate—bumping it up and making the runs more treacherous. "I bet there's still plenty of fresh powder to find if we look hard enough."

At the top of Squaw One Express, James raced past him. Not to be outdone, Paul took fewer turns and quickly caught up. Having skied together all their lives, both worked to outdo the other in their typical rivalry.

Nearing the bottom, they were neck and neck until Paul edged ahead for the win.

"Damn, you're tough to beat." James laughed good-naturedly and glided to the lift.

"That's because I've been up here most weekends and you've been buried in work all winter."

On the next lift, he and James ran into a couple of friends and became a team against the other two. Kevin Barker and Stephen Walters, bankers from the city, were weekend fixtures at Squaw, so trouncing them was challenging. The foursome worked the mountain to find places to race, sometimes hiking up a ways to seek the fresh powder that beckoned.

They eventually broke for lunch, finding a spot on the deck outside to eat. All four wore mirrored sunglasses—Paul used his for the glare, but he'd noticed while going through the deli line, the others had kept theirs on indoors. He smiled, remembering Judith's depiction of the 'good-looking gods of the mountain,' as she'd called them. According to her, the glasses were part of their uniform and made it easier to scope out the terrain without being too obvious.

Stephen and Kevin fit the profile and were eying a couple of women a few tables over. The two were dressed in ski outfits that looked like they'd been molded to their bodies. Neither showed signs of skiing. Their boots were dry and their hair and makeup were fresh, as if they'd just stepped out of a salon.

Paul noted James' interest. "You thinking about chasing snow bunnies?" he asked, nodding in their direction.

James glanced at him, tipping his glasses down to

make eye contact. "I'm thinking about it. Why? What's it to you?"

"Nothing. I'm just wondering about Kate is all," Paul said cautiously.

"Oh? What're you? Her guardian angel? Must've been some weekend for you to go from tearing her down to protecting her," James retorted.

"It's nothing like that." He cleared his throat. "I just never thought you'd cheat on her. No one deserves that."

James smiled. "Well, here's a news flash, little brother. She dumped me." He stretched out his legs, pushed his glasses back in place and moved his eyes back to their original position, on the two women. "So, I'm free to *cheat*," he said, using his crooked forefingers for emphasis.

Paul almost choked on the beer he'd been drinking. Elation surged through him. He quickly schooled his emotions after looking up and catching James' scrutinizing stare. He took a deep breath along with another sip, forcing himself to remain calm. When he could speak without giving himself away, he said, "Really?" He hesitated for a heartbeat. "When did this happen?"

James shrugged. "Last week—at dinner. I still can't believe she did it. But I'm glad she did."

"That's tough," Paul said in his most consoling voice. He waited a few minutes and then asked, "What do you mean, you're glad she did?"

"She deserved better than me." James winced, and even more astonishing, his voice held a twinge of regret. "Considering she wants marriage and I don't. She needs a man who's ready to commit, y'know? I'd been seriously thinking about ending things so that she could move on. It only seemed right. But Kate pulled the plug on us before I even knew what hit me. I should've manned up long before now. In my own defense, she could be a little hard to deal with at times and it was easier just to let things ride."

Nodding, Paul silently studied his brother and mulled over the bombshell he'd just dropped. At the same time, James attention never wavered. Awkward seconds ticked by as they stared at each other.

Eventually, James offered a wry smile and looked away, sighing. "Turns out she met some guy up here last weekend." He chuckled and bent to loosen his ski boot. "Funny, I thought maybe something happened between you two, but I was wrong. She skied with…" He thought for a moment. "Mike…yeah, that's his name. Anyway, he gave her a ride back to San Francisco. I gather she had a date with him after our breakup. I figured he's the reason she broke up with me so fast and without warning. Said she needed to put us behind her—so she could start something new."

Paul's jaw tightened, as his thoughts went haywire. It took a tremendous amount of effort to rein them in. Even still, he couldn't keep his shock from showing, nor could he keep the hurt out of his words. "So, she's dating someone new?"

How could she?

"I'm not sure." James eyed Paul carefully for a long moment. He cleared his throat. "But according to her, she met someone who changed her life." He shrugged. "I assumed it was this new guy. I mean, who else could it be? Something happened. Kate was too set in her pursuit of marriage and nothing was going to stop her. Hence the need to put things right. It was past time."

The rigid line of Paul's shoulders relaxed immediately as he absorbed the information.

James settled back and resumed scoping out the

bunnies.

After a while, they decided to head back to the slopes, but not before James and Kevin made a little side trip to talk to the bunnies. When Paul stepped into his skis, James sauntered up with a wide smile on his face. He grabbed his skis and poles, which had been leaning against the rack. He dropped them on the ground, and proceeded to step into his bindings and lock them in place with a final snap.

He glanced at Paul and nodded. "I'm ready whenever you are, bro!"

"So, I take it you got lucky?" Paul said, noting his pleased look.

James flashed his signature grin, pushing his sunglasses higher on his nose. "Luck had nothing to do with it."

Paul laughed at his audacity, realizing he was probably right. When his brother smiled, the ladies always reacted favorably. "Well, come on, Don Juan. We're burning daylight."

Once in the locker room, after skiing all afternoon, Paul sat as James said, "You're on your own for dinner. I have plans."

"Little Miss Bunny, I take it?"

"You got that right." He sported a wide smile.

"I thought you'd go for the more active type. She's obviously not a skier."

James shrugged. "Dinner doesn't require supreme physical fitness, just a willingness to have fun."

Paul's annoyance flared. "God, James, how could you go so quickly from Kate to her?" He couldn't keep the disgust out of his tone.

"We can't all be saints like you, little brother," James mocked, as he opened the locker.

"Yeah?" Paul sneered, rising to the bait. "It seems to me you could at least show a little sincere regret over breaking up with her."

James' eyes narrowed to slits. "Let me give you some advice." There was no mistaking the heat of anger rising off his body. "You shouldn't stick your nose into things that don't concern you. My relationship with Kate is my business. You know nothing about what went on between us."

"I know she doesn't deserve to be treated the way you've treated her all those years."

James slammed the locker door, his expression turning livid. "Point taken, but who are you to be telling me how to behave? You never wasted any time trying to bring her down a peg with your constant haranguing. So, don't lecture to me about treating anyone the way they deserve. Kate never deserved your sarcasm and cruelty. I should have shut you up back then, because you're right. She deserved better than the two of us." With those words, he snatched his clothes and stalked into the men's room to change.

Paul stared after him, swearing under his breath. He should have kept his mouth shut. Why had it bothered him that James seemed so cavalier about their breakup? It should have made him feel better knowing the two were no longer together. But the thought of James taking Kate so lightly did anger him. James' reaction, once Paul thought about it a moment, made him realize his brother wasn't as unaffected as he'd portrayed.

He gave James a few minutes to cool off then grabbed his stuff to change into and headed for the restroom. He spotted James, who was pulling on a pair of faded jeans. He walked over to him. "I'm sorry. You're right. It is none of my business."

James accepted his apology with a nod. "You hit a nerve." He ran a hand through his hair. "For what it's worth, I haven't slept with anyone—including Kate—in months, and I *was* planning on ending things so she could find the right person. I do feel bad about letting us go on for so long." Then, he snared Paul's gaze, his serious. "So, what about you and Judith?"

"She and I are friends, period," Paul replied truthfully, wondering about the question. "I should've let her go a long time ago too." Sitting on the bench, he leaned over and put his elbow on his knee, cradling his chin with his hand. He blew out his breath in a long sigh. "Man, how did we get to be so pathetic?"

Laughing, James clapped him on the back. "Cheer up, we're getting wiser. Well, I am anyway. Since I'm the one with the date tonight, it's obvious I'm moving on. I suggest you do the same."

Paul watched his brother tuck in his shirt, totally cheered by his words. Somehow, in the past twenty minutes, James had provided answers to several of his questions without being asked. He knew now that James didn't see Kate as his any longer. It was completely over between them. He also learned his brother still cared about Kate, as a friend, not as a lover, and that made all the difference in the world to him.

But Paul wasn't stupid. James had to have a pretty good idea of Paul's feelings for Kate. His question about Judith confirmed this. He was doubly glad that James still cared enough about Kate to make certain Paul wasn't trifling with her.

During the drive back to the house, they each cracked jokes about the day, and both claimed supremacy over the other for their prowess in the snow. Neither mentioned Kate or the topic of James' breakup.

James eventually left for his date with the snow bunny and Paul ate dinner by himself. Afterward, he pulled out his laptop, determined to put the rest of the night to good use. He fought throughout the whole evening to avoid thoughts of Kate, not wanting to dwell on the jealousy lurking over some guy named Mike.

There was nothing he could do about it until he confronted her—and his plans definitely included confrontation. This had gone on long enough. It was time she realized the truth. They belonged together. He'd make sure she understood, so that there'd be no mistaking what they shared.

The next morning Paul was up early. By the time James came slowly out of his room, he was eating breakfast, having already showered and made coffee.

His brother padded over to the pot and poured a cup. He leaned back against the counter and crossed his legs at the ankles. He stood like this for several minutes before finally looking over at Paul and lifting his mug in a silent toast. "I should've stayed home with you last night. Brandie, that's with an *ie*, not a *y*, got on my nerves after the salad arrived." He rolled his eyes. "It's been a while since I dated a bimbo, and that's bimbo with a capital *B*. I'd completely forgotten why I steered clear of them in college."

Paul grinned. "That bad, huh?"

James grunted. "Worse. She even signs her name with a heart over the *i*." He frowned. "God, I hate the dating game." After a long drink, he said, "I realized that's part of the reason why I stayed with Kate so long. That and the fact that even after eight years, she never bored me."

"I hate the dating game too, but I don't expect I'll be playing it again, except with one special person," Paul said in a low voice. "But I'm sure you already figured that out."

James, about to take another sip of coffee, stopped with the cup an inch from his mouth. He eyed Paul thoughtfully, then offered an exaggerated sigh. "What gave me away? I tried to be so careful."

Paul laughed. "Oh, you were. You had me going for a while. Besides, I should be asking you...what gave me away?"

Grinning, James replied, "You know I can't tell you because if I did, you'd learn all my secrets. Damn, I must be getting rusty. But then again, my concern for Kate weighed more on my mind than razzing you. I just wanted to be sure—for Kate's sake. She doesn't deserve another Morrison who can't commit. You do plan to commit, right?"

"Yeah, if she'll have me."

"Are you sure you can handle her?"

"What do you mean?" Paul asked, his eyes narrowing.

"She's a steamroller." James shook his head and laughed. "She's a lot of woman for such a tiny thing—and at times I found it difficult to deal with."

Remembering their few battles, Paul smiled and said with supreme confidence, "Yeah, I know. But we seem to do well together. We understand and respect each other. Or rather I should say, she understands that I'm not about to let her walk all over me."

"Are you saying I did?"

"You're the one who said it was easier to give in."

"Touché." He offered a second toast. "You're a better man than I ever could be." He hesitated and his expression turned more serious. "So you can deal with the fact that we've slept together?"

"Not really," Paul said, grunting. "I want to bash your brains out, but seeing as you didn't bash mine out when I was a jerk to her, I guess I owe you. Besides, you said it yourself. There's a lot of woman in that compact body and I've already proven I *can* handle her, which does make me the better man."

James' head snapped up and his gaze flew to Paul's. Something akin to hurt lurked in those blue eyes, so much like his. Or maybe he just looked lost. James cleared his throat and the look was gone. "I wish you luck."

"Thanks." Paul started for his room. As he passed his brother, he clapped him on the back. "Cheer up. Your time is coming. She just wasn't the right one for you."

"Yeah, well...we'll see." James shrugged and looked away. A few seconds later he asked to Paul's back, "Are you about ready to hit the slopes?"

"Sure," he said over his shoulder. "But I'm driving separately."

"Oh?"

Paul nodded. "I'm heading back to the city early."

"Okay. I'll meet you at the tram when it opens."

Sitting on the KT-22 lift after skiing for several hours, Paul's thoughts were on the same thing he'd been thinking all morning, Kate and this Mike character. He couldn't expel them from his mind, no matter how hard he tried.

He sighed. He really didn't want to ask James about what Kate said, but he felt at this point the need to know outweighed any ribbing he'd attract.

"So tell me about Mike," he said a few minutes later.

James' laugh floated past him. "I wondered when you'd get around to him. You know, if you'd have let me continue my game a little longer you could've found out without humbling yourself now." He glanced over at him with brows quirked. "What do you want to know?"

"What information were you going to let me in on?"

James shrugged. "I don't know much more than what I told you earlier. She skied with him, got a ride back with him, and he invited her to dinner. She made it seem as if he was the reason she was breaking up with me." Then with a sheepish, lopsided grin, he added, "Well, I did nudge her because she ended things so abruptly and I was shocked. I knew then something happened last weekend and your face flashed like a neon sign. My guess is that when I pushed her to find out more, she put up this Mike as a decoy. She gave a good bluff, too. I should've known she was on to my tricks. Then, when I think about it, what was she supposed to say? 'I spent a few days with your brother and we connected so well I want to call it quits?'" He snorted. "You know I don't appreciate hearing stuff like that, and it isn't easy being dumped."

James' expression and words had Paul laughing. "What if I was just one-upping?"

"No way! I'm sure of that, especially after this morning. If I wasn't so relieved, I think my pride would be more hurt. But I'll get over it; you two deserve to be happy."

"What about Mike?" Paul prodded.

"She said she has a date with him tonight. That's the excuse she used to cancel our plans for this weekend." He chuckled. "I thought I had it planned flawlessly...the perfect setup. Have her here and you come in at the end. Just thinking about the scene had my mouth watering."

"Okay, but let's get back to Mike and Kate." Paul made a hand movement to hurry James along. "And their date tonight. Do you think she's really interested in this guy?"

James sighed. "Man, I'm glad I'm not in your shoes."

"Yeah, I got that. Just answer the question," Paul

demanded, getting annoyed.

"I don't know. What I do know about Kate is that she's loyal. If there is something between the two of you, Mike hasn't got a prayer." He stopped and thought for a minute. "You know she did say something interesting the night we broke up. She said she was through being the pursuer. Then she said...and I quote, 'If he wants me, he knows where I am.' I assumed at the time she was talking about this Mike guy, but now I think she was talking about you."

The chair neared the top. As Paul put up the bar and prepared to disembark, he ran through James' comment several times.

He skied off the lift then stopped beside James, who was tightening his boots.

"I'm outta here," he said. "Sorry to leave you hanging, but I need to take care of a few things."

He took off down the path toward the bottom of the mountain as fast as his skis would go.

Chapter 17

Paul raced to the bottom of the mountain and quickly changed. Because he was in a hurry, several friends' attempts to engage him in idle chitchat were met with grunts and his back as he headed to his car and his quest to get back to San Francisco.

Once on the main road, he increased his speed, driving as fast as the car and road allowed. He prayed he wouldn't run into any members of the California Highway Patrol. Not even the threat of a five-hundred-dollar ticket was enough to slow him down.

His luck held. He made the trip back to the city in record time, thankful the seven-series BMW was built for excessive speeds for long periods. He cruised Kate's street. It was Saturday, so he found a spot close to her apartment. Seconds later, he stood at the row of buzzers outside the main door. After jabbing the right button, the intercom came alive with a burst of static.

"Yes? Who is it?"

"Kate? It's me, Paul."

There was a long pause before she asked, "What do you want?" He couldn't miss the note of agitation in the four words.

"Can you let me in?"

"Go away!"

"Come on, Kate, open up. I need to talk to you."

"No. Please, just go away. I don't want to talk to you."

"You're not going to listen to what I have to say?" Paul ground out in frustration.

"There's nothing to say. Please leave. I don't want to see you."

Stilling the urge to hit something, he took a deep breath instead and raked a hand through his hair, trying for patience.

"I can't leave. Not without saying what I came to say." Though he'd brought his anger under control, there was no mistaking the steely edge in his voice. "I deserve that much, don't you think?"

Long seconds passed before the latch clicked. Paul released a breath he hadn't known he'd been holding. He ran up the stairs, taking them two and three at a time. At her apartment, he found the door open about an inch. He pushed it open wider and slipped inside.

Having never been in her place before, he noticed at once how cozy and inviting the large, open room appeared. Kate sat at a table in front of a big bay window overlooking the street. He inched closer until he stood a few feet away, and studied her for a long moment without speaking.

Kate looked up and met his eyes, hers flashing anger. "Well?" Her chin lifted defiantly.

She wasn't making this any easier. He ran a hand through his hair. "Like I said, we need to talk."

"Why? What will it change?"

"What can it hurt?" He bit back a smile when she crossed her arms and glared, daring him...almost goading him.

"God, you are beautiful," he whispered. "Come here."

He reached down to touch her hand and fought harder to restrain the grin breaking free when she leaned away, her expression growing wary. With a firm hold, he gently tugged, pulling her out of the chair and into his arms. The move caught her off guard and he increased his efforts to soothe her. It took only seconds before she relaxed and hugged him back, which told him more than words ever could. Paul only wanted to comfort her. Despite her earlier battle-ready stance, he couldn't stop himself from lowering his head and meeting her lips with his. She looked too adorable, too kissable, too irresistible, and he'd wanted her for much too long.

At first, she stiffened, but he kept his mouth malleable and begging, waiting her out until she softened and opened for him. When she moaned and wrapped her arms around him tighter, bringing him closer, blood pounded in his ears and surged through his system, flooding him with unleashed desire.

Breaking the contact with her lips, Paul spread kisses over her face and eyes. When he neared her ears, he lingered. He caught a whiff of her perfume, the scent reminding him of the last time they'd kissed. His fingers slid underneath her sweater, skimming the underside of her breasts.

Kate's soft moan permeated his brain and seeped into his soul, driving his need to the brink.

"Please, Kate, let me love you," Paul whispered in between kisses. He lifted his head and his expression was pleading. He waited, holding his breath, while several emotions played across her features, the biggest one a yearning he connected with. He let out a sigh of relief. He hadn't been wrong. She did feel what he felt. Yet, instead of giving in to her emotions, she closed her eyes and shook her head. "I can't."

~

Kate pulled out of Paul's arms and took a step back. Noting his stunned look, she spun around and paced, wringing her hands. Her brain refused to function any time he was near. Why had she let him in? And why had she let him kiss her? She was in huge trouble because all she wanted to do was grab him close and never let him go. But she couldn't. He didn't belong to her.

The knowledge seared her soul like a hot poker. The pain brought on tears, and once they started, she couldn't stop them.

Paul reached for her. She felt his lips as he kissed her tears, following them until they reached her mouth, before working his way back up to her eyes.

"Don't cry, Kate. Just tell me what's wrong." He met her gaze and she heard the teasing in his voice when he added, "And here I thought you liked kissing me."

She smiled, her eyes misty, and shook her head, too choked up to speak.

"Then why are you crying?" Paul asked gently.

Kate couldn't talk about it yet. All she could do was shake her head again. The tears continued to fall.

Paul pulled her closer, and she curled against him. For moments, he did nothing but hold her and let her cry, stroking her as if she were a cat he was trying to make purr.

Silence filled the room except for the sound of her sobs.

After a while, her sobbing ceased.

Paul's voice startled her. "You're not going anywhere with Mike tonight."

"What?" She leaned away from him to glance at his expression, not sure she heard him correctly.

"James told me you have a date tonight and I don't see how you can go through with it after what just happened," he said, clearly incensed.

His words and disapproving tone stunned her. How dare he condemn her for trying to move on with her life?

She yanked out of his hold.

"I don't see how it's any of your concern who I date. Who're you to tell me what I can and cannot do?"

"I'm the man who just held you while you cried," Paul ground out, his body stiffening. "And I repeat—you are not leaving to go out with some other guy before we talk this out."

Those words had her chin rising another inch, and she glared at him. "You think a few kisses give you the right to run my life? Think again—I decide who I date and when I date him." Pointing at the door, she turned away. "I think it's time you left."

She felt his eyes on her, but she ignored him and put some distance between them.

"Kate—I didn't come here to fight." He sighed. "We need to talk."

"I think you've said enough," she said, crossing her arms and tapping her foot. But her annoyance only seemed to amuse him. "I don't see anything funny," she huffed.

"I do." His grin widened. "I was just wondering how the woman standing in front of me with such self-righteous indignation can be the same one who melted in my arms only moments ago."

Paying no heed to his suggestive tone, she nodded toward the entrance. "Don't let the door hit you on the way out."

His bark of laughter filled the room. "Damn, even when we're fighting, I find you fascinating." He muttered under his breath, "Why do I have a feeling the challenge of overcoming your objections will be a lifelong battle?"

"What?" He had to be joking, either that or she'd mistaken his comment.

"Nothing." He smiled smugly, lounged back against

the wall, crossing his feet as well as his arms, appearing to make himself more comfortable, which only irritated her more.

"Didn't you hear me? Leave." She glared at him, willing him to go. He was too attractive as it was.

"Not just yet. I told you we have things to discuss."

His words stopped her. She looked at him incredulously, her eyes narrowing. She couldn't believe his audacity. Then she smiled and gave a resigned shake of her head. Why should anything he did surprise her? This was the same man who walked away from her taunting after their snowball fight. She knew he meant what he said. He probably wouldn't leave until he spoke his mind.

"Well?" she prodded, tapping her foot faster, after long seconds ticked by.

Paul's eyebrow lifted. "Well, what?"

Taking a deep breath for control, she waited until she could speak without raising her voice. "You came here to talk, so talk."

Paul's smile spread. He seemed to be in no hurry and was clearly enjoying her distress. "What I had in mind was more along the line of a dialogue—not a one-sided monologue."

Kate sighed. She marched over to the table and sat, but well out of his reach.

Paul chuckled and moved to sit across from her. "As much as I like kissing you, I'm not going to ravish you. I promise."

"Oh, shut up," she snapped, feeling heat seep up her face. She knew he was well aware of his effect on her. "That has never been our problem and you know it."

That comment brought on another bark of laughter. When it died, he sobered and was silent for a while before asking, "And what do you see as our problem, Kate?"

"Come on, Paul. I know you're sexually attracted to me, but I also know your heart belongs to Judith."

His jawed dropped and he stared at her, totally stunned. "Is that what this is all about?"

Blinking back tears over the memory of their parting, she worked to keep the hurt out of her voice. "Can you honestly tell me you don't love her?" What was his game?

He shook his head. "No, but she and I are friends. Period." His expression softened. He reached across the table and placed his hand on top of hers, giving it a gentle squeeze. "Surely you know that."

"What about Judith?" she asked, capturing his gaze.

"We're not a couple any longer." Honesty shone in his eyes. "She'll always have a special place in my heart. I grew up loving her and I can't pretend it never happened. But it has nothing to do with how I feel about you."

Pain engulfed her at his heartfelt words. "Paul, I saw you with her last Tuesday night," she said softly, glancing at their now entwined hands and studying them for a long moment. "I saw the love you two share with my own eyes. I won't be placed in the middle."

He remained silent for a full minute, absorbing her words. Then, he whispered, "Is that what made you cry?"

Tears threatened again. Unable to speak because of them, she just nodded.

"Oh, Kate, I love you. The feelings I have for Judith are nothing compared to what I feel for you. They snuck up on me. I certainly never expected it to happen, but I can honestly tell you that I was ready to give Judith up anyway. She and I weren't meant to be. I finally accepted it."

She considered this a moment before discarding it. "Maybe, but I believe what I saw." At best, she'd become a rebound; at worst, she'd be taking him away from her best friend. "Judith loves you. I can't be the one to take you away from her." And once they were back together, he could really have a laugh over her stupidity.

"She does love me. But only as a friend. We ended things, just like you and James did. So my heart is free and it chooses you." With those words softly spoken, he scooted to the chair next to her and leaned close enough to give her a sweet, comforting kiss. All too soon, heat sparked between them. Right before it got out of hand, he broke contact and said in a tormented voice, "So tell me you're not going out with Mike—not when you kiss me like that."

Kate turned away, wishing she could trust him. He may think he was free, but she knew better. Right now, she *was* his rebound...until Judith realized what she'd tossed away. That thought hurt almost as much as loving him did.

Fighting tears, she stood and said in a resolute tone, "I have to go." She started for her bedroom, beyond the screen.

"What do you mean you have to go?" Paul's confused voice filled the air as he trailed after her. "Why?"

"I don't expect you to understand, but I'm doing it for me."

"No, I don't understand," he shot back, stalking to her front door. As he reached for the handle, he turned. "When you decide you want me and only me, give me a call. I'm done waiting around for what may be. I know what I want. I want you. But that goes two ways. You have to want me just as much. I'm not willing to settle any longer." After his heated outburst, he was out the door quickly, pulling it shut behind him with a little more force than necessary.

Kate sat on her sofa, eyeing the empty space where only seconds ago Paul's tall frame filled the doorway. For the first time in her life, she was unsure how to proceed. She'd always had a plan of action. Right now, however, nothing was going as expected.

Common sense told her she should trust the love and caring she heard in Paul's voice. Paul wasn't James. Why not trust him, or trust her own judgment? Judith's face infiltrated her thoughts and she sighed, her breath coming out in one big whoosh.

She really didn't want to go out with Mike. But the thought of Paul telling her she couldn't just didn't sit right, not after seeing him with Judith.

Mike was a nice guy, and she enjoyed his company. He certainly didn't deserve a phone call with only two hours' notice, canceling their date on the off chance that she and Paul would get together.

What a dilemma!

She didn't move for almost an hour, staring into space. When it was time to get ready, she forced herself into action, trying to forget that her heart was breaking.

Chapter 18

Paul left Kate's apartment with a heavy heart.

At home, he hurriedly put on running gear. Unable to sit in an empty apartment knowing that Kate would be out with another man, he headed for the street.

Remembering her curt dismissal, he ran faster, trying to outrun the pain.

How in the hell could Kate think he'd be able to go back to Judith after kissing her? Nor could he fathom how she could dismiss what was between them so readily.

Maybe he was being irrational. Irrational or not, he was through hiding his feelings. He'd never settle for love without passion again, which is what it amounted to with Judith. He wanted all or nothing.

Was that too much to ask? Of course not.

Didn't Kate want the same? He had huge doubts.

He ran blindly, pushing himself hard for more than an hour. Eventually, his tranquility returned, mainly after coming to several conclusions. The thought of not having Kate in his life seemed unbearable, but he'd survive. On the other hand, having a one-sided relationship with her, like the one he'd shared with Judith, was something he'd never be able to survive. He also realized he had no control over Kate's actions, so he did the only thing one could think of—let go of her.

With the determination he was known for, he put her out of his mind and out of his life, stopping short of locking the door. Only time would allow him to do that.

~

Kate tried to concentrate on the man across from her.

She offered Mike a polite smile after he'd made some comment about his job. He was a sales representative for a major manufacturing firm based in south San Francisco and traveled a lot.

She felt horrible about Paul. She'd hurt him deeply. His angry departure was proof.

"Are you okay?" Mike eyed her thoughtfully. "You seem to be a million miles from here."

"I'm sorry," she said, shoving her thoughts away. Going for a bit of levity, she added, "I think the sugar from all this dessert is wreaking havoc on my mind."

He grinned, clearly taking her excuse in stride. "You sure can put it away. I can't believe you stay so slim with all you've eaten tonight."

"I guess I have good genes." She shrugged, not adding that tonight, eating had been a form of comfort.

"Yeah, you do. I know my sister would love to be that lucky. All she does is moan about how easy it is to gain weight."

"I didn't know you had a sister. Does she live here?" she asked, working at keeping the conversation going. "What about your parents? Are you from the Bay Area?"

He spent the next quarter of an hour talking about his family, before turning the conversation to where in the city he lived.

"The neighborhood's a little on the funky side," he said, of his apartment in an area above the Haight, a district the hippies made famous in the late sixties. "And it's hilly. Gives my clutch a good workout."

She should have stayed home, she realized too late. Her slight smile, as big as she could muster considering her glum mood, urged him to drone on about his work.

Mike had sensed her distraction too many times during the meal, so Kate tried to reciprocate with mention of her shop and some of her business trips. But her heart wasn't in it and the conversation eventually died.

"How about more coffee," the waitress asked, interrupting the uncomfortable silence.

Mike nodded, beginning to mirror her mood. As he drank his coffee, he became as silent and uncommunicative as she.

The waitress cleared the table, leaving behind the check. Mike picked it up and finally spoke. "Why did you come out with me tonight?"

His question brought Kate out of her thoughts and she looked up, unable to keep the guilt out of her expression.

When she remained silent, Mike added, "It's obvious you have other things on your mind and don't want to be here." He shrugged. "I'm curious as to why you came."

Her guilt spread to the heat rising up her cheeks. Unable to look him in the eyes, she drew figure eights on the table with her finger. "I'm sorry. I know I've been lousy company tonight."

Mike smiled. "You want to talk about it?"

Shaking her head, she scrunched up her nose. "I don't think that'd be smart."

"Ah!" His expression turned from knowing to cynical. "How nice. Another guy."

Kate's eyebrows shot up. "How can you be so sure it's another guy?"

"I have eyes and ears," he countered with a self-deprecating laugh. "I'm right, aren't I?"

She took a deep breath, giving up all pretenses. "Yes, I'm sorry. A lot happened after you asked me out, but I didn't feel comfortable canceling."

"Don't you think that would have been better than

putting us both through this torture?"

Smiling sheepishly, she said, "I guess I wasn't thinking."

"Okay—I can accept that, but promise me something?"

"I'll try," she said honestly.

"If this guy doesn't work out, call me and give me another chance." Mike stood and reached for the check. "You're worth another try."

His sincere words lightened her mood. "I would be stupid not to call you." She smiled and nodded at the check. "And because I was such a boring date, I should pay for dinner."

"Don't worry about it." When she was about to disagree, he shot back, "You can pay next time."

They walked back to her apartment in amicable silence.

"I think I'll leave you here," he said, when they got to the outside door of her building. His car was parked a block away. "Will you be all right?"

Nodding, she offered a warm smile. "I am sorry about tonight," she murmured, relieved she wouldn't have to offer any more excuses or explanations. She stood on tiptoe and kissed him on the cheek. "For what it's worth, I really like you."

Mike's laugh was quick. "Yeah, I know...bad timing. Well, I'll see you around, Kate," he said, before he turned toward his car.

Kate watched him walk away before letting herself into the building. Oh, how she hated the dating scene.

She'd never wanted to hurt anyone's feelings. But today, in the course of several hours, she'd hurt two people who didn't deserve it by doing the one thing she shouldn't have done—go out with Mike. Her shoulders slumped at the realization.

As she trudged up the stairs to the second floor, one thought stood out above all others. Paul wouldn't be back. Not without her calling him. Plus, she couldn't discount Judith. But even if Judith gave her blessing, she didn't know if she had the courage to call him, which totally confused her.

What she needed was time to think. Think about what she wanted and where she was going. With these thoughts and more roaming through her head, she pushed her way through the door and walked unhurriedly to her apartment.

Chapter 19

Kate's cell phone rang, waking her from a fitful sleep. She reached across the bed to her nightstand and fumbled for it. "Hello."

"Hey, Kate, it's me, Judith. You want to grab some breakfast?"

A twinge of guilt tightened in her midsection, as Judith's question registered. Almost a week had passed since her date with Mike. She'd been screening her calls, avoiding everyone, especially Judith. But it was time to face her demons. "Yeah, sounds great. Where do you want to meet?"

"How about Ernie's on Chestnut—say, an hour from now?"

"Sure."

Kate disconnected the call, then leaned her head against the pillows and closed her eyes. She hated obsessing over her situation and the only way to keep from obsessing more was to take a break. She'd been busy at the store so she could easily take off two days and go up to Tahoe. James told her the house would be free and that he expected her to use it. Paul usually took Fridays off to her Mondays, so he'd probably gone up yesterday. She worked Saturdays, so if she drove up tomorrow morning, she could easily avoid him. She hadn't heard a word from him, but then hadn't expected to. Well aware the next move was hers, she'd put off dealing with him. Indecision kept her from calling and apologizing. The longer she put off doing something, the easier it became to do nothing.

"Doesn't matter," she muttered, shaking her thoughts and rising to shower. It wouldn't change the outcome.

Forty-five minutes later, Kate was out the door. She arrived at the agreed-upon café a little early. After placing her name on the list, she grabbed a cup of coffee and went outside to wait for Judith. She leaned against the wall and savored the rich brew.

"There's a twenty-minute wait," she said when Judith joined her.

Judith nodded and went to order her own coffee.

When a waitress with menus called out Kate's name, they followed her inside.

At first, Kate didn't see Paul or James seated at a corner table near the window. Too late to turn back now, she kept her eyes straight ahead, praying Judith wouldn't notice. As the two neared the empty table the waitress indicated, James looked up and waved.

Kate cringed inwardly when Judith glanced their way, then nudged her. "Look who's here. Paul." She started in their direction.

James scooted back his chair and stood. "Hey, guys, why not join us?"

Judith smiled at Paul and ignored James. "That'd be great."

"Yeah, great." Avoiding looking at Paul, who'd stood to kiss Judith's cheek, Kate sighed, wondering how this was going to go over. She'd never told Judith about her breakup with James or her attraction to Paul, so her friend had no idea of the undercurrents going on around them as she sat down beside Paul. Left with little choice, Kate sat next to James and gave Paul a slight nod. He returned the gesture, but didn't look at her.

Kate opened her menu, ignoring James' perplexed expression. His silence spoke volumes.

Since Paul acted as if Kate didn't exist, she followed his lead and pretended he wasn't there—which had been the norm before their weekend in Tahoe.

Looking as if he were wishing he'd never asked the two women to join them, James finally found his voice. "So, how's work?"

"Fine." Kate shrugged and added, while perusing her menu, "How's the architecture business going?"

James chuckled. "It's still there."

Judith, who was used to Paul and Kate ignoring each other, seemed to think nothing of carrying on a conversation with Paul, without the other two intervening.

Kate flashed James a grateful smile when he made small talk with her. To anyone watching, it appeared as if four friends were enjoying themselves, but Kate knew better.

When Paul finished, he threw some cash on the table and stood. "I'm sorry, but I need to leave you ladies. I have an appointment." Then, he bolted for the door, not looking back.

James rose, offering an apologetic smile. "Ladies. It's been nice, but I have to talk to Paul about something." He added his cash to Paul's, then turned and said in a louder voice, "Wait up. I'll join you."

Judith stared after them, looking totally confused. "I wonder what that was all about?"

Kate cleared her throat and studied her food intently. Finally, she gave a negligent shrug. "I wouldn't know— Paul is unpredictable."

"Don't start," Judith warned, nailing her with an accusing gaze.

"What? I'm not starting anything."

Judith sighed. "Look, Kate, I know you don't like

Paul, but he's my friend and I'd appreciate it if you'd at least be civil to him."

Incensed, Kate asked, "What did I do?"

Shaking her head, Judith rolled her eyes. "I thought the two of you became friends after Tahoe. What happened to change things?"

"You thought we became friends? What gave you that idea?"

"I don't know. Paul just seemed to accept you more. Seeing as how you're my best friend, I'd really like it if you both got along when you two are around each other."

The words tore at Kate. Had Paul been wrong about Judith's feelings? It sounded like she was more serious about him than she let on...like she was thinking long term. No matter how outrageous the thought seemed, Kate had to know. "Are you two engaged?"

Judith laughed. "Heavens no! Whatever gave *you* such an idea?"

"Well, you have been talking about marriage. It sounds like you've changed your mind."

"I haven't. I love Paul, but he's not the one. Thank God, I didn't have to end our friendship to get him to see that. Now that he's finally realized all we will ever be is good friends, I would really appreciate your cooperation on being civil. Is that too much to ask?"

"No." Kate's relief bubbled up into a nervous laugh. "I'm sorry. I'll try harder to be nice to him."

Judith nodded. "Thank you. I'm tired of playing referee."

~

Ignoring passersby, Paul headed toward his apartment at a good clip.

"Hey, Paul! Wait up," James shouted behind him.

He slowed his pace. James caught up at the corner.

The two walked in silence for another block.

"What the hell's going on?" James finally asked.

"Nothing." His denial rang in the air and he kept walking until James grabbed his arm and pulled him to a stop.

"Bullshit," he said. "Tell me what happened."

Paul glared at him. He really didn't want to get into it. But noticing James' unyielding expression, he figured he had to say something. James wouldn't give up until he got an answer.

"Let's just say things ended before they even got started."

"What?" Confusion clouded James' eyes as they met Paul's. "The last I knew, you were hot to get back here to see Kate and now you won't even look at her."

"She kept her date with Mike."

"So? What's the problem?"

Paul looked out across the street, unable to keep meeting James' direct gaze. "Damn it all, you don't understand."

"Make me."

"I can't," he muttered. "So, let's drop it."

"No."

Paul didn't respond, just stared at a distant point, rubbing the back of his neck in agitation.

James prodded, "I only want to help."

"We were this close..." He stopped and shook his head. "No one can help. I just need to forget her," Paul said, the words coming out in one long, aggravated breath.

"Wait a minute—you're all worked up and talking about forgetting her because she kept a date she made days before?"

"Yes. I asked her to break it but she said she had to

go out with him."

James snorted. "You probably *told* her to break it."

"What difference does that make?" he shot back indignantly.

"I thought you said you could handle her."

"I *can* handle her." Paul's jaw clenched and his spine straightened.

"Well, you're doing a lousy job. Hell, even I wouldn't have done that."

Glaring at him, he ground out, "You're not helping."

James let the comment pass and tsked. "And here I thought you were the sainted one when it comes to understanding and dealing with women. Obviously, you had me fooled."

"I know how I feel." Paul notched his chin higher and curled his hand into a fist, as the knot in his stomach tightened. "I'm damn sure not waiting around for anyone to figure out who she wants."

"I can't believe what I'm hearing." James shook his head. "Think about it. You may have something special with Kate and you're not even willing to fight for it."

Stunned by the truth in the words, Paul hesitated, as doubt crept into his thoughts. But, the idea of Kate with this Mike guy ate at him. "My feelings meant nothing to her." He caught his brother's stare, one so much like his own and said, "Now do you understand?"

"Yeah, but do you?" he asked in a gruff voice. "Are you sure your feelings meant nothing, or is it your ego or jealousy coming out?"

"I'm not sure of anything anymore." Paul sighed. Studying a point on the horizon, he mulled over James' question. He didn't want to accept the bit about ego, nor did he want to admit to being jealous. But he couldn't deny the truth.

"If you and Kate had some kind of a connection, you can damn sure believe that this Mike character didn't stand a chance with her. She's not the type to lead guys on and I doubt she'd start now." He remained silent for a few long seconds before urging, "Look at it objectively. Try to see it from her side. Maybe she had reasons for keeping the date. Did you ever consider her intentions might not have been to hurt you?"

That all made sense. Paul rubbed the back of his neck. "I guess I need to look at this from another angle," he finally acknowledged.

James grunted. "While you're at it, consider this. If you're in it for the long haul, running away at the first sign of trouble solves nothing. I'm sure there'll be plenty of times when you'll hurt each other. Sucking it up and working it out is the only way you two will survive."

Paul smiled, his first one in days. "How did you get to be so wise?"

James laughed. "I can dish it out. I just can't take it." He clapped him on the shoulder. "Talk to her. Don't let her go without a fight."

~

"There you go, Mrs. Stone," Kate said, handing the woman a receipt. She looked up when the bell over the door jingled and was surprised to see James sauntering toward the counter.

She smiled and nodded. "I'll be with you in just a minute."

"No problem." James took off his sunglasses and stuck them in his pocket. "I have nothing but time."

"I can't wait to see how that chest will look in my bedroom." Mrs. Stone stuffed the receipt into her purse and snapped it closed.

"Let me know how it works out."

"I will." She stopped at the door. "I'll take a picture and email it to you."

"Great." Once she left, Kate glanced at James. "So what brings you slumming to my neck of the woods?"

"It's nice to see you, too." He walked up to the counter and did a three-sixty, taking in her shop. "Wow, the store's changed since the last time I was here. A lot of new stuff. Looks like business is booming."

"Thanks. Sales are strong." She tapped the keyboard on her laptop to bring up the account she was reconciling. "So, what's up? I'm sure you didn't drive all this way to ask about business."

When he remained silent, her eyebrows shot up. "Well? I'm a little behind."

He smiled and leaned against the counter. "Okay, since you're obviously too busy for idle chitchat, I'll get to the point." He paused for the longest time, as if searching for a way to begin.

After more seconds, Kate prompted, "Today would be nice."

"Damn, you're annoying sometimes," James said. She started to object and he put up a hand. "I'm here on a goodwill mission, so sheath your claws, woman."

When she flashed *get to it* with her eyes, he offered an innocent grin. "Okay, this is me getting to the point. What's going on with you and Paul?"

"That's personal." She kept her expression neutral so as not to reveal her shock. How did he even know there was anything between her and Paul, let alone have the nerve to ask about it?

James' smile didn't quite reach his eyes. He shook his head and waved a forefinger in front of her. "Ah, ah, ah, wrong answer. I thought we decided to be friends."

"Oh, and you think that gives you a right to dig into

my personal business? If so, think again." She snorted and, closing her laptop, she picked it up and turned toward the back room. "I'm really behind," she added, while walking. "So, you'll have to excuse me."

"I never took you for a coward, Kate."

How dare he call her a coward? She stopped dead in her tracks and spun around. "This doesn't concern you."

"When you hurt my brother, it concerns me a lot."

"Does Paul know you're coming to his defense?"

"No, I'm definitely butting in. I don't like it that you're trifling with him."

"Trifling?" Fuming, she went rigid and lifted her chin. "I'm not the one who's trifling." Nodding at the door, she said, "I'd go before you say too much and really tick me off."

"You know, Kate," he said, making no effort to leave. In fact, his stance was now combative. "I always thought the problems in our relationship were all because of me and my inability to communicate or to commit. But now I'm not so sure." He waited a heartbeat before adding, "What's more, I think you're running scared, which *is* cowardly in my book."

His words stung. "Why are you doing this?" she whispered, hating the thought that he might be right. "I'm not a coward. The fact that I took your shit for eight years proves it."

"Yeah, and you never had to take the final step to commitment either, even though that's what you always claimed to want. Only, now I'm starting to doubt you really wanted it to begin with."

Tears seeped into her eyes as she denied hotly, "That's not true. I want commitment." She wiped her eyes and glared at him, daring him to disagree.

James eyed her for a long minute. Then, he asked,

"Who is this Mike? What's he to you?"

"Why me, Lord?" she muttered, looking toward the heavens, knowing James wasn't going to leave without some answers. "Just some guy I met at Tahoe."

"From what Paul's said, I gathered you two started something." At her stony silence, he prodded, "Am I right?" When she offered a slight nod and looked away, he added, "So how could you let *some guy* come between that?" He waited until she made eye contact again. "It's not like you to flit from man to man. Why start now?"

She laughed. "I'm not flitting from man to man. I like Mike." Then, she weakened and shook her head, closing her eyes to block out the pain. She opened them and blinked, staving off the tears that built. "I've really mucked things up." She wiped the moisture out of her eyes. "Oh, James," she said, finally letting down her defenses. "I have no clue what I want any more. Everything's gone haywire. Three weeks ago, I hated Paul and you were my universe. Now, you and I are done and I love Paul but he hates me. I don't know what to do about it."

James caught and held her gaze, not letting go for what seemed like an eternity. "You know what to do about it." He offered a knowing smile. "I'm just not sure you want it as much as you say you do."

"You're wrong." She lifted her head, but couldn't maintain eye contact and had to look away.

"Prove it," he taunted. "You need to be willing to go beyond your fears and grab the brass ring. You aren't even reaching for it, and it disappoints me."

He took his sunglasses out of his pocket and put them on before turning and walking out of her shop without a backward glance.

Staring dumbfounded through the window as he

climbed into his SUV, she wanted to run out and yell that he didn't know what he was talking about. But his words held too much merit. And like a scratched CD, they replayed over and over.

If only she could find the Off switch.

Chapter 20

Kate stalked to the door and flipped the dead bolt, not caring that she was closing two hours early. After reliving James' parting shot in her mind for the thousandth time, she was ready to scream. She had to get out of here. She darned sure couldn't continue pacing, going back and forth and round and round, while trying to rationalize her actions.

James had been on target with his assessment and it chafed. Who would have guessed James—the guy she least expected it from—could have such insight?

Her lips curled in bitter amusement. It was better than crying over the truth. She was a *coward*. And scared. Of facing her emotions and living up to Paul's expectations. He'd been so adamant about what he wanted. So sure of himself and his purpose. She hadn't believed him when he tried to explain about Judith. She should have listened, not turn her back on his certainty or his love. She should have grabbed on to the chance at love and never let go.

The thought of life without Paul galvanized her into action. She headed for her car. It was time to apologize and beg for his forgiveness.

At her street, she rounded the corner. A man sat on the ground in front of her apartment building with his back against the brick wall. He watched her approach. It took a few moments before she recognized Paul's lithe form. Joy rose up in her heart and her steps quickened.

He stood and brushed off his pants. Their eyes caught.

She ran the rest of the way and slipped into his open arms. "I'm so sorry. I love you. Please give me another chance." Tears slipped from her eyes.

"Shush. It's okay." Paul wrapped his arms around her, hugged her fiercely, and covered her face with feathery-light kisses. In between them, he murmured, "I love you, too."

Happiness burst inside her heart. Returning his kiss, she focused on one thought. *He came back.*

Paul lifted his head and whispered, "We're giving the neighbors a show. Can we go inside and talk?"

Letting go of him, she smiled, realizing how close to the truth he was about getting off the street before they created a scene.

Like two kids on Christmas morning rushing to open packages, they raced upstairs to her apartment.

Once inside, Paul reached for her as he kicked the door shut behind him.

Heat flashed the moment their lips connected. This was surely heaven, Kate thought. Despite the excitement racing through her body, she felt more than that. A sense of peace enveloped her. A sense of urgency spurred her on, and a sense of his total acceptance had her trusting him completely. How had she lived so long without Paul's love?

"Can you feel how much I want you?" he murmured into her mouth.

Kate moaned in response when he stepped closer. How could she not feel what grew between them? This was Paul. He was hers, just as she was his. She was right where she belonged. In his arms.

As if sensing her overwhelming need, Paul picked her up and headed behind the screen.

He gently placed her on the bed and knelt down so

that he was above her.

Her half laugh of glee erupted. He caught her smiling lips in his own. The tender kiss was full of love and teasing, but soon changed to something deeper. More vital.

He broke their connection, then met her gaze and said, "Kate, I need to know you're mine." As those words faded to silence, he held her eyes captive for what seemed like forever. Sincerity shone in those intense pools of blue. "If you make love with me now, I'll consider it a commitment between us and will expect nothing less than one hundred percent of you. Do you understand?"

Her heart soared. She nodded. "Oh, Paul, I love you." A lump of emotion lodged in her throat and barely let her get the words out. "I have no intention of ever allowing anyone to come between us again." She reached up and pulled him closer, sealing her promise with a kiss. Sensations of well-being and longing set off sparks of pleasure. She kissed her way to his ear. "I'm glad you came back," she said, nuzzling. "I needed to know you cared enough," she admitted, in between kisses. "I needed to know that I was worth the effort."

He chuckled and recaptured her mouth. His slow and thorough kiss wiped away her earlier doubts. He nipped at her chin. "Kate...Kate...Kate," he said, adding a nip in between each word. "Until our weekend together, I had no idea what true love was. Now that I do, I'll love you forever." If he hadn't already owned her heart, those words would have cinched the deal.

Then, his lips covered hers again. His kiss left her spinning with need and want. She felt a sense of loss when he bent to take off her shoes and socks. He methodically spent long seconds rubbing and massaging each bare foot before reaching for the snap on her jeans.

His touch was soothing. Erotic.

He tossed her jeans aside and concentrated on her sweater. His lips were warm and wonderfully enticing as they moved over her body in slow motion, kissing and baring her skin all the way to her neck before he lifted the garment off her shoulders. She closed her eyes trying to hold on to the sensations cascading over her.

When he touched her chin and waited, she finally peered at him with eyes at half-mast. His gaze scorched her with its intensity, saying more than words ever could that she was essential to his existence. Her feelings were reflected in her face; how she wanted him inside her. Wanted more of his kisses. Wanted him for a lifetime.

After he slipped off her bra, baring her to him, she reached for him. He jumped off the bed and said with a boyish grin, "Patience." Still, he rushed, shedding his clothes in seconds and was soon lying close to her.

Having him right where she wanted him, she wrapped her arms around him. He smiled lovingly and lowered his head, but not before teasing, "Okay—where were we." His smile turned devilish. "Oh yeah! I remember," he murmured into her mouth.

Heat and need slammed into her. Nothing in her life prepared her for the emotion filling her as Paul entered her. Kate knew she'd never be the same again. She'd belong to him forever.

~

Later, Paul kissed the top of Kate's forehead and adjusted so that she could lay with her head in the crook of his shoulder. Holding her close and basking in the aftermath of their lovemaking, he stroked her arm with his free hand.

"I'm sorry I left without fully understanding your motives for going ahead with your date," he finally said, disturbing the peaceful silence. "But I'd like to know why you felt you had to do it."

"Does it really matter?"

"I think so…so humor me."

"I'm not completely sure why it seemed important." For several seconds Kate drew figure eights on his chest. Then, she sighed. "It seems kind of silly now."

"Feelings are never silly." He stilled her hand. "We have some really strong ones between the two of us and we need to be able to deal with them."

"Don't I know it! Every time I'm around you, I'm overwhelmed. What I felt scared me and my best guess is that I needed the date with Mike to shield myself from feeling too much or getting hurt." She rose up on an elbow to look closer into his eyes. "Then, there is the fact that you can be somewhat bossy and I've never liked anyone telling me what to do."

He smiled at that. "Kate, have you ever thought that I have to be firm to deal with your personality, one that tests me at every turn?"

"I don't test you."

"Yes, subconsciously you do. You have a strong will that I find exhilarating and challenging. But if I let you, you'd walk all over me."

She thought about his comment. "Okay. I'll admit it. I can be a little tenacious at times."

"Just a bit," Paul agreed. "But, I also realize it goes both ways. I'll try and remember that." He remained silent for a lengthy moment before picking up her hand. He kissed it. "Let's promise that when either of us hurts the other, we'll talk it over instead of lashing out and creating more hurt."

"I never wanted to hurt you." Tears welled up in her brown eyes, making them appear larger and more beautiful. His heart did a somersault.

He put a finger to her lips. "It's ancient history. Let's worry about the future."

Nodding, she flashed him a warm smile. "I promise to talk to you and tell you how I feel, if you'll do the same."

He weaved his fingers with hers and bestowed another kiss on her hand. "It's a deal."

She hesitated, her smile wobbling a little. "What about Judith? I know you've both said you are just friends, but I worry about her reaction when she finds out."

"Don't worry. I'll break the news to her as gently as I can." Paul sighed. "And if there is a reaction, I'll deal with it."

"We'll deal with it together," she said, squeezing his hand. "You've been hers for so long. I can't help feeling like I've taken something that belongs to her."

"Then, I'll be doubly careful." He exhaled a long sigh. "But after seeing the two of us together, she'll probably figure it out on her own. James sure picked up on it quickly enough."

"Yeah, he did," Kate agreed. "And he stuck his nose where it didn't belong."

Paul laughed. "Well, I for one am glad he did. I owe him big-time."

Her gaze narrowed. "Oh? Care to elaborate?"

"No." He shook his head. "Just something between brothers." Then, to change the subject, he said, "I gather you're going skiing tomorrow—want some company?"

Sighing contentedly, she stretched. "Yeah, I was planning on it, and I would love the company."

Paul smiled. Now that they'd covered all the necessary topics of conversation, he had more important things on his mind, all centered on making Kate scream with pleasure. Only this time, they'd go at a slower pace, if that was possible.

He captured her lips and moved his mouth and tongue over hers in unhurried, drugging kisses that left them both reeling and wanting more.

Her soft moans drove him to the brink and Paul steeled himself for control, trying to draw out her pleasure for as long as possible. But when her hands roamed lower, he lost the fight. He wondered if he was ever going to be able to control the passion that flashed between them when they kissed. That was his last conscious thought and it was all Paul could do to hang on for the ride until they jumped off the precipice together into oblivion.

~

After a whirlwind couple of months, Paul asked Kate to marry him and she didn't hesitate to say yes. At that point, she felt like the luckiest person on the planet. He accompanied her to Chrissie's wedding in Chicago where she proudly introduced him to her family as her fiancé.

Only family and a few friends were invited to their August wedding. The small ceremony would be held at Lake Tahoe—the place it all began.

~ The End ~

About The Author

Sandy Loyd is a Western girl through and through. Born and raised in Salt Lake City, she's worked and lived in some fabulous places in the US, including South Florida. She now resides in Kentucky and writes full time. As much as she loves her current hometown, she misses the mountains and has to go back to her roots to get her mountain fix at least once a year.

She spent her single years in San Francisco and considers that city one of America's treasures, comparable to no other city in the world. Her California Series, starting out with Winter Interlude, are all set in the Bay Area. Her series consists of fun, heartwarming stories about crazy friends who, like single people everywhere, are seeking that someone special to share their lives with among thousands of eligible candidates.

Email her at sandyloyd@sandyloyd.com or visit her website at www.sandyloyd.com.

Thank you for reading *Winter Interlude*. If you enjoyed this story, please help others find it by posting a review on Goodreads, or Amazon, or Barnes & Noble— wherever you bought it—share a link, tweet about it, Facebook it... Everything helps in this new internet world.

LINKS TO OTHER BOOKS BY SANDY LOYD

Contemporary Romances
The California Series
Winter Interlude – Book One –
http://www.amazon.com/dp/B008OYT28A
Promises, Promises – Book Two –
http://www.amazon.com/dp/B008UT76ZA
James – Book Three –
http://www.amazon.com/dp/B008UYPFXA

Second Chances Series
Tropical Spice – Book One
http://www.amazon.com/dp/B009UZGC08

Romantic Suspense
D.C. Bad Boys Series
The Sin Factor – Book One -
http://www.amazon.com/dp/B009TROEXE

Running Series
Running Out Of Fear – Book One – Due out
November 15, 2012

Printed in Great Britain
by Amazon